Praise for
The Montgomery Brothers
Series by Samantha Chase

"Chase's three-dimensional characters leap off the page, encouraging readers to sit down, put their feet up, and enjoy…charming."

— *Publishers Weekly* for *Until There Was Us*

"Longtime Montgomery fans will appreciate the opportunity to catch up with the other members of the family."

— *Publishers Weekly* for *I'll Be There*

"Sweet and sexy."

— *Omnivoracious: The Amazon Book Review*
for *I'll Be There*

"High on humor and romance, *Meant for You* by Samantha Chase makes the perfect summer read, all year-round!"

— *Tome Tender* for *Meant for You*

"[A] charming tale."

— *RT Book Reviews* for *Meant for You*

"[A] sweet romantic tale that feels as warm as melted chocolate with a hint of spice."

— *Tome Tender* for *Return to You*

"A moving tale of reunion and redemption."

— *RT Book Reviews*, 4 Stars for *Return to You*

Also by Samantha Chase

One *More* Moment

SAMANTHA CHASE

sourcebooks
casablanca

Published by Sourcebooks Casablanca, an imprint of Sourcebooks, Inc.
P.O. Box 4410, Naperville, Illinois 60567-4410
(630) 961-3900
Fax: (630) 961-2168
sourcebooks.com

Printed and bound in Canada.
MBP 10 9 8 7 6 5 4 3 2 1

This book more than any other gave me an extensive and eclectic playlist that got me over many bouts of writer's block. And with each song, not only did the words come, but so did the smiles. So many memories came to mind from a time so long ago and the friends I've been blessed to have. The summer of 1987 where "Slippery When Wet" played on a constant loop will always be one of the best.

You all know who you are.

This book is for them, and for the readers who have loved this series and the men of Shaughnessy. I hope I did them justice.

Prologue

ON ANY GIVEN DAY, JULIAN GRAYSON CONSIDERED himself to be a big fan of music. Any music.

Not today.

Right now, the strains of classical harp music were grating on his last nerve and it took every ounce of strength he had not to scream out to stop.

He chuckled softly to himself at the image. After all, how would it look if the groom threw a fit while standing at the altar as he waited for his bride? The lighted garden of the Hotel Bel-Air was set up for their evening nuptials, and Julian felt it was only right that he refrain from doing anything to upset his guests or his bride.

Another laugh—only this was mirthless.

His bride. Right. Dena was many things, but *his* seemed the least fitting. It was an odd thing to be going through his mind on his wedding day, but there it was.

Standing to his left were his four closest friends—bandmates Riley Shaughnessy, Matt Reed, Dylan Anders, and their manager, Mick Tyler. Julian had hit the jackpot where these guys were concerned. Not only were they a tight unit within their band, Shaughnessy, but he genuinely liked them and knew—no matter what—each of them would have his back.

"You sure about this?" Riley asked from beside him. "It's not too late to back out."

Julian's back instantly stiffened. To any onlooker,

they were five smiling men facing the front of the garden where the bride would appear at any moment. The road to the altar had been rocky, to say the least, and the guys all knew it. He wasn't proud of it and he knew most people wouldn't understand why he'd stuck it out for so long or put up with so much.

Honestly, neither did he.

"Jules," Riley murmured without breaking his smile or turning his head. "I'm serious. Say the word and—"

"I'm good," Julian said quietly but firmly. He knew exactly what to say and how to say it to make sure people didn't argue with him. Between the tone and his six-foot-two frame, people knew better.

Looking around the garden, he had to admit he was impressed. It felt intimate, and yet there were two hundred and fifty people sitting and smiling at him.

Dena had insisted on booking this space, and the staff had been beyond accommodating. No one had batted an eye at any of their requests—which came in the form of menu changes, lighting suggestions, and privacy clauses.

And then there was today's last-minute addition.

Julian had to hide a satisfied smirk. He wasn't a man who left anything to chance and he almost never did things on the spur of the moment.

But today he had.

And he couldn't wait to see the look on Dena's face when he surprised her.

The ceremony was set to begin, and as the music changed to the "Wedding March," Julian straightened and turned his head briefly to look at his buddies. They all thought he was crazy—had told him so on numerous occasions—and yet they all stood beside him to support him.

Mick caught his eye and gave the barest of nods, and for some reason, that small gesture calmed Julian's last-minute nerves.

Everyone stood and turned to watch Dena float down the aisle on her father's arm. She looked beautiful—like an angel in miles of white satin and lace. Her blond hair was long and curled, and even from where he was standing, Julian could see her signature pink-glossed lips. She caught his eye and gave him a beautiful smile, her blue eyes gleaming.

She was everything.

She was perfect.

She was…he couldn't find the words.

Swallowing hard, Julian moved to take her arm as she stepped up beside him. They waited for her father to take his seat before facing the minister, who smiled serenely at them.

"Dearly beloved," he began, "we are gathered here today to witness the union of Julian and Dena in holy matrimony, which is an honorable estate. It is not to be entered into unadvisedly or lightly, but reverently and soberly." He paused and looked at Julian. "It is my understanding you have a special presentation for the bride that you would like to make before we begin, is that correct?"

Julian forced himself not to turn and look at Dena even as he heard her soft gasp. She didn't like surprises. She had orchestrated and planned every detail of this wedding down to the second, and was probably more annoyed than curious at his messing with her schedule.

"That is correct," Julian said.

With a curt nod, the minister stepped to the side as

a large projection screen was revealed behind him. For a minute, Julian was seriously impressed with how the staff had disguised it behind strategically placed greenery and flowers.

"Julian," Dena whispered with a hint of annoyance, but he simply removed her arm from his as he took a step to the side—close to Riley—and waited for the images to play on the screen.

The sound came on first, and you could have heard a pin drop in the garden as the guests listened in stunned silence.

Heavy breathing.

"Oh, just like that."

"You like that, don't you, babe?"

"So much…you're so good…so perfect…"

"Better than Julian, right?"

Female laughter.

"So much better…always so much better."

An image finally appeared on the screen. It was a little dark, a little grainy, but not so much that you couldn't see what was going on.

A couple in bed.

There wasn't any chance of disputing who the woman was.

And the much younger guy was a studio technician who had worked on the last three Shaughnessy albums.

And was currently a guest at the wedding.

"Why are you marrying him, babe?"

She stopped moving and smiled at him, stroking his cheek. "Because he's Julian Grayson and he's rich," she said simply. *"And I want to be rich."*

"I'm rich."

"No, your father is rich," she corrected. *"You're just living off his name."*

"Isn't that what you'll be doing with Grayson? And besides, money isn't everything."

"Oh, please. Yes it is," she snapped. *"And don't worry, you'll be able to enjoy it too after I'm married. Julian gives me whatever I want no matter what I do."*

"That's just cold, Dena. Even for you."

She shrugged and went back to moving with her lover. *"Agree to disagree. I want it all and I want Julian to give it to me."*

The screen went black and Julian finally allowed himself to look at his bride. He forced a smile and willed himself not to fall for the shocked look on her face.

How many times had her tears worn him down? How many times had he believed she was sorry for the things she'd done?

"You want it all, sweetheart?" he asked as he took a menacing step closer. "I guess you'll get it from your latest fling."

Turning, he looked at his buddies, who were all trying to hide their own shock and amusement. Only Mick looked serious. Reaching into his pocket, he pulled something out and tossed it to Julian. "Everything's out front," he said.

Nodding, Julian grabbed the keys Mick had thrown and stalked up the aisle as chaos broke out in his wake.

Chapter 1

DIRTY, DUSTY, AND MORE THAN A LITTLE SWEATY, Julian tossed his keys on the table and stood in the entryway of the home he hadn't seen in three months. He'd say it was good to be home, but he wasn't a liar.

With a mixture of dread and curiosity, he forced himself to move. He'd been told what to expect, but if he'd learned anything over the last five years, it was that there were some things you just couldn't prepare yourself for.

Stepping into his massive living room, he froze. The place looked completely different—void of anything personal. It could have been a picture out of a decorating magazine, and as much as he hated it, he couldn't help but let out a sigh of relief.

Every trace of Dena and their life together was gone. *Good riddance.*

The entire room was white—the couches, the rug, the curtains. The back wall was made of windows, and with the sun shining through right now, it was almost blinding. Looking down at himself, he knew there was no way he could even walk further into the room—let alone touch anything.

He kept waiting to feel something. Anything. But after three months of riding his motorcycle around the country, he supposed he had dealt with most of his feelings on just about everything.

Maybe.

After walking out on the wedding, Julian had found a car waiting in front of the hotel and a valet holding the door open as if he'd known exactly when Julian was going to need it. Then he had gone to Mick's place and picked up the motorcycle he'd dropped there the previous day and the duffel bag that was already packed with things he'd need for however long he wanted.

Amazing how when the band traveled on tour, he required half a dozen pieces of luggage, but for this particular trip he had managed to condense it down to one duffel bag. And he'd made it work. He'd looked like hammered shit most of the time, but it worked. It fit his mood, and really, the only one he'd been hanging out with was himself, so what difference did it make?

There wasn't a doubt in his mind that most people thought he was crazy for what he'd done. Not just taking off on his bike for three months, but the whole wedding thing. Looking back, he knew it was the only way for him to do it. For years, Dena had been playing him, and he'd been so blinded by love and loyalty that he kept taking whatever she threw at him. So many people had warned him and tried to talk him out of staying in the relationship, but Julian wouldn't listen. Couldn't. He'd been too determined to make things work.

It wasn't until a week before the wedding that he'd been confronted with the truth—some things were never going to work no matter how much you wanted them to. And some people weren't worth wanting.

It was easy to say, not so easy to make himself believe.

Hence the three months on the road.

Julian wasn't stupid. Well, maybe he had been stupid,

but after spending so much time in his head these last several months, he'd learned a lot about himself. For starters, he knew he'd stayed in a toxic relationship way too long. It didn't matter how much counseling they had or how much they had talked through their problems, Dena had always found a way to make him feel like her behavior was somehow his fault. He worked too much, didn't give her enough attention…on and on it had gone. And he'd believed her.

When that video had surfaced—and he had thanked Mick and the private investigator he'd hired for it— Julian had been hit with the hard truth.

It didn't matter how much or how little he worked.

It didn't matter how much attention he gave her.

Dena didn't love him. Probably never had. He was a means to an end. She wanted fame and money and he was her ticket.

Her words on the video had devastated him, but he couldn't help but be thankful for them as well.

Given his tendency to cave where Dena was concerned, Julian knew the only way he was going to stay strong was to put some major distance between the two of them and not let anyone know where he was. He'd periodically checked in with his family, along with Mick and the guys, but other than that, Julian had spent the better part of the last ninety days on the back of his motorcycle and sleeping in some of the crappiest motels he had ever seen. It made staying under the radar and not being recognized a whole lot easier.

As if on cue, Julian's phone rang. Pulling it from his pocket, he grinned and answered. "You adding ESP to your list of skills, Mick?"

A low chuckle was the first response. "Nah, just know that you're punctual if nothing else. You said you'd be at the house at two. I figured I'd give you ten minutes to get in the door and get your first look around." He paused. "Everything okay?"

"I made it as far as the living room."

"My decorator, Joanie, did a fantastic job, don't you think?"

Julian shrugged even though Mick couldn't see him. "It's very…white."

"White's in. It's classic. Trust me, in time you'll love it."

"Maybe." Not that it mattered. Now that Julian was back, he had no intention of keeping the house. He thought back to how Dylan had felt after completing his stint in rehab—the first thing to go had been his house.

"My Realtor will be over to meet with you tomorrow," Mick said with a sigh.

Now it was Julian's turn to chuckle. "How'd you know?"

"Please. I know you better than you think. Just like I know Riley, Matt, and Dylan better than they think. Personally, I was surprised you didn't want me to sell it before you got back."

"I thought about it, but I need to have my own closure."

"Makes sense."

They were silent for a moment and Julian almost willed his manager to tell him something—anything— even if it wasn't what he wanted to hear.

"She's back in Phoenix," Mick said solemnly.

It was where Dena had been born and raised, so it wasn't really a surprise. "And?"

"And he's no longer employed."

"You mean with the label? Encore?"

"No. I mean anywhere," Mick clarified. "Word spread pretty fast after…well, after. Let's just say as of right now, he's not welcome at any of the big labels. In time, I'm sure he'll find work again, but for now, not so much."

The kicker was that Julian had actually liked the guy. He'd always been nice to everyone and was easy to work with, and even though they hadn't had a lot of interaction, Julian couldn't find a bad thing to say about his work.

On a personal level? That was another story.

Right now, all he wanted to do was sit down, but all the white furniture gave him pause. With a muttered curse, he walked into the kitchen and sat on one of the leather barstools by the massive granite island.

"So now what?" Julian asked with a sigh. "Do I need to be prepared for anything? Is Dena gonna come sniffing around? Does everyone think I'm the bad guy for the way it all went down?"

Mick laughed. An honest-to-goodness hearty laugh. "Julian, you're joking, right?"

Raking a hand through his black—and seriously overgrown—hair, Julian stiffened. "What?"

"I have been fielding calls about this since it happened—people wanting to interview you and get your story."

"And that's funny…why?"

Mick sighed loudly. "Because you had given me a heads up about what you were planning, I had things in place."

"What kind of things?"

"Things like talking to our legal team and our PR people. I knew Dena would immediately go to the press to play the victim, and I needed to make sure that didn't happen."

"So, what did you do?"

He let out a low chuckle. "It's not important right now. What I need to know is what you want to do from here. I have a house that's available for you to rent for the next three months if you want it. No pressure or anything. But if you want out of that place and you're not ready to go house hunting, this could be a solution."

He really didn't want to deal with house hunting or anything else right now, and even though, from what he could see, there was no trace of Dena in the house, it didn't matter. His brain remembered her everywhere in the space—new furniture or not. This offer was really a blessing.

Julian had known he would have to come home and deal with his life, but he certainly didn't have to stay and let it mock him.

"Text me the address," he said.

———∿∿∿———

There was efficient, and then there was Mick-efficient. As Julian stood on the deck staring out at the ocean two hours later, he had to admit his manager had outdone himself.

The rental house was right on the beach in Malibu. It was prime real estate and the house itself was magnificent. Three bedrooms, four bathrooms, and decorated for people who wanted to live in the house rather than use it for display. The moment he walked inside he had felt at home.

Something he hadn't felt in a long time.

Along with the address, Mick had informed him that the place was only lightly stocked, but there would be a housekeeper coming in tomorrow to do his shopping—all he had to do was give her a list of the things he liked. On top of that, she would come in twice a week to clean and would cook for him too if he wanted.

Not a bad deal at all.

Living here for the next several months certainly wasn't going to be a hardship, but he also knew he would have to start giving some serious thought to his future.

Part of the problem was how much he had isolated himself since walking out on his wedding. It was a completely selfish thing to do—after all, he did have a commitment to the band and they had all been talking about getting back into the studio. But even after all his soul-searching, he wasn't feeling much like making music. If he were honest, he would just admit that he was burned out. Besides all of his years with Shaughnessy, he had pulled double time trying to help Dena launch her own music career—which had failed. And on top of all of that, if it hadn't been for this career of his—his fame and notoriety—Julian wouldn't be in this position right now. Not the standing in a five-million-dollar home on the beach, but realizing how people weren't real or genuine. People would use you and betray you all because of who you were.

There was no way he was going to open himself up to that again.

Ever.

He'd made his fortune and invested well. There wasn't a doubt in his mind—especially after the past few months' nomadic life—that he could live comfortably for the rest of his life without stepping into a recording studio or up on a concert stage again. He knew he'd catch a lot of crap for it and he'd be disappointing some of the greatest people he'd ever known, but at the end of the day he needed to have peace for himself. And stepping back into the limelight meant he would always be looking at the people around him with suspicion and wondering who was going to stab him in the back next.

The guy in the video with Dena had been one of many, but he was the only one Julian could look at and know with any certainty who he was. How many others at the label or in his circle of friends and acquaintances in the music business had done the same thing with her? And what was worse, how many had looked him in the eye and lied to his face while sleeping with his girlfriend?

So yeah, he wasn't too keen on going back to his music career, because that trust was broken and he knew he had to be some sort of laughingstock. He prided himself on being a good person—an honest person—and the type of man who would be there for anyone who needed a hand. And just knowing that people knew—really knew—what Dena had been doing…well, it was almost too bitter a pill to swallow.

Had people warned him? Yes. Had anyone been willing to give names? No. Julian thought of his wedding day and how Riley had asked him if he was sure about going through with the ceremony. He sighed when he realized all the guys had been asking that for years—not about the wedding but about the relationship in general. How many conversations had they had as a group or one-on-one where they wondered why he would opt to stay in a relationship that was so clearly toxic?

Good question.

How many times had he asked himself the very same thing while riding across the country? And how many times had he come up with no real answers, only excuses?

The truth of the matter was that Julian had been raised to not be a quitter—to go after what he wanted and fight for it. He'd done it with so many different aspects of his life that when he met Dena and felt like he had been hit with love at first sight, he knew he'd do anything to make it work.

And he had.

To the point of turning into a damn joke.

It didn't matter how much you loved something, and whoever came up with the old adage *If you love something, set it free* was a true genius. If Julian had listened to that sooner, he could have saved himself a lot of pain and a lot of embarrassment. He could have saved himself from having to change his whole lifestyle so he wouldn't have to feel that way ever again.

With one last glance at the ocean, Julian turned to go back into the house. Entering the living room, he sat down and turned on the TV.

For several minutes, he simply channel surfed. That was something he hadn't done in ages. When he was home and not on tour, Julian spent his spare time either playing or writing music. He found that he hated being idle.

But right now, he didn't want to think.

He didn't want to feel.

And if he had his way, he wasn't going to any time soon.

The sun was coming up and Julian didn't remember seeing it go down. He'd been watching all kinds of boring documentaries since he'd first turned on the TV. Slowly he rose from the couch and stretched. With a quick glance around he spotted a clock and saw it was barely six a.m.

"To sleep or not to sleep," he murmured, walking toward the kitchen. "That is the question."

It didn't take long for him to realize he hadn't eaten anything the night before and there really weren't any options that were appealing for him to make now.

His body ached, and after three months of either camping out or sleeping in crappy motel rooms on lumpy beds, he needed a decent night's sleep in a real bed.

With a shrug, he slowly made his way to the master bedroom, stripped down, and slid beneath the sheets. Everything in him began to relax. He had forgotten what Egyptian cotton sheets felt like or how incredibly satisfying a soft pillow was.

It was the little things he was learning to appreciate, and as he closed his eyes, he felt at least a small sense of contentment.

But after three hours of tossing and turning and willing his brain to shut off, Julian gave up the fight to get some sleep. It was annoying as hell to realize that after staying up for over twenty-four hours straight, he just couldn't relax enough to sleep. Off in the distance he heard his phone ring and kicked the sheets off. Naked, he stalked to the living room and grabbed the phone from the coffee table just as it stopped ringing.

"Son of a bitch," he hissed. A minute later a text came through.

> **Mick**: Housekeeper not coming today. She'll
> be there Wednesday.

So much for the hope of just hanging around and not having to be responsible for anything. Just what he needed on top of his mental and physical exhaustion. Now he had to leave the house and actually go back into the real world.

To buy groceries.

If this was the start of his new life, it seriously sucked.

The line in the coffee shop was longer than usual, and Charlotte Clark was thrilled that she had no place pressing to be until later in the afternoon. It would have been even more thrilling if she didn't have to work on a Sunday, but that was the way it went. Being a vocational rehabilitation counselor had her working more hours than she would have imagined, and sometimes those hours weren't conventional.

Some of the people she found jobs for were fresh out of rehab or even prison, but most of the time they were simply people who were down on their luck.

Sort of like the guy standing in line in front of her. His clothes were rumpled, his hair was unkempt, and he looked like he hadn't shaved in a week. Silently she cursed herself for being judgmental. Maybe he was just a guy who didn't care about his appearance. That certainly wasn't a crime and she'd known many people like that, but everything about this guy had all of her senses on alert.

With a background in social work, Charlotte had learned to read people and notice things about them that maybe they were trying to hide or simply didn't want to share. If she had to venture a guess, she'd say this guy was tired and a little agitated. His posture and the way he kept shifting from one foot to another...and then the way he sighed—loudly—multiple times. Maybe it was the long line or the fact that the line wasn't moving that was bugging him, or maybe it was something else.

She shook her head and reminded herself that she needed to quit analyzing people so much. The guy was simply here to grab a cup of coffee, just like she was. End of story. And even if it wasn't, it wasn't any of her business. There was no way she could help everyone, and there certainly was no way she would approach a total stranger. How could she walk up to him and ask him if he realized that he needed to fix himself up a little bit?

Bad Charlotte! Ugh...she hated when she couldn't get out of this mode. It was a beautiful day outside and she should be thinking about finding something fun and relaxing to do. Later she'd need to go over to the homeless shelter in Santa Monica and meet with her group to see about setting up interviews for the coming week.

The line moved forward and she was relieved to see that she was almost to the front. Unkempt guy stepped up to order and she couldn't help but listen.

"Large black coffee," he snapped. "None of that overpriced fancy crap. Just your basic, regular coffee. Three sugars." He paused. "And let me get a blueberry muffin and...actually, make that two."

"Anything else?" the cashier asked.

He shook his head and waited.

At that point, Charlotte put her own focus on the menu board and thought a blueberry muffin sounded good too. Originally, she had only planned on getting herself a coffee—one of the overpriced fancy ones—and a fruit cup, but now that the idea of the muffin was there, she knew she'd be changing her order.

In front of her, the guy reached into his back pocket and cursed.

Loudly.

"Um…cancel my order," he told the cashier, his voice so low and deep it was almost a growl. "I forgot my wallet."

Without hesitation, Charlotte stepped forward and smiled at the young cashier. "Hi, Carly," she began, reading the girl's nametag, "if it's okay, you can add his order to mine." She was feeling pretty good about herself and her gesture, but when she turned and looked up at the man she was helping, she couldn't help but gasp.

Jet-black hair and silver eyes—which were currently glaring at her. There wasn't even a hint of a smile, and if anything, he was borderline snarling.

"What do you think you're doing?" he asked.

Charlotte had met enough people who were down on their luck to know that sometimes pride was a huge deterrent to them accepting help in any form. "I heard you say you had forgotten your wallet and just figured I'd help."

"Why?"

Her shoulders relaxed even as her smile grew and she laughed softly. "What do you mean, 'why'?"

"Ma'am?" the cashier asked. "What can I get you? The line's getting backed up."

"Oh, right. Sorry." Although she was a little miffed at being called "ma'am." At twenty-seven, she didn't consider herself old enough for *that* title, but she'd deal with that later. "I'll have a tall mocha Frappuccino and a blueberry muffin, please." Then she handed her credit card over before looking back at the angry man.

"I don't need anyone to buy me coffee," he growled.

Undeterred, she smiled and accepted her card back from the cashier. "Oh, please. I know I get cranky when I can't have my coffee, and you look like you could use it. It's not a big deal. Really." She stepped around him to go wait at the other end of the counter for their order. For a minute, she didn't think he would follow, and she had to hide her smile when he finally did.

"I could have just gone and grabbed my wallet and come back," he argued. His voice was low, but there was still heat in it.

She shrugged and offered him a smile. "Now you don't have to."

They stood in silence until their order was placed on the counter, and Charlotte thanked the barista and then smiled at the man. He still hadn't picked up his coffee or muffins, and she wondered just how stubborn he was going to be.

"Look, if it bothers you that much, just…pay it forward," she said.

"Pay it what?"

"Forward. You know, next time you're in line and notice someone in need of a hand, help them out." Her smile broadened even as he looked at her as if she were crazy. "Anyway, enjoy and have a great day!"

Without waiting for an answer, she walked out of the coffee shop and across the street toward the park benches, where she could sit and see the beach and enjoy the fresh air. It was a beautiful day out and there was no way she wanted to waste it sitting inside.

Sitting down, she pulled the muffin out of the bag and was about to break off a piece when someone sat down beside her.

Her unkempt man.

With her sunglasses on, she was certain he couldn't read her surprise, and she did her best to sound casual as she asked, "Would you like to join me?" For the life of her, she had no idea why she would even suggest such a thing. It was obvious he was annoyed with her, and really, just because she tended to be trusting didn't mean it was always the right thing to do. For all of her speculation, she had no idea who this man was.

"What is your deal?" he asked a little suspiciously, but not snarling or growling nearly as much as he had been inside the coffee shop.

"My deal?"

He nodded. "Why'd you buy my breakfast? What's it to you if I didn't have my wallet?"

For a moment Charlotte could only stare. Was this guy for real? Here she was doing a nice thing and he was giving her crap for it?

"It was just coffee and a couple of muffins," she reasoned pleasantly. "It wasn't a big deal, and like I said, just pay it forward."

That should have been the end of it, but considering he didn't move or say anything, she figured it wasn't.

Now she started to feel a little uneasy.

Looking around, she tried to see how many people were nearby. It was early and people were out walking on the sidewalk and down on the sand, so she relaxed. She could handle this.

"What is it you want from me?" he finally asked, his scowl back in place.

Charlotte frowned at him. "Excuse me?"

He sighed in agitation. "You heard me. What is it you want? You want me to sign something?"

Sign something? What the...?

"Look, Mr....?" She paused and waited for him to fill in the blank, but when he didn't, she was the one to sigh. "I'm Charlotte, by the way. Charlotte Clark. I'd prefer not to keep calling you 'angry guy' in my head." And when he still didn't answer, she stuffed her muffin back in the bag, grabbed her coffee, and stood. "I honestly didn't mean to offend you, okay? I just thought it would be a nice thing to do and then we'd both be on our way—me feeling good and you feeling thankful. Obviously, I was wrong. So... I'm sorry if I was mistaken, and if you'll excuse me, I'm going to go and enjoy my breakfast elsewhere."

Her heart was hammering in her chest as she moved around him and walked back along the sidewalk to the crosswalk in hopes of finding someplace else to sit and eat. The whole time she complained in her head, because she seriously enjoyed sitting and watching the waves crash and all the sights and smells of the beach.

Stupid angry guy messing with my good morning.

Standing on the corner, she waited for the signal to change when she felt someone walk up beside her. She didn't even have to turn her head to know it was him.

"Julian," he said gruffly and Charlotte had to hide her smile. She was used to dealing with some belligerent people, and it was always satisfying when they had that moment where they started to trust her.

This was that moment for her.

Looking up at him, she said, "It's nice to meet you, Julian." A last name would have been nice, but for now she'd take what she could get.

He nodded. "So…are you going back to eat by the coffee shop?"

"Well, I normally sit and enjoy my coffee while watching the waves crash, but…"

Another nod. "Sorry I ruined that for you. You should go back and do that. I…" He paused and Charlotte got the impression he wanted to say more but didn't know how.

Unable to help herself, she was instantly in social-worker mode. Touching his arm gently, she shifted so she was facing him. "If you'd like to join me, that would be okay."

It was clearly the wrong thing to say, because he stiffened and the snarl was back.

"Or not," she quickly added and stepped away. And without another glance at him, she turned and walked back to the bench. She primly sat down and took a sip of her coffee before pulling out her muffin and taking a huge bite.

Normally, she would pick at such a large item, but she was annoyed and frustrated and just… *Gah!* Why did people have to be so distrusting? It was just a friendly gesture; why was she being punished for it?

Her jaw almost hurt from chewing so hard and fast and when she finally swallowed, she had to force herself to take several deep breaths—to let herself simply inhale the sea air that she loved so much—and relax. Closing her eyes, she let her head fall back and willed some of the tension to leave her body.

When she straightened and took another sip of her coffee, she felt more like herself. Overhead the seagulls flew and made their noises, in front of her people walked and talked and laughed, and in the background were the waves—the glorious sound of the waves, which never ceased to calm her.

Out of the corner of her eye, she saw Julian slowly walking toward her. A few minutes ago, this would have pleased her, but right now she wanted to tell him to go away. And she totally could—he wasn't one of her clients. She didn't owe him anything. As a matter of fact, *he* owed *her*. And when he went to sit down beside her, she held up a hand to stop him.

"There are, like, a hundred other places for you to go and sit," she said curtly. "And I would appreciate it if you would."

He was a big man—easily over six feet tall—and with his broad chest and muscled arms, he could have been some sort of linebacker. Add the scowl into the mix and he was beyond intimidating. Standing at only five-six herself, she knew better than to get up and try to intimidate him into moving away.

But she was tempted.

"Can we just…start over?" he asked.

Now? Now he wanted to start over?

"Please," he added, and that was when he had her. She was a sucker for someone who seemed to know when they were wrong and tried to make amends. Everyone deserved a second chance and Julian was no different. Without a word, she motioned to the space beside her, but immediately went back to her meal—opting to pick at the muffin this time rather than biting into it again.

They sat in silence for a solid five minutes as they each ate and sipped at their coffees. She heard him groan with appreciation several times, and she had to wonder if it had been a while since he'd had a decent meal. So many questions sprang to mind—things she asked all of her applicants—but she was afraid to voice any of them and risk upsetting him again.

Beside her, Julian put the muffin wrappers back into the bag they'd come in and gulped down the rest of his coffee. Charlotte figured he was done and would get up and leave and that would be the end of it.

"Thank you for breakfast," he said quietly, looking at the waves, just as she'd been doing.

"You're welcome."

"I'll pay you back if you want. I don't live far from here."

That was surprising. They were in Malibu—one of the nicest communities on the coast—and he lived here? Looking like this?

Stop judging! she admonished herself.

"It's fine. Really," she said. "We've been over this."

Silence.

Deciding to let herself admire the view for a few more minutes, she finished up her muffin and placed the wrapper and napkin back in the bag, and then slowly sipped her coffee.

Unfortunately, her mind wouldn't shut up and she couldn't help but start talking again.

"You looked like you needed it," she said and glanced over at him. "I could tell you were annoyed at the long wait and you look tired and…I don't know. It just seemed like it was one of those situations where it was kind of a big deal to have to cancel your order."

And for the first time, she caught a hint of a smile on Julian's face.

Aha! she thought.

"Let's just say it was par for the course," he said after a minute.

I knew it.

"Sometimes it certainly feels like that," she agreed. "And it's usually the little things that can set you off, like not getting your morning cup of coffee."

"You have no idea."

"But I do!" she replied earnestly. "I deal with this sort of thing all the time."

"You often miss your morning cup of coffee and want to snap?" he asked with a small grin.

She laughed. "No, but I work with people who feel like everything is working against them and just need a little help to get back on their feet."

He looked at her oddly.

"I'm a vocational rehabilitation counselor."

"Um…I have no idea what that is," he said flatly.

"I help people find jobs—homeless people, some who have just gotten out of rehab or prison—that sort of thing." She paused. "When I meet them, they're all overwhelmed and feeling like they don't know what to do or where to begin, and sometimes it's the little things that throw them off the ledge, if you know what I mean."

Nodding, Julian studied her for a long moment. "That

sounds like it can be a challenge. Do you always find these people jobs?"

"Usually I do. They're not always permanent jobs, but I get them working. That gives them the confidence they need to rejoin society. Having a job is so important— not just for financial reasons but for our self-esteem and mental well-being too."

He shrugged. "Maybe. But jobs aren't always the answer."

"For the people I work with, they are," she countered. "When someone needs to put a roof over their head or feed their family, a job is always the answer."

He didn't look convinced.

"Do you have a job, Julian?" she asked.

There was a flash of something in his eyes, but it was gone before Charlotte could begin to analyze it. "I'm in between jobs right now," he said stiffly.

She *knew* there was a reason she was drawn to him. He needed help and he was too proud to ask for it. It was as if she was divinely put in his path today!

"There's no shame in that," she said compassionately, reaching out and touching his arm again. They were nice arms—sculpted and tanned and…strong. Immediately she forced herself not to focus on that, because as attractive as Julian was, she wasn't going to help him by flirting with him. That wasn't what he needed. What he needed was someone who could help him find work and get his life back on track. "I meet people in the same situation all the time. If you're interested, I'm working with a group later this afternoon. We'll be going over job listings and talking about how to apply for specific types of jobs, and then we'll be doing some brief training."

"What kind of training?"

"Today we're working over at the homeless shelter in Santa Monica. We'll be helping unload trucks for the food kitchen, and it's mostly manual labor and cleaning. But it's an honest day's work and will leave you with a sense of accomplishment."

Julian looked at her as if she were crazy. "You're asking me if I want to work at a homeless shelter?"

Nodding, Charlotte explained, "And I can help you look for jobs in your area of expertise. What is it you used to do...you know...before you got laid off?"

His eyes went wide. "Who said I got laid off?" he asked defensively.

"Well, you said you were between jobs. I just assumed..." And then she stopped. "Sorry. That was wrong of me. I don't know why it is that you're between jobs." And then she waited for an explanation that never came.

"Santa Monica's about twenty miles from here," he said finally.

"We offer a shuttle if you need it, or I can give you bus fare. If you really want to go, that is."

Those gray eyes were still wide. "Now you're offering me bus fare?"

Charlotte couldn't help but laugh. "Oh... I guess after seeing how you reacted to the coffee and muffins, I should know better, right?"

Luckily, Julian laughed with her. "You would think."

"Well, I'll tell you what," she began and reached into her purse and pulled out a pen and a business card. Writing down the address, she handed it to him. "This is where I'll be today at four. If you'd like to come and join us, great. If not, that's fine too. On the front is my business number, and if you would like help with your job search, please feel free to call."

Standing, she finished the last of her coffee and felt much better about how the morning had gone. Turning toward Julian, she smiled. "I need to get going. I'm sorry we got off on the wrong foot, but I'm glad we met." Reaching out her hand to him, she added, "It was nice meeting you, Julian, and I wish you luck with finding a job. If there's anything I can do to help…"

Just then he stood and took her hand in his and—holy crap.

His hand was huge and warm and it completely wrapped around hers. Charlotte knew she wasn't a particularly petite woman, but this man certainly made her feel that way.

"Um…" she stammered and tried to pull her hand gently from his. "Maybe I'll see you later today."

Julian didn't release her right away and when he did, her fingers grazed his palm; his skin was rough. She had to wonder what it was he used to do for a living.

Liar. You're curious how that rough skin would feel on other parts of your body.

Okay…maybe.

He didn't respond other than to say, "It was nice meeting you, Charlotte," and then he turned and walked down toward the beach. Part of her wanted to follow him and see where he went. He certainly wasn't dressed for the beach—not that there was a required wardrobe or anything—but she was still curious about what his story was.

Walking over to a trash can, she tossed her cup and

bag and walked closer to the steps leading down to the sand to watch him for a little longer. He was heading down toward the more residential side of the beach. She looked down and sighed at the sight of the houses. They were magnificent but frivolous, she thought. All that money could go to so many other things—things that would help the less fortunate.

Then again, wouldn't she love to wake up to the sound of the waves every day if she could? The answer was a very enthusiastic "Hell yes!" So really, who was she to judge? For all she knew, the owners of those houses donated to charity and did volunteer work in their spare time. Just because she couldn't personally afford to live in that kind of luxury didn't mean she should begrudge those who could.

With her eyes still down on the sand and watching Julian in her peripheral vision, she gasped when he stopped and turned around and seemed to look right at her. It wasn't really possible to tell from this distance, but she could almost swear he was smirking—as if he knew she'd still be standing there watching him. While it would have been easy to pretend she hadn't seen him and turn and walk away, she couldn't make herself move.

And when he started walking back toward her, she knew she definitely couldn't walk away. Had he changed his mind about the bus fare? Did he have a question about accepting her help in finding work?

When he came off the last step, they were about ten feet apart. Julian looked at her with amusement—she knew it!—and said, "I thought you said you had to go?"

"I…I do," she said nervously. "But I was just enjoying the view."

He quirked a dark brow at her and she realized how that sounded—especially since she had been watching him.

"I mean… I was just about to leave when I saw you heading back this way. Did you need something?"

Stepping closer, he said, "I guess I wanted to know more about what you do."

Relief washed over her. He wanted her help. He trusted her.

She'd only said she had to leave earlier because she didn't want to push or overwhelm him. There were still many hours until she had to leave for work.

"What would you like to know?"

With the serious look she was coming to associate with him, he considered her for a moment. "Would you like to walk on the beach while we talk?"

Ooo…walking with her toes in the sand was her second-favorite thing to do, after listening to the sound of the waves. Not wanting to sound too giddy, she shrugged. "Sure. That sounds fine." This was just like one of her interviews, except it was the first time she was conducting one while doing one of her favorite things.

It felt odd and yet…right.

Julian motioned toward the steps and they climbed down. At the bottom, Charlotte slipped off her sandals and stepped into the sand.

"Mmm…"

Her hand almost flew over her mouth when she realized she'd made the sound. How professional of it was her to be making noises like that?

Beside her, Julian smirked. "Like the feel of the sand between your toes, huh?"

Laughing softly, she said, "Guilty."

They began to walk and Julian spoke first. "So, how does one become a vocational rehabilitation counselor?"

Okay, that wasn't what she expected, but she was more than willing to talk to him about it if it meant he was going to trust her.

"I started out as a social worker," she began. "Actually, I went to school to be a psychologist and ended up in social work. So many of the people I met had the same issues—their lives would just seem better or would get better if they had a job. Now, there are employment agencies out there and that's all fine and well, but it's not always as simple as 'You're hired,' you know?"

Julian nodded.

"I just have a passion for this sort of thing. When I was growing up, my father got laid off and it took him years to find work. We struggled and had to go on public assistance, and I watched my once-confident father transform into this meek and almost pitiful person. His self-esteem was gone, and he went from making a decent living and supporting his family to doing menial labor and feeling ashamed. I don't want to see that happen to someone. There should never be any shame or guilt for working to support your family. Every job is an honest job."

"Well, that's not entirely true," he argued lightly. "There are some pretty shady job choices out there."

"True, but I'd like to think that with the right support network in place, people have the opportunity to avoid having to make those choices."

They strolled at a leisurely pace, and Charlotte knew she had to wait Julian out. If he was going to share anything about himself, it would be when he was ready. She went for idle conversation—the weather, the number of people on the beach, that sort of thing. As they got closer to a cluster of houses, she couldn't help but sigh.

"Something wrong?" he asked.

She shook her head. "Not really. It's just…" She motioned to the houses. "Look at them. I mean, I can only imagine the cost to live in someplace as magnificent as that—and these aren't even the really exclusive ones."

"Really exclusive?"

"You know, the ones with private beaches that cost probably ten million dollars and you're not allowed to look at them because you're not rich enough," she said with a laugh.

Beside her, Julian laughed too. "Somehow I don't think it's quite like that."

"Probably not, but you know what I mean. It doesn't seem possible that people actually live like that." She paused before adding, "Why do they get the best views of the beach when us mere mortals can't?"

When Julian didn't respond, she figured he probably felt the same way too, but it wasn't something that was of any real concern to him.

"So, what about you?" she finally asked, her curiosity getting the better of her.

"What about me?" he asked slowly, quietly.

"What is it you used to do before you found yourself between jobs?"

Silence.

They kept walking, but Julian looked straight ahead without uttering a word. Okay, message received; he wasn't ready to talk about it yet.

Up ahead Charlotte spotted a sandcastle someone had obviously put a lot of time and effort into before having to leave it. "Ooo…look at that," she said in awe. It stood about three feet high and had a lot of details—although some of it had collapsed since its completion. "I've always wondered how people can do this. It takes such skill and patience." She looked over her shoulder at him and smiled. "Something I certainly lack at times."

"I would imagine patience is an important part of your job," Julian commented.

"That part, yes. I kind of have the patience of a saint. At least, that's what my parents tell me," she said lightly. "I'm not artistic at all. I am an analytical thinker. I like solving problems. But to create something with my hands? Totally not my thing."

"Have you ever tried?"

This time her laugh was loud and hearty. "More than you know! Oh my goodness…I've tried pottery, painting, quilting, knitting—both of my grandmothers were fantastic knitters and they tried for most of my life to teach me—but I'm not coordinated enough for it. Or anything like it, apparently."

"Maybe you just haven't found your medium," he said as he walked around and examined the castle. "Not everyone figures it out when they're young. My mother always thought she wasn't artistic, but we were on vacation a couple of years ago and she started taking pictures. She mentioned that she thought photography looked interesting and I encouraged her to try it. Now she takes the most amazing pictures. And I'm not talking about just snapping shots of friends and family. She can go anywhere and capture something that no one else probably noticed and make it look beautiful."

Charlotte straightened and looked at him. The way he

spoke, the passion in his voice, told her how much his relationship with his mother meant to him. She could hear the affection and pride even if he wasn't aware of it. It sounded like they had an amazing relationship.

"Thank you for sharing that with me," she said softly.

In that moment, Julian seemed to realize what she meant and he looked away almost as if he hadn't meant to tell her so much.

She looked out at the ocean and inhaled deeply. If she could, she'd sit out here all day and not think about anything except how good the breeze felt, but that wasn't going to happen. At least not today.

Pulling her phone from her purse, she checked the time and knew she was right. By the time she walked back to her car, stopped at the grocery store, and went home to start her laundry, it would almost be time to head to work.

Maybe there'd come a time when she wouldn't schedule herself for these weekend sessions, but right now she really had nothing else to do with her time. Her parents had moved to New Mexico last year, her siblings were all married and scattered all over the country, and she wasn't currently dating anyone. So, while she had the time and there was a need, she didn't mind doing it.

Looking at Julian, she saw he was studying her again. His gaze was intense, his brow furrowed. She couldn't help but wonder what he'd look like if he actually relaxed and smiled.

She'd bet good money that he had a great smile.

"I should get going," she said finally, explaining all the things she needed to do. "You have my card and if you'd like some help with job placement, please don't hesitate to call me."

He nodded.

"And if you have the time and a way to get there, we could always use the extra help at the shelter today."

Another nod.

Conversation clearly wasn't his thing.

Stepping closer, she held out her hand to him again. "Thanks for the walk on the beach."

This time when he nodded, there was a small smile to go along with it.

Baby steps.

He took her hand in his, and just as earlier, it was big and warm and…yummy.

And it was completely inappropriate for her to be thinking about *that*.

"Take care of yourself, Julian," she said, and slowly removed her hand from his.

"You too, Charlotte," he said, and something about the way he said her name made her inappropriate thought of a moment ago seem tame. His voice was deep and rich and a little rumbly and…yummy.

She was going to blame the use of that word on the muffin and the fact that his breakfast order had prompted her to have sweets for breakfast—something she rarely did—but she knew she was only kidding herself. The man was yumminess personified. Not that it mattered; if she did happen to see him again, it would be in a purely professional capacity and she needed to remember that. She'd never been faced with this kind of situation where she found herself attracted to a client, but she was fairly certain there had to be rules about such things.

With a smile and a wave, Charlotte forced herself to turn and walk away. It wasn't until she was almost back to the steps that she allowed herself to turn around one last time.

And gasped softly when she saw Julian was standing exactly where she'd left him—watching her.

Chapter 2

WHAT THE HELL AM I THINKING?

Five hours later, Julian found himself standing outside the outreach center in downtown Santa Monica asking himself that—and not for the first time since he'd decided to go.

But there'd been something about Charlotte Clark, with her long, wavy brown hair and brilliant blue eyes. When he'd first seen her at the coffee line, he had found himself momentarily tongue-tied. And more than a little stunned that he would feel such a strong pull of attraction to anyone right now.

At first, he'd thought there was no way someone would step up and pay for his breakfast without wanting something from him. It wasn't possible. It had happened too many times before—a beautiful girl wanting to buy him a drink in hopes of endearing herself to him. He thought she had recognized him and hoped by paying for his order he'd be so grateful that he'd do something for her—an autograph, a picture, or who knew what else. He'd heard and been asked for it all before.

But she didn't ask for a damn thing. If anything, she had seemed so genuinely concerned about him that he couldn't quite comprehend it. Once he mentally counted to ten and got his initial rage under control, it didn't take long for him to realize she didn't have a clue who he was. That did happen from time to time—as the drummer in a band, Julian was sometimes in the background. Honestly, not being front and center in Shaughnessy was a perk for him. Especially while he'd been on the road for the last several months. Very few people recognized him now.

And that's when he decided that maybe—just maybe—he could let down his guard a little bit.

Before life had gotten so complicated—or maybe he should say before he was forced to accept all the ways his life had gotten so out of control—Julian never had a problem with being suspicious of everything and everyone. Early in his career with the band, it had been fun when people wanted to buy them a drink or dinner. Unfortunately, once they hit it big, things like that were no longer a friendly gesture; they were the means to an end. Riley, Matt, and Dylan never seemed to have a problem with it, but after a while it had started to grate on Julian's nerves. He didn't care if someone wanted something from him, he just would prefer they be honest and up front about it.

"Because he's Julian Grayson and he's rich—and I want to be rich."

Yeah. That one statement played on an almost constant loop in his head no matter how hard he tried to stop it. There was honesty for you. It wasn't honesty to his face, but it had ended up there anyway.

Maybe there'd come a time when he'd get over it—not just Dena's words and actions, but his near-obsessive distrust of pretty much everyone. Man, he hoped so. The constant tension and negative energy was slowly making him insane. The isolation wasn't bothering him, but not even being able to relax enough to enjoy it was.

Pacing away from the building, Julian pulled out his phone and decided he needed a minute to get himself under control. He needed to calm down before going inside and doing…he still didn't know what.

Scrolling through his contacts, he pulled up Riley's number and hit it.

"Julian!" Riley said excitedly as he answered. "You're back!"

Unable to help himself, he laughed, because it felt good to know there were people who were genuinely concerned about him and his well-being. He'd been so determined not to feel anything for so long that it was a little weird to feel this good about his friend's reaction.

"Yeah, man. I'm back," he said gruffly as he kept walking.

"So, how are you? You doing okay? You back in LA?"

"Actually, I'm staying in Malibu right now."

"Ah," Riley said knowingly. "Mick mentioned he had a place on hold for you there."

There was no point in bringing up his reasons for moving; Riley was fully in the know about all of that. "I was relieved to have the option. I didn't think it was going to be a big deal to be home, but…"

"It was," Riley finished for him. "And I can't blame you. I remember Dylan saying the same thing. Maybe some people can just go back and pick up where they left off and reason how it's just a house, but it's not. It's a place that holds memories—good and bad."

"Exactly."

"But seriously, Jules, how are you?"

He shrugged even though his friend couldn't see him.

"I thought I was doing okay," he admitted honestly, "but…now I'm not so sure."

"Uh-oh. What happened?"

Julian explained about his meeting with Charlotte this morning. Looking back, he realized it was wrong to be so evasive with her. After all, the last thing he needed was a…what did she call herself…a vocational rehabilitation advisor? He didn't need a job and he didn't particularly want one.

So what was he doing here?

And that's exactly what Riley asked him.

"Maybe I'm just bored."

Riley laughed.

"What's so damn funny?"

"Because you're never bored. In all the years we've known each other, you're the one who is always doing something. There were times I felt exhausted just watching you or listening to all of the things you would do— writing music, playing music, producing music. I swear, for the longest time I thought you couldn't possibly be human because it seemed like you never slept. So really, I don't think you're bored, exactly. If anything, you hate to just sit and relax."

"I've been doing nothing but sitting and relaxing for three months," Julian reminded him.

"Not really. You've been running away from your demons. Not the same thing."

That was one way of looking at it, he supposed. Still… "Not without good reason. But that's neither here nor there. Now that I'm back, I'm sort of unsure what I want to do."

"Why don't we get together and hang out tomorrow?

I'll call Dylan and he can join us, and I know Matt's back in North Carolina right now, but maybe he can fly out one day next week and we can all get together and jam. What do you think?"

He thought the way his heart was hammering that he was going to pass out.

Even though Julian had felt fairly certain he was ready to walk away from this part of his life—playing music—telling his bandmates wasn't going to be easy. And he didn't even want the temptation of getting behind a set of drums right now. He didn't want to think about doing it again—playing, opening himself back up to the type of people who had betrayed him—and yet he didn't want to hurt Riley's feelings. Or Dylan's, or Matt's, or even Mick's. Although he was fairly certain their manager suspected it was coming.

He just didn't want to get into it all right now.

"How about we just deal with tomorrow and we'll talk about the rest?" he said after a minute.

"I understand."

And while Riley was probably the most levelheaded guy Julian had ever known and he'd dealt with his own anxiety where music was concerned, there was no way he could fully understand what Julian was dealing with. It was impossible. Mainly because he couldn't explain it himself.

"So let's get back to what it is you're doing right now," Riley said, interrupting his thoughts. "Why are you there at this homeless shelter? I mean, not that it's a bad thing—volunteer work is awesome—but somehow I don't think this is all about you doing your good deed for the day. What made you decide to drive to Santa Monica for this?"

His immediate response—even though he didn't say it out loud—was Charlotte. She just…

Raking a hand through his hair, he sighed. There was something about her that made it impossible for him to just walk away and never see her again. And besides, it wasn't like he had anything to do today. What was the harm in volunteering at a homeless shelter? There were worse ways for him to spend his time.

"I don't know. The chick seemed so passionate about what she was talking about that I was curious."

It wasn't a total lie.

"Okay, so this is about doing a good deed," Riley said casually. "There's nothing wrong with that."

"I know," Julian replied, a little defensively.

Riley chuckled. "You seem a little on edge for a guy just looking to do something nice. You sure that's all there is to it?"

"What else would there be?"

"Jules, how long have we known each other?"

"Over a decade."

"Exactly. Granted, for the second half of that decade you were involved with Dena and I spent most of the time scratching my head wondering what you were doing, but overall I think I know you pretty well."

"Is this going anywhere?" he asked, hoping he sounded bored and not annoyed.

"I think maybe it's about the girl a little more than it's about the deed."

There were so many things on the tip of Julian's tongue and yet he couldn't get the words out. Riley was right. This was about Charlotte, and it freaked him out more than it should. He knew that, but he didn't know why.

With a huff of agitation, Julian said, "Look, I should go. We'll talk about this tomorrow."

Luckily Riley didn't push him and they agreed on a time, and when he hung up, he had to wonder if he'd have any answers by then.

Julian looked up and down the street and realized this wasn't a particularly great part of town. He'd parked several blocks away at a parking garage because...well, partly because this wasn't a great part of town and partly because he knew if Charlotte saw his Mercedes SUV she'd have some questions for him.

And he wasn't prepared to answer them just yet.

Not that he owed her—or anyone—an explanation. He was here to do a good thing and that's all that mattered.

Slowly he made his way back up the street and stood in front of the center. It was a rundown-looking place—faded brick facade, dirty glass windows and doors. The small green space in front was neatly manicured, but other than that, it didn't look all that welcoming. Maybe that was intentional—this was a functional space to help people temporarily and they didn't want it to look so appealing that you'd want to stay for the long-term. Although he couldn't imagine anyone wanting to stay homeless. Sometimes that was the unfairness of life: you were thrust into circumstances beyond your control and ended up living the life you never imagined.

Fortunately, there were places like this and people like Charlotte to help you. He was taken from his reverie by the door opening, and much to his surprise, Charlotte stepped out. Her blue eyes widened, as did her smile when she spotted him.

"Julian," she said with a hint of surprise. "I'm so glad you decided to come." She looked up one side of the block and down the other before looking back at him. "Did you have a hard time getting here?"

"Not at all," he replied. *GPS makes getting anywhere easy.*

"I'm so glad. We're just waiting for a few people, but you're more than welcome to come inside and get something to eat and drink. We've got some coffee and doughnuts set up for the meeting, so please help yourself."

"I'm good," he said. "But thank you."

"I was just coming out to see if anyone else had arrived. We're due to start in five minutes."

There really wasn't anything he could say to that so he just stood with her and waited. After a minute he asked, "So…how does this all work? Do you unload the truck first or do your class first?"

Tucking her hair behind her ear, she looked at him and seemed pleased that he was initiating the conversation. "We'll start out with the class. We have a room set up with a conference table and a whiteboard, and computer stations around the perimeter. We'll spend the first thirty minutes talking about the progress everyone's made in the last week, and I'll answer any questions the first-timers may have. Afterward, we'll spend an hour applying for and setting up as many interviews as possible. Once the hour is up, we'll head back to the loading dock and help with the truck and whatever else is needed."

Julian was about to ask her if he could just skip the class and go directly to the labor, but she started talking again.

"I think you'll find the class very helpful. Part of the problem so many people struggle with is looking for the kind of job they want." She paused when he looked at her like she was crazy. After all, what was wrong with going after the kind of job you want?

Then she continued. "Sometimes it's important to start with something you might be overqualified for just to get back into the workforce. And then—in time— build up to a job that is maybe more on your level."

"Seems to me you're asking people to sell themselves short," he commented. "Why not encourage them to apply for a job they're qualified for that offers training so there's a chance for advancement?"

"Because right now most of the people I work with are homeless or don't have a wardrobe or even transportation to get them to and from a job. I don't want anyone to get discouraged or have any excuses. If they can start at something—anything—and start collecting a paycheck, soon they'll be able to look into buying the clothes they need to go on interviews with a place that is maybe more on their level of expertise. Not everyone who comes here is ready to go to work in the corporate world."

"I suppose."

"Believe it or not, it's taking the first step that truly is the hardest. We tend to build up these scenarios of self-doubt in our minds and think we can't possibly overcome the hard circumstances and it paralyzes us."

"Us?" he asked.

She smiled and laughed softly. "You know what I mean. I'm speaking figuratively, not literally. The fear of failure truly stops so many people from doing what needs to be done. For example, you take a family who is homeless due to the husband losing his job. He'll struggle with a lot of emotions over that and his family having no place to live. And for some people, they can't move past that to take the step to find another job."

"Why?"

"Mainly because they think they have to find a job exactly like the one they had before. Pride has a lot to do with it," she explained. "But with some counseling and guidance, we have a great success rate. It may not be exactly what they had before, but that's something they can work toward if they truly want to."

It made sense when she explained it like that. Julian had never been poor and his family had never struggled with unemployment, so this was all foreign to him. His father had worked as an accountant for thirty years and his mother had been a stay-at-home mom for most of his life and was now enjoying being a photographer. One career for each. And before the band had hit it big, Julian had worked for a landscaping company. He'd never been fired or laid off—he simply left when the band got a recording contract.

"So how do these people live? I mean, let's say you help them find a job but they're living here at the shelter. How do they make it work when they have to start over from scratch? I would think that in itself would be overwhelming."

"Oh, it is! But we're lucky we have a donation center where people donate everything from clothing and furniture to dishes and all kinds of housewares. It's available to everyone, and by the time most people are ready to sign a lease on an apartment, we have enough here to help them at least begin to furnish their new home."

"But what if they need more? How can they possibly do it all if they're working at a fast food restaurant making minimum wage and have a family to support?"

Julian had no idea why he was asking so many questions, except now that this kind of situation was brought to his attention, he was curious. Although, knowing what Charlotte thought about him, he was pretty sure she believed he was asking for his own personal reasons.

Before she could answer, three men turned the corner, and he saw by the way Charlotte seemed to relax that these were the ones she was waiting for.

"Carl! Derek! George! I'm so glad you were able to come!"

And with that, they all walked inside for class.

It wasn't like her to be so distracted, and yet Charlotte was.

It didn't matter what she was doing or saying, she could feel Julian's eyes on her. He didn't ask any questions and he didn't offer to answer any of hers, so she just chalked it up to him wanting to observe. That was fine and well, but she couldn't help sneaking glances his way and every time she did, he caught her doing it.

Focus, Charlotte!

After she had spent the first part of the class talking, she assigned everyone a computer station. She'd offered one to Julian and he'd sat down at it, but she noticed he didn't search or apply for anything. Maybe he was nervous, because it couldn't be that he didn't understand the instructions. It had been her intention to go and sit with him and ask if he needed help, but it seemed like tonight was the night of a million questions from everyone else. And each time she happened to glance in Julian's direction, he was watching her intently.

When the timer on her phone went off, letting her know classroom time was over, she almost sagged with relief. At least now when they went to help out with the truck, she would be too busy to be so aware of him.

Only…if anything, now she was even *more* aware of him.

The man had muscles and he wasn't afraid to use them.

He could have unloaded the truck by himself. There didn't seem to be anything he couldn't—or wouldn't—do. He was mesmerizing to watch, and although she had at least a hundred things she could be doing, she found herself stopping to watch Julian lift and carry boxes.

And wishing there was a second truck to unload.

"CeeCee!" someone called out, and Charlotte immediately turned around. "What time do you need the room on Thursday?"

Hank Carter ran the center and she knew he had her schedule—she always gave it to him a month in advance—but he had a tendency to seek her out to confirm and reconfirm. Walking toward him, she gave him a patient smile. "I'm planning to come in at two on Thursday, Hank," she said. "I believe we already have a dozen people signed up for the workshop but there is plenty of room for more, so if you know of anyone and want to send them my way, please do."

"You're such a blessing to the people here, CeeCee," he said warmly. She wasn't fond of the nickname, but she never argued over it. "We had three new families arrive last night, and we gave them all of your information so you should be expecting to hear from them, possibly before Thursday."

For the next fifteen minutes, he gave her a brief overview of each of their situations. The wheels in her mind were already turning as she thought of ways to help them immediately.

"Have them reach out to me first thing tomorrow," she said, feeling hopeful. "I'll be in the office at eight and we'll get right to work on their cases."

"You're amazing," he replied. "I wish everyone was as involved as you."

"Thanks, Hank." With a smile and a wave, Charlotte went to go and check on the progress of the truck being unloaded.

Or maybe she was just going to look at Julian.

"Charlotte!" someone else called out as soon as she began walking toward the loading dock. Why did she think she could just go and stare at someone when her time at the center was usually spent talking to the residents and staff and helping put out fires seemingly everywhere?

For the first time in years, she almost resented the intrusion. She had her own work to do just like everyone else, and yet it seemed to her like nothing got done until she was here on-site. It was something she'd been dying to talk to Hank about, but she didn't know how to do it without it sounding as if she was trying to tell him how to do his job.

Which, let's face it, I would.

For the next two hours, she spoke with one of the new families, set up appointments for some one-on-one career counseling, and had more than enough to do to keep her from checking on Julian or the progress of the truck. By the time she was finally able to get back to it, the loading bay door was closing and the only one around was Hank.

Darn. Had she missed saying goodbye?

"Hey, CeeCee," Hank said as he turned and walked toward her. "Great job tonight. We got so much accomplished. The new guy who joined your group— Julian?—he was a tremendous help."

"Really?" she asked, wanting to be pleased, but she was also curious.

Nodding, Hank explained. "He helped unload the entire truck, and when that was done, he helped Gladys and Mark move all the boxes of donations that arrived yesterday. It required quite a bit of rearranging in the back storage room. We just told Julian what we needed, and he did it."

Brow furrowed, Charlotte had to wonder where the heck everyone else was if Julian was doing all the work. Which was what she asked Hank.

"Oh, the other guys all helped with sweeping up and breaking down the pallets and boxes from the food delivery. This is the best this place has looked in a while."

And it made her smile. It was nice to know she could do something to help make a difference, and she instantly felt bad for feeling so put-upon earlier.

"So what's his situation?" Hank asked. "How long has he been out of a job?"

Charlotte shrugged. "Honestly, I have no idea. He hasn't said. I just met him this morning and mentioned what we were going to be doing here tonight. I was kind of surprised when he showed up." She paused.

"Normally I can get a good read on people, but he's not an easy case at all."

"Some people are like that." Hank studied her for a moment with a patient smile. "You know you can't work miracles with everyone. And not everyone has so many layers that you need to take it upon yourself to go through."

"Maybe…"

And while she knew Hank had a point, she didn't think it applied to Julian. She knew enough about people to know when there was more there than met the eye, and that was exactly what she felt in this situation.

And then there were some blurred lines in her reasons why she wanted to know more about him. It wasn't solely for professional reasons, and it was the first time she'd ever had to deal with that kind of conflict. From the moment Julian had turned around in the coffee shop this morning, she'd felt more than a professional interest in him.

No matter what she tried to tell herself.

Charlotte was about to wish Hank a good night and say goodbye when something occurred to her. "Did Julian happen to mention what kind of job he was looking for?"

Hank shook his head. "It didn't come up. If anything, I got the impression he doesn't like to talk about himself. Any time we started talking about job prospects, Julian would ask what else needed to be done." He chuckled softly. "That was kind of how we ended up getting so much done. You know we never turn down an offer of help."

Which meant the topic of job prospects must have come up a lot.

"Oh. Okay. Thanks." This time she did say goodbye

and walked to the office to get her purse. On her way out, she glanced around and noted how the place did look a lot better than it had in a while—cleaner, less cluttered. She wished she could have thanked Julian, but he was nowhere in sight.

She stepped outside, foolishly hoping she'd find him outside just as she had earlier, but he wasn't there. The sun was going down, and as she wondered where he might be, her stomach growled loudly. It was only then that she realized she hadn't had anything to eat since her coffee and muffin that morning with Julian.

Julian...

With a sigh, she walked toward her car and wondered again what it was about him that had him so firmly planted in her mind. Did she want to help him? Yes. Did she need to know he was going to be okay? Absolutely.

Did she also want to run her hands up his muscular arms and touch him and then have those same arms wrapped around her?

She hung her head and shook it.

Yes.

It was right then when she knew if she did happen to hear from Julian again, she was going to have to ask one of her colleagues to help him.

She was already too emotionally invested in him, and not in a strictly professional way.

As Charlotte drove home, she forced herself to think about something else. Anything else. And surprisingly, it wasn't hard to do. By nature, she was a list-maker, and once she pushed all thoughts of Julian aside, she realized how much she had to do in the coming week.

Going out with friends had become a bit of a

challenge in the last six months because the last of them had gotten married and now everything was suddenly a couples' event.

Every. Blasted. Thing.

Even their once-a-month brunch had all the husbands horning in. It was impossible to have any serious girl-talk with five men sitting there!

As much as she'd like to blame it on the guys for ruining their time out, it was also the way everyone was looking at her, wondering out loud why she wasn't dating, asking when she was going to settle down and why she didn't want a family.

She did! More than anything Charlotte wanted to get married and have kids and a dog and a house with a white picket fence, but it wasn't so easy to find! Listening to her friends, however, you'd think it was. Each of them had met their Mr. Right, and when they told the story, it was as if they'd just opened their doors one day and said "Oh! There you are!" and that was that.

Um, yeah. That had never happened for her. If anything, she'd opened her door and found Mr. I-Have-Issues. She'd invest months in helping him, only to have him walk away and be someone else's Mr. Right.

"Ugh…maybe I need to get a fish," she said as she made her way to the kitchen and pulled out a bottle of water.

Most people would contemplate getting a dog or cat, but not her. The ever-practical side of her knew she should start small and work her way up. Sure, a fish couldn't snuggle with her, but she was a firm believer in not overwhelming herself when she tried something new. Fish would be easy to care for, and it wasn't like she was going to invest in a big aquarium. Maybe just a goldfish for starters.

And how pathetic was it that she was actually starting to feel a little excited at the prospect of getting a goldfish?

———

"And nobody recognized you?"

Julian shook his head. "Nope. No one. I'd say it was weird, but I was just on the road without it happening so...maybe I'm used to it now." He was sitting pool-side at Riley's house along with Dylan and telling them about his night working at the homeless shelter.

"So, here's my question," Dylan began. "Why? I mean, why go? You talked to this woman and she just assumed you needed help—which we'll get to later—and that was the end of it. You never had to see her again, so why bother going?"

With a shrug, Julian reached for the bottle of water in front of him. "What else have I got to do?"

Riley and Dylan looked at each other and then back at him. "I would imagine after three months away you'd have a lot to do," Riley said. "You've been away from everything and everyone. I would have thought you'd want to reconnect with your friends and your family, Jules. Your first night home and you're out unpacking a truck in Santa Monica. It just seems a little...odd, that's all."

"It was my second night," he corrected. "I talked to Mick, I'd been in contact with my folks the whole time I was gone, and now I'm here with the two of you. I'm meeting with a Realtor later today about the house, and I'm going to put most of my stuff in storage until I find a place of my own."

"You may find someplace pretty quick," Dylan said. "Paige and I did. It was the first house we went to and we just fell in love with it."

Riley nodded. "That's how I felt when I saw this house. Savannah and I talk about moving, since this was my place from before we met and it's getting a little crowded with two kids, but we just love it."

Julian couldn't help but smile. If ever there was a family man, it was Riley Shaughnessy. It wasn't just the fact that Riley came from a big family; he really seemed to have hit his stride since becoming a father.

"How's the baby doing?" Julian asked. "I noticed it was pretty quiet in the house when we arrived."

Riley's grin spoke volumes. "He's doing great. Savannah's parents are flying in today and she took the kids to meet them at the airport. Her mother would be devastated to have to wait even an extra minute to see them."

"Speaking of kids," Dylan said, and Julian noted the slightly goofy grin on his face, "we just found out Paige is pregnant!" There was a flurry of congratulations, and Dylan's smile grew. "Can you believe it? Me! I'm going to be a dad!"

"That is amazing news, Dylan," Riley said. "How is Paige feeling?"

"She's great. I mean seriously great. I was going to wait until Matt got here next week to tell you guys, but…I couldn't," he said with a laugh. "We knew as soon as we bought the house that we couldn't wait to have kids and I'm so freaking excited it's happening."

"Good for you, man," Julian said and he meant it. Dylan had gone through so many years of battling his demons that it was good not only to see him clean and sober, but also so happy. Then he glanced over at Riley and realized how his friend hadn't gone through anything even remotely as dark as the rest of the band, but he'd overcome a great deal after his mother's death so long ago, and here he was loving life too. And no doubt when he saw Matt he'd notice the same thing. So it was possible to find happiness after the lowest points in your life.

At least for other people.

Somehow, Julian didn't think it was going to happen for him. He doubted he would ever be willing to open himself up to the possibility ever again.

Been there, done that, bought the T-shirt.

"I'd say let's make a toast," Riley said with a small laugh, "but it feels weird to be doing it with bottled water."

But that didn't deter Julian. "Doesn't matter what we're drinking, the sentiment is there." He raised his bottle of water and looked at Dylan. "Here's to you and Paige and baby Anders. We can't wait to see what kind of hell he puts you through!"

They all laughed and drank, and for a few minutes, the conversation was all about babies. Julian sat back and pretended to listen. It certainly wasn't in the cards for him, and no matter how happy he was for his friends, he was surprised at the pang of sadness that hit him at that realization. He was happy for Dylan—and Riley and Matt—and the last thing he wanted to be was the downer of the group. Especially on a day like today with Dylan's big news.

"So, where do we want to play next week when Matt gets in?" Riley asked. "Normally I'd suggest here, but with Savannah's parents I think it would be too distracting." He looked over at Dylan. "Is your space ready to use or should we book space someplace else?"

"I've been waiting for a chance to christen my studio," Dylan said excitedly. "I've played in it alone a couple of times, but I've been dying to get you guys all together and jam. This is gonna be awesome!"

Julian's heart pounded like the drums he usually played. *Now*. He had to tell them now and pretty much kill the mood. If he didn't, it would just be that much harder next week.

"Listen…" he began hesitantly, "I'm not sure."

"No," Dylan said firmly. "No way. Uh-uh. This is in no way a professional commitment. This is just four friends getting together to jam. Nothing more, nothing less."

Then Riley chimed in. "We're not rushing you, Jules. When you're ready to get back in the studio with us, you just say the word and we're all there. But you just got home and you've got to work things out in your head. We get it."

"Just know," Dylan added, "if you said getting back in the studio would help you, we'd all be there in an instant. But this is your call."

He wanted to relax—he seriously did—but no matter how supportive they were being, it wasn't going to help. There was no way he was returning to Shaughnessy and the whole rock star lifestyle. That chapter was closed for good.

Riley's phone rang and he held it up to show them Mick's name. He put the phone on speaker as he answered. "Hey, Mick. What's up?"

"Is everyone there with you?"

"Everyone except Matt," Riley said. "What's up?"

"Just got off the phone with Robert Hayward— the president of Encore Records. They're going to be celebrating their twenty-fifth anniversary on January fourth, and all of their clients are performing. So I wanted to give you a heads-up and say that this will be the perfect way to get Shaughnessy back in the spotlight and maybe announce a tour. We'll meet next week to talk about it when Matt's here."

"Wait, wait, wait," Dylan said. "That's like three months away. Why the last-minute hoopla?"

On the line, they could hear Mick sigh. "It's not last-minute. It was just that we—meaning Shaughnessy—were in crisis mode when word was released and I didn't think we needed to add this into the mix. Now that Julian's home, we can get back to business."

Riley and Dylan looked at Julian. If he ground his teeth any harder they'd disintegrate. All the tension he'd been tamping down was back at the surface. As if sensing it, Riley looked at the phone. "Sounds good, Mick. Let me call you later, okay?"

Without missing a beat, Mick said, "Talk to you then."

Riley put the phone down and looked at Julian. "I swear I think he's watching us all the damn time. It's like he knows exactly when to call and what we're talking about."

"He's freaky like that," Dylan agreed and then nervously looked at Julian.

He wasn't ready for this. Any of it. He'd thought he was. Thought that the time away would be enough time to get his head together.

But it wasn't.

Standing up, he said, "I need to go and meet the Realtor. Call me when Matt's here." And without anything more than a slight wave, he walked back into

Riley's house and straight out the front door as if the hounds of hell were chasing him.

In his car, he sped out of Riley's neighborhood and onto the freeway. He actually had several hours before he had to meet with the Realtor about the house, so there was no place pressing he had to be. So he drove.

Straight to Santa Monica and the homeless shelter.

It was doubtful Charlotte would be there. But he knew how much help the shelter needed and…it had actually felt pretty damn good just to lend a hand.

Driving around the block and over a few more, he parked in the lot he had last night and then walked over to the shelter. Inside he spotted Hank and strode over to him.

"Need a hand today?"

—◆◆◆—

For the next several days, that had been Julian's pattern—get up, pretend he was just going to stay home, and eventually end up back at the shelter. He hadn't talked to anyone about donating money; for now this was simply about giving his time and doing what he could in a hands-on way.

By Thursday afternoon, he had helped unload trucks, sort through donations, move furniture, and even paint several rooms. It had been a long time since he'd done anything quite so physical and he found he enjoyed it.

It also meant he was thankful to be able to go home and stand under a hot shower or soak in the hot tub to ease his sore muscles.

"Julian!" Hank called out. Julian looked over and saw him motioning to come over to his office. Once they were inside, Hank closed the door and studied him for a moment. "How's everything going today?"

With a shrug, Julian sat down. "Good. The paint is done in the rec room and I secured the wire shelves back in the pantry."

Nodding, Hank walked around and sat at his desk. "We really appreciate all you're doing, Julian."

There was something in his tone that had Julian stiffening a little—like he was about to say something to him that wouldn't be particularly well received.

And he was right.

"You're Julian Grayson."

Shit.

Unsure of what he was supposed to do or say, Julian waited him out. The unspoken question was out there and sure enough, Hank answered it by sliding a newspaper across the desk toward him. It was open to the entertainment news and a picture of the band.

SHAUGHNESSY SLATED TO PLAY AT
ENCORE'S 25TH ANNIVERSARY BASH!

He was going to strangle Mick when he saw him.

Hank leaned forward a little and rested his arms on the desktop. "It's not my place to ask what you're doing here. Personally, I'm just thankful for the help and the fact that you were willing to do it."

"But?" Julian prompted.

"But…I take it no one else knows who you are or that you're here?"

Nodding, Julian replied, "It really isn't anyone's business what I do in my free time. I came here and saw you could use some help and I wanted to do it. End of story."

There was a long, awkward silence while Julian waited for Hank to comment. "Charlotte doesn't know who you are," he began, his tone suddenly way more serious and solemn than it had been a moment ago. "She is under the impression you're in need of our help and her services."

"I never told her that," Julian argued mildly.

"Maybe not, but that's what she thinks."

This wasn't news. But now that he was here, he knew he was going to have to clear up the misunderstanding.

"I can appreciate your concern, Hank. But I can't control what conclusions Charlotte drew."

And for the first time, this mild-mannered man seemed to get pissed. He straightened a little in his chair as if he was going to try to intimidate Julian. "Do you know that by now she's probably already started a file on you? Even if you didn't give her any information, the fact that you came here and sat in her class, she's probably already making calls on your behalf just in case she sees you again?"

Julian didn't respond.

"Charlotte is the kind of person who wants to help everyone. It doesn't matter if they want her help or not, she goes above and beyond, and there are tens of dozens of families who are thankful for her and for the help she gave them. And you know what she gets in return?"

"A paycheck?" Julian responded snidely.

Hank ignored the comment and glared at him for a moment. "She gets to maybe take a breath and then starts all over again with the next group of people who need her. She gets verbally abused by people who are belligerent and angry about their circumstances. She cries with them, she encourages them, she feels for them. And you can be sure she's already feeling for you, because that's the kind of woman she is. So if you're going to sit here with that kind of attitude, I'll say thank you for your help and ask you to leave."

For a moment, Julian could only sit and stare. Seriously? They were going to ask him to leave even though he had been busting his ass to help, all because he didn't want to have an awkward conversation with Charlotte?

Slowly, he came to his feet and held out a hand. "It was a pleasure meeting you, Hank," he said evenly. Hank stood and shook his hand, and Julian turned and walked out the door.

—⁂—

The moment Charlotte walked into the center that afternoon, she noticed the changes. Her first thought was how the help Julian gave on Sunday must have motivated the staff. And it was pretty hard to hide her disappointment that she'd missed seeing him.

Fortunately, she didn't have much time to think about him because there were several new families who needed her attention. So for three hours, she talked and coached and advised and set up appointments to help these families get back on their feet. By the time she was done and ready to go, all she wanted was to go home, have a glass of wine, and not think. Cases like the one she'd dealt with today, where there were small children who just looked sad and scared, took a lot out of her.

"You calling it a day, CeeCee?" Hank asked as she stepped out of the meeting room.

"I am," she said with a weak smile. Their routine was to talk and compare notes when Charlotte was done meeting with people. Tonight she just wasn't in the mood for it.

"Do you have a few minutes to talk?"

She hated to disappoint Hank, but Charlotte knew her head just wasn't in it right now. "Actually, Hank, I have a bit of a headache and really want to head home. We'll catch up next week, okay?"

"Of course, of course," he said. "Feel better."

"Thanks." Making her way to the door, she was riddled with guilt. It wasn't like her to lie. For all she knew, there was something important he had to share with her. And just as she was about to change her mind and turn around, someone called out for Hank.

Thank God.

Stepping outside, she let out a small sigh. Tired and a little hungry, Charlotte began to plan how she was going to spend the rest of her day. Should she stop for takeout on the way home? Stop at the grocery store for something to cook? And once she got home, would she read or watch something on Netflix? So many questions…

She'd only gone a few steps when she spotted him.

Julian was leaning against the front of the building looking as if he was waiting for her.

Or maybe it was just wishful thinking.

"Hey," she said casually, surprised to find him there, since from everything she'd heard earlier, he had left hours ago. "I hear you were a real hero in there this week."

Pushing away from the brick wall, Julian moved toward her with a careless shrug. "Just doing what needed to be done."

She liked that he was a little bit humble. "Yes, but it's been needing to be done for a long time. So thank you."

He nodded.

"How has your week been?" she asked.

"Good."

"Anything new and exciting happen? You know, other than all the work here at the center?"

"Nope."

His lack of conversation skills was really starting to annoy her. It was on the tip of her tongue to mention how important communication skills were in the job market when he surprised her.

"Would you like to go and grab something to eat?"

Her soft gasp was her only response before Julian started to chuckle.

"I figured I could pay you back for that breakfast."

Her shoulders sagged and all Charlotte wanted to do was stomp her foot with annoyance, but she didn't. "Julian, I told you it wasn't necessary."

"You said to pay it forward."

"With someone else." She didn't hide her exasperation very well.

His gaze held hers for a long moment—almost in defiance. "I was going to suggest grabbing some burgers or something and just sitting and talking. It's not a big deal. I'll still pay it forward for the coffee and muffins, if it makes you feel better."

Now she was in quite the predicament. She wanted to go out with him and get to know his story a little more, but there was no way she could feel comfortable about him spending money he probably shouldn't.

"I'll go, but under one condition."

Julian arched a dark brow at her—something he'd done before and Charlotte found it was a rather sexy gesture.

"I pay for myself," she said firmly, forcing herself to stop thinking of him in terms of sexiness and instead remember he needed her help.

"Charlotte—"

But she held up a hand to stop him. "It's not negotiable. Either I pay for myself or I don't go." Then she wanted to kick herself because maybe he was only inviting her so he could pay her back, and now that she was taking that off the table, he would simply tell her good night and walk away.

It was a possibility.

But she really hoped he wouldn't.

Swallowing hard, she did her best not to look away from his intense gaze. He was quiet for so long that she started to squirm—it was like a staring contest and she was afraid to be the one to look away first. Why? She didn't know. But it seemed important not to back down.

"Fine," he said finally, through clenched teeth.

Charlotte let out the breath she didn't realize she was holding and smiled. "My car is parked right across the street. There's a great burger place around the corner we can go to."

"Why don't we head back toward Malibu? There's a great burger place right down the block from the coffee house."

She knew exactly the one he was referring to. "That

sounds great. Do you need a ride? Did you take the bus here?"

Shaking his head, Julian replied, "I'm parked around the corner. You go ahead and I'll meet you there."

"Sounds good."

Charlotte noticed that he stood where he was until she was safely in her car and driving away. It was a very gentlemanly gesture, she thought. And she wondered how on earth she was going to get him to share a little more about himself so she'd know how to advise him.

Now that she thought about it, however, she realized he actually had yet to ask her for help.

Odd.

So, what did it mean? And how long was she supposed to sit around and wait him out?

"As long as it takes," she answered out loud.

Chapter 3

IT WAS AFTER SIX, AND AFTER ONLY HAVING A BOTTLE of water since lunch—which seemed like years ago— Charlotte was more than ready to eat. Part of her was excited about joining Julian for dinner, but then she recalled why exactly it was that he was here and she had to remember her place. This wasn't a date; this was an opportunity to help someone. And that's what she forced herself to think about as she drove back to Malibu.

As she sat in traffic, her mind wandered to some of the positions she knew were available that she could suggest to him and then—

She stopped and cursed.

Charlotte remembered her decision from Sunday to refer Julian to someone else in her office. "Okay," she murmured. "So I won't set anything up for him, but I can certainly give him some direction."

Feeling mildly satisfied with her solution, the remainder of the drive was spent focusing on traffic and what other topics of conversation they could cover over dinner. Her curiosity was killing her. What kind of man was Julian? Where did he work before? What was... She stopped and realized she didn't even know his last name! How had that happened? How had this man consumed so many of her thoughts when she didn't even know anything as basic as his last name?

"Well, that's question number one."

Okay, maybe not number one, but Charlotte was determined to get to know more about Julian personally—for strictly professional reasons, of course.

She knew how to talk to get people to respond, and now that she wasn't on any time restriction, she had no doubt that with the right questions, she'd be able to learn more about him. Was he married? Did he have any kids?

Gasping, she realized it should have been one of the very first things she'd asked. What if she'd been sitting back doing nothing except sort of daydreaming about him when he had a family…somewhere, and he was trying to take care of them?

Then he wouldn't have asked you to join him for dinner.

Okay, that was true, and she needed to relax and just get a grip.

Something else she had to remind herself of as traffic crawled along.

So rather than fret about it, she'd go into this dinner with him with no expectations and see where the conversation led.

Charlotte didn't blink an eye when Julian suggested they take their dinner and eat out on the beach. She had a blanket in her trunk, and if anything, she seemed more than a little excited at the prospect.

Personally, Julian couldn't care less about the picnic part. He was more concerned with not sitting in the middle of a crowded restaurant and being recognized. He'd been back home for less than a week and it hadn't happened, but he was fairly certain it was only a matter of time.

He wasn't ready for it.

And he certainly wasn't ready for it to happen in front of Charlotte.

There was no way he wanted to talk about his sensationalized failed trip to the altar and the aftermath. Not with anyone. And there wasn't a doubt in his mind that when it happened—when someone recognized him—it would be the first thing they'd want to bring up.

So, what was he doing?

He didn't owe anyone anything, he reminded himself. If he never saw Charlotte again, he'd live. Life would go on. Just like he didn't have to go out and grab a burger for dinner. He'd had his groceries delivered and was perfectly content to hide out back at the beach house.

And yet here he was. Instead of hiding, he was sitting on the beach with a woman he'd just met who seemed to be under the impression that he was in need of a helping hand. True, he could just tell her she was mistaken and put an end to it. Do as Hank suggested and simply open up. But there was something about her that was intriguing to him. There was an honesty to her, a goodness, that he was finding almost too good to be true. Even without Hank's word, he'd known it. So for now, Julian wanted to stay under the radar and get to know more about her before she found out who he really was.

Beside him on the blanket, Charlotte sat with her sandals off, her long hair pulled back in a ponytail and a serene smile on her face. Everything about her body language said shc was happy and content—all with a decent burger, better-than-decent fries, and a blanket in the sand.

It almost seemed beyond comprehension.

Did this sort of simplicity really make people happy? Could someone honestly find enjoyment in things like this?

In Julian's experience, they couldn't. How many people had he known—especially since his career had taken off—who only seemed happy when they were dining at five-star restaurants or traveling to exotic locations for vacations, living in multimillion-dollar homes and driving expensive cars. That was his world. That's what seemed to be the norm for what it took to make a person happy and content.

"I love this, don't you?" she asked, breaking into his thoughts.

"The burgers?"

She let out a small laugh as she turned to look at him. "Well, the burgers are really good, but I'm talking about this—the beach, the waves, the smell of the ocean." She inhaled deeply and let her breath out slowly. "I'm telling you, if I could, I would set up my office right here in the sand and be totally fine with it."

He couldn't help but chuckle at the image. "I'm not sure you'd get much work done."

"Probably not, but it would be worth it. It would be like constant mental health therapy. I bet I could totally make that a thing."

"Or you'd find yourself living here—and not in a good way—because you wouldn't be able to pay your bills." He said it teasingly but she seemed to sober instantly. "What? What did I say?"

"Okay, look," she began seriously, "I'm really trying not to pry but…"

"But…?" he prompted.

"Are you okay?" she asked, reaching out and placing

her hand on his arm. They both seemed to stiffen at the gesture even as she paused. "I mean...do you have a place to stay that's safe? Because I know of other shelters that are closer than the one in Santa Monica and I can get you in if you need it."

Wait a minute...on top of thinking he was just down on his luck, she thought he was homeless too?

"Listen, Charlotte, I think you misunderstood—"

She interrupted before he could go any further. "I don't usually just blurt out something like that. I try to be more sensitive and wait until someone wants to confide in me about what's going on in their life, but I feel like you're struggling with this—and that's totally fine! But you need to know that it's okay and that there is help for you."

For a while, all he could do was stare. In his entire life, Julian couldn't remember a more awkward moment.

Ever.

And that was saying something, considering the conditions when he'd essentially walked away from his life three months ago.

"Seriously, Charlotte, you need to listen."

But she wasn't listening. She was rummaging through her purse and pulling out her phone and scrolling in search of something. "We can find you a place to stay. I mean I know you have a car, but I really hope you're not sleeping in it. There are so many options, and if you come to my office tomorrow, I can have you working by the end of the day. I promise." Her eyes were huge and she was so passionate about what she was saying that Julian had no idea what he was supposed to do or say.

The truth would certainly help...

And it would, but it was going to be embarrassing to them both when he admitted why it was that he didn't need her help.

Dammit, this really wasn't the way he wanted all of this to go down.

All he wanted to do was have a simple dinner and just have a conversation with her. He wasn't looking for drama, and he certainly wasn't looking to open the can of worms he'd been trying to keep closed for three damn months.

Unfortunately, he didn't have a choice.

Tossing the rest of his dinner back in the bag, he stood up. She looked up at him in confusion and with a myriad of emotions in her eyes that almost drew him in and forced him back down beside her.

Then he remembered another pair of expressive eyes he'd always caved to, and vowed to stand his ground.

"I need to show you something," he said gruffly and watched as she cleaned up her dinner mess and slowly climbed to her feet. He helped her fold up the blanket, took their trash and tossed it in the nearest can, and slowly began walking down the beach toward the houses.

They walked along quietly, but he knew it was only a matter of time before Charlotte asked questions.

He figured he'd beat her to the punch.

"I'm not homeless," he said, keeping his gaze trained straight ahead. "When we met on Sunday, I know you got the impression that I was a guy in crisis—and I am— just…not the crisis you seem to think."

Beside him, Charlotte looked at him with her brow furrowed. "I don't understand. You said you were between jobs and you couldn't pay for your breakfast."

"It wasn't that I couldn't pay because I was broke, I just didn't have my wallet."

"O-kay…"

Julian stopped in front of the first of the houses that overlooked the beach. "You see these houses?"

Wordlessly, she nodded.

"This is where I live," he said flatly, still not looking at her.

"You live in that house?"

"Not that one, but the fifth one down is mine for the next few months."

She was silent for so long that Julian thought he'd go crazy. When he couldn't take it any longer, he forced himself to face her. "I was simply a guy who forgot his wallet that morning. I didn't mean for you to jump to any conclusions."

But she wasn't looking at him, she was staring up at the houses, and when he looked a little closer, he saw her trembling slightly.

"I really am between jobs," he said quickly, unsure why he suddenly felt the need to explain himself. "It's just—"

"It's not really an issue," she finished for him in a soft voice, almost sad.

He saw her swallow hard before she looked down at the sand and he knew she had to be embarrassed. He sure as hell was.

"Charlotte…"

Then she turned and looked at him. "Why didn't you correct me?" she said with a little snap in her voice this time. "I mean, if I was so off-base—and clearly I was—why not just tell me the truth? Why come to the shelter and sit through my class? And why keep going back there and helping out? I never had to know, Julian! You could have just walked away on Sunday and paid it forward like I asked you to!"

"I know," he said and suddenly felt like he was being reprimanded as if he were a child. He'd done a lot of stupid things in his life—particularly in the last five years where Dena was concerned—and no one had ever called him out on it quite like this. Now here he was standing on the beach with this woman calling him out on something as minute as a misunderstanding over why he didn't have a wallet.

She continued to stare at him as if waiting for more of an explanation, and as much as he kept telling himself he didn't owe anyone anything, for some reason he felt like he owed Charlotte at least the truth.

With a weary sigh, Julian raked a hand through his hair. "I'm Julian Grayson," he said and waited for her to recognize it.

But she didn't.

Not a big deal, but—

"I'm the drummer for Shaughnessy," he explained.

Still nothing.

This time his sigh was more one of agitation.

Then he spilled out the story of his life: the band, his relationship with Dena, the wedding, and his road trip to escape it all.

"So now I'm back, and when you offered to buy my breakfast that day I thought you had recognized me and wanted something from me," he said, beyond irritated that he'd been talking for the better part of fifteen minutes without her uttering a single word. Now that he was done, he was certain she'd offer some sort of apology

for all he'd been through or for not recognizing him or...
something.

Instead, Charlotte stiffened her spine and tilted her
chin at him. "It was nice to meet you, Julian Grayson,
and I wish you luck with your life."

And she turned and walked away.

Julian blinked, too stunned to move. That was it? That
was all she had to say? Even if she didn't offer him any
sympathy—or ask for an autograph!—she could at *least*
have offered him some sort of professional advice. She
was a social worker who—from everything Hank had
told him—wanted to help everyone. Well, he needed
help, dammit! Why wasn't she concerned with him?

*Charlotte is the kind of person who wants to help
everyone. It doesn't matter if they want her help or not.*

More of Hank's words came back to him, and rather
than making him feel bad, as they had earlier, this time
they pissed him off. Granted, he hadn't been honest with
her, but he hadn't out-and-out lied either. She misunderstood the situation and he just hadn't corrected her soon
enough. That didn't make him some sort of criminal
or someone who wasn't worth her time, for crying out
loud. She even worked with reformed criminals, so what
made him so undeserving of help?

By the time he got out of his own head and focused
on his surroundings, Charlotte had blended into the
crowds enjoying sundown on the beach.

Dammit.

You know what? he thought with a shrug. *Screw it.*
He was fine exactly the way he was, and he didn't want
her help or guidance or advice, none of it.

Good riddance.

That attitude lasted until Saturday morning, when Julian
opted to go out for coffee and found himself in line behind
Charlotte. He'd like to say it was a coincidence, but maybe
he'd lingered around outside until he saw her go in.

Maybe.

If she noticed him walk in, she wasn't letting on. She
was reading something on her phone and from what he
could tell, she was fairly oblivious to anything going
on around her. Sure, she moved when the line moved,
but other than that she kept her head down. It left him
wondering what he should do.

And if he did happen to say hello, then what? What
could he possibly have to say after that?

"Hey, Carly," Charlotte said in front of him, effectively pulling him from his thoughts. "Can I get a caramel Frappuccino and a parfait please?"

For some reason, Julian felt like this was his opportunity. "Can you add a large black coffee and a blueberry
muffin to that?" he asked as he stepped forward and
pulled his wallet out.

"That's not necessary," Charlotte quickly interrupted,
looking only at the cashier. She pulled out her own
wallet and had her credit card out before Julian had his.
"Just for mine, please." Then she gave him the side-eye
before returning her attention to the transaction.

"Seriously?" he asked, more than a little annoyed.
"Why is it okay for you to pay for my order and I can't
pay for yours?"

With a smile and a word of thanks to Carly, Charlotte
stepped down to the end of the counter to wait for her

order without uttering a word to him. Fortunately, he was able to pay for his quickly and was standing beside her a minute later. "Well?" he demanded quietly.

"That was different," she hissed. "You couldn't pay for your order. I am perfectly capable of doing so."

Leaning in a little closer, he smirked at her. "And here I was just trying to pay it forward."

She rolled her eyes. "No, you're trying to clear your conscience, and I don't appreciate it. If you want to do something nice for someone, do it for a stranger."

"You're kind of a stranger. I mean…other than your job, I don't know anything about you," he said simply, enjoying the light feeling this banter was giving him.

The barista called out Charlotte's name and she stepped away to pick it up. With another word of thanks, she turned and walked toward the exit and away from him.

With a huff of frustration, Julian hung his head. "This shouldn't be so damn difficult." His order came out immediately and he made his way out of the shop. It took him all of ten seconds to spot her walking across the street toward the benches where she could watch the waves.

Rather than jog after her like he was inclined to do, he made his way slowly over to the benches and sat down beside her—not too close, but close enough to hear her huff of annoyance.

"If paying for my coffee will put an end to this, you can just give me five bucks and go," she said, but her lips twitched as she said it and that's when Julian knew he had her.

"Uh-uh-uh. For all I know you'll spend that money on something you don't need. Face it, you're going to have to let me buy it for you myself." He took a sip of his coffee and felt victorious. When he lowered his cup, he grinned at her.

"Why are you like this?" she asked, but there was no heat behind her words.

"Like what? Friendly? Considerate?"

Her eyes went wide. "There are many words that come to mind when I think of you, Julian, but friendly and considerate aren't two of them."

"But you do think about me."

She laughed out loud and it was an amazing sound. Laughter was something he hadn't heard a whole lot of in a long time and he realized just how much he missed it. It seemed like every time he was around Charlotte, she made everything seem just that much…lighter.

Which should have annoyed him, considering how much he wanted simply to bask in his anger and misery. That worked for him and he was comfortable with it. This whole happy, sitting-on-the-beach-laughing thing felt weird and completely unfamiliar.

"Are you working today?" he asked.

Charlotte shook her head. "I finally have a day off."

"You're up and out early for your day off. I would imagine you'd want to sleep in and relax."

She looked at him oddly. "Why? This is how I love to start my day. It's a bit of a drive to get here, but once I am here, it fills all of my senses. I can clear my mind and relax and then I just have a better attitude and outlook for the rest of the day." She took a sip of her coffee and pointed out toward the sand. "You see that group of people over there?"

"The ones with the mats?"

Nodding, she said, "Someday I'm going to be brave enough to join them."

Julian looked out at the group and noticed they were all doing matching poses, then freezing, changing poses, and freezing again. He looked over at Charlotte. "Why the hell are there so many poses?"

"I've never taken a yoga class, but I keep telling myself that someday I'll learn enough about it where I can join that one and not make an idiot out of myself."

He studied the group again. "Doesn't seem too hard. Just looks like a lot of bending and then staying still."

"There's more to it than that."

"Not from here there isn't."

"Anyway…what about you? Why are you out here so early?"

He shrugged and took another sip of coffee, then held out his cup to her. "They make a great cup of coffee and I don't. Plus they have muffins. It was either come here or have a bowl of soggy cereal and sub-par coffee."

"Poor you," she murmured.

They sat in companionable silence while Julian took a couple of bites of the muffin and Charlotte took a spoonful of her parfait.

"What do you do on your day off—you know, other than not doing yoga on the beach?" he asked.

"Today I just planned on doing stuff around the house—laundry, vacuuming…nothing exciting."

"I'll say," he murmured.

"We can't all have housekeepers," she said under her breath.

Draping his arm along the back of the bench, he shifted toward her. "What if you did?"

"Did what?"

"Had a housekeeper and you didn't have to go home and do all that crap. What would you be doing today?"

"Kind of a moot point considering it's not an option," she stated and took another prim spoonful of her parfait. She was looking straight ahead, almost as if she were ignoring him, but Julian wasn't going to let that happen.

"But what if it was," he said softly in a teasing tone, leaning in a little closer. "Just pretend, Charlotte. If you had a day without any responsibilities, what would you do with it?"

And that's when he noticed she was getting tense— her back stiffened and her expression went from carefree and relaxed to strained.

Totally not the reaction he thought he'd get.

"You know what—"

"I'd sit on the beach and read," she said, interrupting him. "I would set up one of those big umbrellas and a chair and a blanket and have a little cooler with snacks and drinks and just sit and read all day." Then she turned to him with a hint of sadness in her eyes. "It's not exciting, but it's two of my favorite things to do."

"So why don't you?" he asked, confused how her simple admission made her so emotional.

With a small shrug, she looked away. "Because it's not a productive use of my time. It's a little selfish and the only one benefiting from it is me, so…"

Now he fully shifted on the bench to face her. "Everybody needs some time like that, Charlotte. Hell, I just took three months to do it."

"And did it help?"

The question brought him up short. Had it? Yes, it

had. It had been a good distraction, and he wasn't completely delusional. Taking off the way he had hadn't solved anything, but it had given him time to think, to breathe, to relax. Eventually Julian knew he was going to have to deal with the situation and the aftermath, and he'd be stronger for having taken some down time.

"It did," he admitted. "At the time it was a necessity. In your case I think you—more than anyone I know—deserve a mental health day. From what I hear, you do more than your share of work to help those in need."

Her head tilted as she looked at him curiously. "Where'd you hear that?"

"Hank talked about you quite a bit. From his point of view, you practically walk on water. And even if he hadn't said a word, I watched you in action on Sunday. You take on a lot. I would imagine hearing the things you do on a daily basis, and dealing with people who are essentially in crisis mode are mentally and emotionally draining." He paused and finished his coffee. "And that's why you need a mental health day."

She blinked at him, didn't say anything for a long moment, and then shrugged again. "Maybe some other day. I wouldn't even know where to begin to make that happen today. By the time I gathered all of those supplies, it would be late and I'd be too stressed out from wasting time to fully enjoy it."

Unable to help himself, Julian laughed. "You've got to be the only woman I know who would feel stressed out by doing what you need to in order to relax."

Finishing her coffee, Charlotte stood and gathered her trash. "I can't help it, it's how I've always been. If I happened to have a beach umbrella or one of those low chairs hanging around, maybe it wouldn't be such a big deal. But I don't. So…again, moot point."

"Agree to disagree," he replied, coming to his feet.

"What does that even mean?"

Together they walked over to the trash can and tossed their cups and bags in, then began walking back toward the coffee shop.

"It means I think you're making excuses. I think it would be easy to get those things and be back here in an hour—tops," he challenged.

"Clearly, you've never had to do these things for yourself, Julian. I'm sure a man in your position just has to mention that he wants these things and people scurry around to make it happen. Well, news flash. In the real world, it doesn't work that way."

So much for the mild-mannered social worker. When there wasn't a case file between them, he found that Charlotte had a bit of a snarky side to her.

"Care to test that theory?"

She studied him for a long moment. "I'm listening."

"One hour," he began, "and I'm not making any calls. We'll get everything you need and have you on the beach—and relaxing—in an hour."

The laugh she let out was part derision and part pure amusement. "Doubtful, but I think I'm honestly good with putting off my housework just to prove you wrong."

Julian held out a hand to her. "You're on."

―⁓―

An hour later and she still wasn't sure how it happened.

Umbrella? Check.

Blanket? Check.

Cooler full of snacks and drinks? Check and check.

And with her Kindle in her hand and her toes in the sand, she was still stumped.

Beside her, Charlotte heard a beeping sound and glanced over to see Julian grinning as he looked at his phone. "Time's up," he said with a little more giddiness than she thought he had in him.

As soon as she'd shaken his hand earlier, he sprang into action, taking the divide-and-conquer approach. Charlotte had gone home to grab her Kindle, a blanket, and to change her clothes, while Julian had gone for snacks, drinks, chairs, and the umbrella.

"I guess this is where you're going to gloat and say 'I told you so,' right?"

Shaking his head, Julian relaxed in the chair beside her. "I have to admit, it feels pretty good to be right, but this wasn't all that hard to do only because most of the stuff we needed was just up the beach at the house."

Right. His million-dollar home overlooking the ocean.

She wanted to hate him a little bit for that, but she was feeling too relaxed right now. "That was kind of cheating."

He leaned in closer until their shoulders were almost touching and whispered loudly, "Technically, but considering you didn't have to go out and buy anything either, I'd say we're even."

Well, drat. He had a point.

"Fine."

They sat quietly for a few minutes and she watched as Julian pulled a tablet out of the bag beside him. Glancing over slyly so he wasn't alerted to her curiosity, she tried to see what he was reading. What kind of stuff did a rock star read? Or more specifically, what kind of stuff did *this* particular rock star read?

"The latest James Patterson," he said mildly as he swiped a finger across the screen.

Busted.

"Is it good?" she asked, keeping her gaze firmly focused on her own screen where she was reading the latest J.D. Robb thriller.

"So far. I just started it two minutes ago."

Placing her Kindle down, she looked at him. "You don't have to read just because I'm reading, you know. Honestly, while I appreciate you helping me out with this setup, I wouldn't be offended if you didn't want to stay."

Julian continued to read quietly for another minute and then swiped across the screen again. "I'm curious about how relaxing this whole thing could be. Personally, there's a little too much conversation going on, but...that's just me."

She started to sputter and rebut and then thought better of it. He wanted less conversation? Well, fine. She could do that.

For thirty minutes, Charlotte allowed herself to get sucked into the story as her toes flexed in the sand and she let the sounds and smells of the beach surround her. Her stomach began to rumble, and before she could make a move, Julian handed her a giant chocolate chip cookie. That's when she realized he had a stash of his own snacks and they were much better than hers. All she had was fruit and cheese and some bottled water, but the cookie was definitely going to be hers.

"Thank you," she said softly. She knew he must have gotten it—and the one he was eating—from the coffee shop, and it was pure bliss on her tongue. The chocolate was just a little melty and she had to lick her fingers several times as she went. When she was done, she reached into her cooler for a bottle of water, grabbed a second one, and handed it to Julian. He thanked her and she realized they were like one of those couples who've been together for years—they were completely in sync with each other and it felt…nice.

Really nice.

Not wanting to go there, she stretched in her seat and went back to the story. Over the next hour they shared some fruit as they read, and Charlotte realized this was just as glorious as she'd always imagined it would be. Maybe even more so. When she finally couldn't sit any longer, she stood and put her Kindle down.

"The ocean's calling," she said. "I need to put my feet in it for a little bit."

Julian nodded but didn't look up from the screen.

The first wave of cool water washed over her and she sighed happily. Swimming in the ocean was totally not her thing, but getting her feet wet and walking in it a little was the perfect compromise. In her practical one-piece bathing suit and floral sarong wrapped around her waist, she fit right in. She walked up the beach a ways and looked out at the people who were doing the same thing—camped out in their spots with friends and families—and when she turned to go back, she noticed Julian watching her.

He wasn't smiling and maybe he just happened to be looking in this direction, but her heart gave a little kick in her chest at his gaze. There were many things she'd noticed about Julian in this last week, mainly how intense and serious he was. After he'd explained to her about his life and his current situation, she could understand it. Still, she wondered what he would be like if all of that hadn't happened to him.

Would he smile more? Laugh more? Would he flirt with her?

Yeah, she was going to have to figure out exactly what she was doing here. Why was she still hanging out with him?

And vice versa.

Slowly, Charlotte made her way back to their spot and sat back down in her chair.

"How was the water?"

She couldn't make herself look directly at him because she had a feeling he'd be able to tell exactly where her thoughts had been. "Good. It was good. It felt really…"

"Good?" he asked.

"Um…yeah."

With a small smile and a nod, Julian went back to his book, and Charlotte took a moment to look at him and try to get a read on him. Again. He was a bit of an enigma and he was possibly the first person she couldn't figure out.

Settling back comfortably, she picked up her tablet and checked the Wi-Fi connection, and hid a smile when she saw she had one. It seemed odd now that she hadn't done this before but she tilted the screen so Julian couldn't see it and did a search on him.

Julian Grayson, drummer for Grammy award-winning band Shaughnessy…age 35…single…

After that was a description of the band and a list of their biggest hits and albums. A bit further down it came to the personal information about his very public wedding stunt and subsequent disappearance. According to this article, he hadn't been seen in public since that day.

Clearly, they're just not looking hard enough, she thought, because he was hardly disguising himself. She pulled up a page full of images of him, and other than the perpetual five-o'clock shadow and his need for a haircut, he looked pretty recognizable. And from what else she could tell, there wasn't anyone lurking around trying to get a picture of him. Even here on a fairly crowded beach, no one was coming forward and talking to him, so maybe…maybe… Hell if she knew. Was it a good thing or a bad one that he was forcing himself into seclusion?

This was where her psychology degree came into play.

But why? Why did she even care why he was in seclusion? It was his right to do what he wanted and how he chose to handle his anger and grief over a failed relationship.

She glanced at him again, careful to keep her tablet facing away from him. "Can I ask you something?"

"Sure," he said, but he didn't look at her.

"Now that you're back from…you know, are you going to start playing with your band again?"

Julian didn't answer. Instead he turned off his tablet and put it in his bag right before he stood and stretched. She figured he was just ready to move, but then he looked out toward the ocean and said, "I think I've had enough of the beach today. Feel free to stay here as long as you want. I'll come back for the stuff later."

Seriously? Standing up, she got right in front of him until he was forced to look at her. "You can't just leave this stuff here. Someone will take it."

He shrugged. "Then I'll replace it."

The man was beyond infuriating. "What is your deal?" she asked with irritation. "I mean, we were just sitting here and everything was fine and now you're just going to jump up and leave rather than answer my question?"

"Pretty much."

A dozen questions and retorts played in her mind, but she couldn't get the words out. He wanted to leave? Fine. There was no way she was going to stay, however. She'd take her own stuff and go and she seriously hoped someone stole his.

With a huff, she moved aside and watched him walk away with nothing but the bag that held his tablet. For a full minute, she didn't move, and when she realized he really was leaving, she had no choice but to collect her stuff. Staying and relaxing was no longer possible, so she did her best to grab as much as she could and try to move it to the car. Julian had helped her earlier, but there was no way she was going to call out and ask for his help now.

Clumsily, Charlotte started to walk across the sand toward her car. She'd gone all of ten steps when her bag slipped from her hands. When she picked it up, her blanket fell. Letting everything drop to the sand, she growled with frustration. And just as she was about to bend over and start again, Julian was there beside her. Wordlessly, he picked everything up and started walking ahead of her.

She wanted to be annoyed with him, but right now she was just relieved not to have to carry everything herself. Following behind him, her mind raced. Every time she was ready to write him off as a self-centered jerk, he did something to prove her wrong and she had no idea what to make of it.

And she was getting tired of trying to psychoanalyze him.

It was getting to be a full-time job.

Normally it would have felt awkward to spend so much time without speaking, but it seemed the safest way to go right now. At her car, Charlotte almost cringed. As a rule, she wasn't ashamed of her car—it was a ten-year-old Toyota—but right now she wondered what was going through Julian's mind when he saw it. Without knowing too much about him, she had no way of knowing if he was one of those snobs who looked down on people who had less than he did, but her gut told her he wasn't.

Then again, her gut had told her that he was a homeless guy who needed help, and look where that had gotten her.

Slamming the trunk shut, she finally looked at him. "Thanks. I appreciate the help."

As usual, he didn't say anything, and while part of her wanted to rail at him and demand to know what he was thinking, the other part of her was just…done. He clearly had issues or some sort of personality disorder, and she dealt with enough of that on a typical work day. Having to deal with it on her day off was just asking too much. With a sigh, she said goodbye and turned away.

"Charlotte," he said gruffly when she opened the car door.

With her head down, she didn't turn around; she simply waited. After a full minute of silence, she spun around. "What?" she snapped, unable to help herself.

He seemed as frustrated as she was, and Charlotte secretly hoped he was just as confused too. Raking a hand through his hair, he stared at her and there was annoyance as well as vulnerability in his eyes. "I don't like talking about my life," he finally said.

"No kidding," she murmured.

"Maybe it's not logical or practical, but there it is. My life's a freaking mess right now, and if I don't talk about it—"

"Then it's still going to be a mess," she finished for him, instantly going into social worker mode. Taking a step closer, she went on. "You went through something that was devastating to you and you took off to avoid dealing with it. Or," she quickly said when he made to interrupt, "that was how you chose to deal with it. Either way, Julian, you can't just pretend it didn't happen and you can't go on not talking about your life. I don't care if you don't talk to me about it, it's really none of my business. But I have a feeling you're not talking to anyone about it."

"It's no one's business," he said, teeth clenched.

"Really? What about your friends? Your bandmates? I would imagine at some point you're going to have to talk to them about this. Your leaving affected them too, you know. As much as you want to claim you're the wounded party here—and no one's doubting that—your actions after you walked away from the wedding had an effect on everyone there."

He looked like he was about to say something and then thought better of it.

"Have you thought about talking to someone?" she asked. "A friend, a clergyman, or a therapist?"

"No one needs to hear about my problems. There are people who are far worse off than I am."

"Oh, I agree. But it doesn't mean you don't need to

talk to someone and figure out how to move forward from here." She paused and tried to organize her thoughts. "Julian, you had a life before that day, and a career. You can't just let it all go because of one incident."

With a mirthless laugh, Julian turned and paced away before coming back toward her. "I wasted five damn years," he growled, his voice louder and more intense than she'd ever heard him speak. "I'm a joke in the industry! No amount of talking to someone is going to change that, Charlotte."

Her heart broke for him. His pride as well as his heart had been damaged by this woman. There was no way she could try to make light of it or tell him everything would be okay. She had no idea if it would. In her life, she'd never been so deeply in love or so devastatingly betrayed, so she had no experience to draw from. All she could do was understand that he'd been hurt and accept him exactly where he was at.

With a small nod, she met his gaze. "I'm so sorry she did this to you," she said quietly. "I wish there was something I could do or say that would help, but…there isn't." Reaching out, she took one of his hands in hers and gently squeezed. "I hope someday you'll smile again, Julian, and that you'll find some peace." When she went to pull away, he held her hand tightly in his. She gasped softly and her eyes widened.

"Why?" he said, his voice deep and gravelly. "Why do you even care?"

"It's just in my nature," Charlotte admitted. "It's who I am."

"So I'm like a case to you," he stated, sounding bitter about it.

She shook her head. "No. You're not. That first day? Yes. But now that I know a little more about you, it's not how I see you at all." Her heart beat wildly at the admission, because she knew exactly where that statement would lead.

"How do you see me?" His voice was softer now and somehow the space between them was disappearing.

Swallowing hard, she decided she had nothing to lose. "I see you as a man, Julian. A very sad and hurt man." With her free hand, Charlotte reached up and caressed his cheek. "And I wish there was a way I could ease your pain and make you smile."

When Julian continued to stare at her, she thought she'd said too much, that she'd said something wrong, because his expression became closed, guarded. The last thing she wanted to do was push him away—not that she saw this going anywhere, anyway, but at the least she wanted him to think of her as a friend.

"When I'm around you, I do smile."

Her own lips twitched at his admission. "Behind my back? Because most of the time you're pretty serious-looking."

Then his expression did relax and his lips softened into a small smile.

And he was even sexier when he did that.

Between his incredibly handsome face, his hard, muscled body, and the sheer size of him, he had Charlotte practically in a puddle at his feet.

"Are you always this sassy or is it just with me?" he teased.

"Just you," she said, meaning for it to come out

lightly, but somehow her voice was a little breathless and a lot more serious.

Her answer seemed to please him as he wrapped an arm around her waist and pulled her in close to him. "Just me?" he whispered and Charlotte could only nod at the intensity in those two simple words. "Good."

It was the last thing he said before leaning down and capturing her lips with his.

Chapter 4

WHAT THE HELL AM I DOING?

Yeah, that seemed to be a common question for Julian where Charlotte was concerned, but her sassy mouth was quite the turn-on. He couldn't resist kissing her even if he tried.

And it surprised the heck out of him how responsive Charlotte was in his arms. Her lips were as soft as her curves and she smelled like the ocean and sunshine—which were now two of his favorite scents. Her hands glided up his biceps and over his shoulders to rest against his nape as she pressed even closer.

Why on earth had he opted to do this in the middle of a public parking lot? Right now, he wanted someplace to lay her down and touch her as he continued to kiss and taste her. Her tongue skimmed along his bottom lip and he groaned with need. The kiss went from tentative to sweet to *holy crap* in the blink of an eye and Julian cursed their location.

His hands cupped her bottom to hold her close to him, and the urgency he felt to explore her was something he'd never expected to feel again. Only...

He'd never felt this kind of urgency with Dena.

Ever.

And that was the single thought that caused him to break the kiss and take a step back.

Charlotte's eyes were closed, but they slowly

fluttered open as she looked at him with wonder. Her lips were wet and her cheeks flushed. The only thought he had was how he'd love to see her look like that while sprawled across his bed.

He took another step back.

"Um…yeah," he said, his voice rough. He scrubbed a hand along the back of his neck and had no idea what he was supposed to do or say right now.

"Please don't apologize," Charlotte said quickly. "I mean, even if you are sorry or you regret it, please don't say it." She moved back to the open car door and glanced inside as if suddenly remembering it was there. "I—I should go."

All Julian could do was nod.

"So…um, take care of yourself," she said nervously and then turned to climb into her car. He knew he should say something—anything!—to her, but his voice just wouldn't work. Instead he stood back and watched her pull out of the parking spot and drive away.

It hit him then that he was shaking. "What is going on with me?" he murmured. Charlotte's words from earlier came back to him.

It doesn't mean you don't need to talk to someone and figure out how to move forward from here.

With the weight of the world on his shoulders, Julian made his way back to the beach, where he grabbed up the chairs and umbrella and made the awkward walk back to the house. He should have done it in two trips, but he knew what he needed to do and the last thing he wanted was to put it off any longer.

Once inside, he immediately grabbed a bottle of cold water from the refrigerator and then pulled out his

phone. Sitting down on the large sectional that faced the
wall of windows overlooking the ocean, he brought up
Dylan's number and hit Call.

"Jules!" Dylan said happily. "To what do I owe this
honor?"

"Honor?"

Dylan chuckled. "Yeah, you never reach out and call
anyone. We're usually the ones hunting you down. And
considering we only talked a week ago, I'm feeling kind
of special here."

"Don't be an idiot."

"Don't ruin this for me," Dylan deadpanned.

Julian laughed quietly. "Fine. I won't."

"So, what's up?"

"I kissed Charlotte," he blurted out and then cursed
himself.

"Social worker Charlotte?"

"Yeah."

"And?"

"What do you mean, 'and'? Isn't that enough?"

"Um…no," Dylan said. "I'm not seeing what the
problem is here."

Julian sighed and began to second-guess making this
call. "I shouldn't be out there kissing anyone or even
thinking about it."

"Why not?"

"Seriously? You know why. Earlier this year I was
about to get married and—"

"And you dodged a bullet!" Dylan said loudly. "Jules,
listen to me—what happened with Dena sucked. We all
know that. But that whole situation doesn't mean you're
not allowed to get involved with anyone ever again. If

anything, I would have thought you'd be sleeping your way across the country. You're not supposed to live like a monk for the rest of your life."

"That was never my style—sleeping around just for the sake of sleeping around."

"Please," Dylan said with a snort of derision, "we all did it in the beginning and you were no different. It was fun for a while and then we all grew up."

"Still, it's not who I am now."

"Come on—you're telling me that while you were on the road these last months…?"

"Okay, fine. I wasn't exactly a monk, but it wasn't—I mean, it didn't…"

"Yeah," Dylan said. "I know. Sometimes it's just something to pass the time."

"Exactly. And afterward it just felt…wrong. And I didn't feel like it did anything except offer a physical release and it wasn't even all that satisfying."

"Well, that sucks."

"Tell me about it. And that's what I'm trying to avoid, Dylan. I don't want that emptiness, that shallowness. I don't want to be that person who goes for the casual to pass the time."

"Okay, then good for you, man. Really. I think that's great. But it sounds like you're freaking out over this Charlotte chick. Why?"

That was the million-dollar question.

Again.

What was it about her?

"I'm not looking to get involved with anyone. Like, ever again," he admitted.

On the other end of the line he heard Dylan sigh.

"You think that now, but believe me, you're going to change your mind."

"No, I'm not," he said obstinately.

"Dude, let me tell you something. When I got out of rehab, I was determined to live my life like a choirboy. I didn't want anyone to think I was the same guy I was when I went in and that included sleeping with the kind of women I used to."

"It's not the same thing, Dylan."

"It's exactly the same thing. When I met Paige and realized I was attracted to her, I was convinced I wasn't good enough for her—that I *couldn't* be good enough for her. And I told myself I could resist her. But I couldn't. And believe me, I fought it for a long time and the only thing I was doing was making myself crazy."

"I'm not looking to change like that. Our situations are completely different. You were trying to change your image. I'm unwilling to let myself be in a situation like I was with Dena ever again. I don't want a woman having that kind of hold on me. I refuse to be made a fool of twice."

Another sigh. "Julian, you have to know that Dena was a freaking head case. She was a manipulative bitch. And if you can get past some of your issues, you'll admit that. She was like that from the beginning—you and I had this conversation not long after I got out of rehab. I never understood why you stayed. Why you were so convinced she was the one and you had to put up with all her crap."

Julian was coming to realize at least part of the reason why, but he wasn't ready to admit it to anyone yet, either. It would just add to everyone's perception of him as a joke.

"It doesn't matter. Not anymore. The fact is I was hanging out with Charlotte and...I don't know, it just happened and it freaked me out." The only reason he chose to call Dylan was because he knew that of all his friends, he'd be the one who might understand. Not that their situations were the same, but there were enough similarities in the aftermaths of each of their rock-bottom moments.

"I get it. I do. Like I said, with Paige? Damn. Did I ever tell you that she came on to me first?"

Julian chuckled. "That sweet girl hit on someone like you? No way."

Dylan took the teasing and laughed along. "True story. And that was a total test of my self-control. I did turn her down because—like I said—I didn't think I was good enough. And then when I did give in? Yeah, it freaked me out. I walked away and then cursed myself for doing it. Luckily, she was persistent," he added lightly.

"Yeah, yeah, yeah, and the rest is history," Julian mocked just as lightly. "I'm overreacting, right? I mean, I kissed Charlotte. So what? It doesn't have to mean anything other than I'm a man and she's an attractive woman and I got caught up in a moment. Right? That's a thing, isn't it?"

"Sure. Definitely. So, you're saying you don't want to go there again? Like if she knocked on your door right now, you wouldn't act on it?"

Right then an image of Charlotte standing in the doorway flashed in his mind. She'd still be wearing that clingy bathing suit that had tormented him all day and the filmy sarong he wanted to untie with his teeth. Her hair would be loose and windblown and her blue eyes issuing all kinds of promises. There was no way he'd be able to resist her if that happened.

But it wouldn't. Of that, Julian was certain. Charlotte hadn't been chasing after him; if anything, he'd been the one pursuing her.

"I can't act on it," Julian said roughly. "Look, I had a lot of time to think while I was on the road and I know what I have to do with my life to keep myself sane."

"And?"

"It doesn't matter. I know what I have to do and I need to know that you guys are going to respect that."

Dylan cursed. "You're going to take off again, aren't you? You're gonna blow off the music, the band, your freaking life all because of what one messed-up chick did? How is that fair? Why are you taking a bad situation and making it worse?"

"It's not like that!" Julian said defensively. "Do you think this is how I envisioned my life? I'm never going to be able to walk around the city and see people I know and not think about how they all knew! They *knew!* And no one said a word. How many guys did we work with who slept with Dena? How many friends, business associates, acquaintances were there?" He paused and caught his breath because he was beginning to think he was having a panic attack. "I can't do it. I can't live with that kind of thing on my mind every time I turn around. It's too much."

Dylan was quiet for a long moment. "And so you're willing to give it all up?"

"I don't have a choice."

"You do, Jules. You really do. Don't let her win."

"She's already won. She's been paid off so she got

the money she always wanted." And just saying it out loud almost made him sick to his stomach. "She got my money and my pride. I've got nothing left to give."

"You have everything left to give! You didn't give her every penny you made! You gave her an amount to make her go away. End of story. Now she's gone and moved on and you need to as well. Trust me, dude. It's gonna get better."

But Julian was shaking his head. "No."

Dylan was quiet for a moment. "Will you just do me a favor and promise me something?"

"Maybe."

"Matt's flying in on Friday. Will you just come and hang with all of us and talk? Please?"

Julian wanted to say no—to let Dylan tell Riley, Matt, and Mick what he'd just said. But he couldn't. He owed them more than that.

"Fine."

"Thank you," Dylan said, sounding relieved. They were silent for a minute before Dylan added, "So this social worker? Is she a good kisser?"

Julian burst out laughing, and even though he'd never go into detail over how hot their brief encounter was, he had to give his friend props for asking.

"How about you tell me how Paige is doing and how you're spoiling her during this pregnancy instead?"

It was almost as if he could hear Dylan's smile. "Deal."

—⁓—

Monday morning, Charlotte was sitting at her desk unable to focus on a darn thing. How was it possible that one kiss could affect her this much? Granted, it had been pretty hot and unexpected and if they hadn't been in the middle of a public parking lot, she would have been totally on board for taking things a little further.

Not that it mattered. It seemed like Julian was having regrets about it even before they were done.

Not the greatest ego boost in the world.

"Hey, Charlotte, you got a minute?"

Looking up, she saw her supervisor, Jennifer, standing in the doorway with an armload of files. She wanted to groan and tell her to go away, but maybe diving into some cases would help clear her mind of Julian.

And his fantastic kissing skills.

Three hours later, she realized there may not be enough case files in the world to do that.

At lunch, she sat in the break room with the salad and fruit she'd packed for herself and it all tasted like sawdust in her mouth. Looking around the room, it felt as if the walls were closing in. She was restless and twitchy and needed to get outside for a bit and just... breathe.

Tossing her food in the trash, she grabbed her purse and walked through the office, straight out the front door. The building wasn't in Malibu or even near the beach, but Canoga Park was an area where there was always something to see that piqued her interest.

But right now, she really wished she had her toes in the sand. Oversleeping that morning meant she'd had to skip her trip to the coffee shop and her few minutes of beach bliss, and now she was really feeling it. She walked up and down the block and tried to clear her mind, but it refused to cooperate.

When she went back into the office, she was greeted

with a handful of phone messages and a waiting room full of people needing to be seen.

Typical Monday.

By the time she left for the day, it was after seven and she was nearly frantic for something substantial to eat. No frozen entrées or salads, she needed a real meal. Thoughts of burgers and fries ran through her mind and they made her think of Julian. Stopping at the coffee shop for a premade sandwich and maybe a brownie for dessert was another option. And that made her think of Julian.

"Gah!" she huffed as she climbed into her car and headed for the supermarket to get something to make—maybe some salmon or something else that was easy to prepare and was real food rather than processed.

Did she drive past the burger place thinking she might see him?

Yes.

Did she detour to go by the coffee shop in case he was there?

Yes.

Was she starting to feel a little like a crazed stalker who needed to get professional help?

Um...definitely yes.

Luckily by the time she arrived at her place, her stomach was growling loud enough to block out anything else and Charlotte was more than happy to give it the attention it clearly needed. The salmon, steamed veggies, rice, and a glass of wine were the perfect meal. When she was done and sitting on her couch with her Kindle, she felt thoroughly satisfied.

Seriously? The food is what you're feeling so good

*about? Wouldn't some time alone with a man feel a
whole lot better?*

She was seriously getting tired of her inner self
mocking her. Charlotte had no issues with being alone.
Not really. But after spending some time with Julian, she
realized just how long it had been since she'd gone out on
a date. And since dating Julian wasn't an option based on
how cagey he was, she knew she'd have to do something
else about ending this being-alone streak she was on.

"Note to self, call the girls this week and start putting
out feelers for a blind date." Even saying the phrase made
her cringe a little. She'd never had any luck with getting
set up. There was never any spark or attraction or even a
second date. Unfortunately, this was where she was at.
Maybe she'd catch a break this time and meet a nice guy.

"Doubtful," she murmured and then cursed herself
for immediately being so negative. Maybe the problem
wasn't the guys. Maybe it was her.

With a groan, she put her tablet down and opted for a
second glass of wine.

By Friday, Charlotte felt a little more in control. She'd
had a particularly crazy week and had spent extra time in
Santa Monica at the homeless shelter. With the weekend
wide open ahead of her, she drove home that afternoon
with a sense of excitement at having two whole days to
herself.

She'd opted for a group text to the girls to see about
someone finding her a date and amazingly enough, she
had one on Saturday night with a guy who sounded…
normal. Oliver. Yeah, the name didn't do much to

inspire her or make her think of some big, sexy guy, but
that didn't mean it was the case. If anything, there was
no big sell on him, no over-the-top promises; he just
seemed like a decent guy who—like Charlotte—was
looking for the chance to meet someone new.

So she was hopeful.

All week she'd been hoping to catch a glimpse of
Julian, without any luck. Deep down, she knew it was
for the best. Even if he wasn't recovering from a bad
breakup, what would someone like him—a world-
famous musician—want with a small-town social
worker? There wasn't one glamorous thing about her,
and he was living in million-dollar-plus homes and
probably had more than one of them.

And multiple cars too, no doubt.

They were as opposite as any two people could be.
When he was comfortable enough to get involved with
someone again, he'd more than likely gravitate toward
someone in his own social circle.

And that definitely wasn't her.

Never had been, never would be.

Which was kind of depressing. Didn't most people
dream of living the lifestyle of the rich and famous? Was
there ever a time when she had?

"Of course," she murmured as she stepped into her
apartment. Growing up, she'd always imagined what
it would be like to be rich and live in one of those
houses—well, just like Julian was living in right now.
Growing up in Malibu, she wasn't immune to being
around the wealthy set. And while her parents were
both highly respected business professionals and considered upper middle class, they'd never reached the

house-on-the-beach level. Even after her dad had gotten back on his feet and had steady employment again.

It was funny how Charlotte had—for the most part—grown up in a very comfortable environment where she had never known poverty. Even during the time when her father had been unemployed, they hadn't lost everything or been forced to start over. Their struggle had been emotional and psychological, and yet it made such an impact on her that it was what she'd gravitated toward as a career. All these years later and her parents still thought it was an admirable profession but an odd choice for her.

Some days she agreed.

How much easier would it be to work in a more glamorous and less gritty environment? Maybe then she wouldn't be so aware of the differences between herself and the Julians of the world. Maybe she would have a little more confidence in herself where he was concerned and then she'd feel totally at ease with seeking him out.

It wasn't as if she didn't know where to find him. She remembered their conversation from their dinner on the beach when he'd pointed it out to her.

The fifth one down is mine for the next few months.

If she was a bold kind of woman, she'd simply drive down to the beach and walk until she found the house, climb up the back steps, and—what? What on earth did she think she'd do? Ask him out? Jump him? Seriously, what would she do?

"Nothing," she said with a weary sigh. "I'd do nothing because I'm *not* the kind of woman who walks up the stairs to a man's home and does anything."

And right now, she wasn't so sure if that was a good thing or a bad thing.

Ugh. Why was she doing this to herself? It didn't matter about the what-ifs. The fact was that she was going out with a very nice man tomorrow night and she was happy about it. They were meeting for drinks at one of her favorite wine bars down by the Santa Monica pier and with any luck, they'd go for a walk either along the pier or on the beach and she'd like him enough to want to go out with him again.

It was a totally attainable goal, and Charlotte was the queen of helping people make a list of their goals and then reaching them.

Go Charlotte!

It was a lot different when she was making the list for herself.

"Obviously I'm no good at practicing what I preach," she murmured as she walked into the kitchen. Rather than get Chinese takeout, she'd decided to make something herself and enjoy a late dinner on her tiny balcony.

All in all, not a bad way to spend the evening.

When her mind tried to correct her on a better way to spend the evening, she immediately shut it down and went to work on the dinner.

To block out any further chances of her mind wandering where it shouldn't, Charlotte hooked her iPod up to her mini speakers and hit one of her favorite playlists, one she normally listened to if she went for an early morning walk.

And wouldn't you know it, the first song to pop up was by Shaughnessy.

How could she have forgotten that song was on there?

It was okay, she could listen to the lead singer's voice and not focus at all on the drums playing in the background.

Only…that made her focus on the percussion sound and an image of Julian playing them.

Focus on something else! she admonished herself. There were so many other things she could be thinking about—how she wanted her chicken…was this too much broccoli…did Oliver play an instrument…

"Dammit," she hissed, more than a little annoyed with her wayward mind.

Looking around her kitchen, she spotted the bottle of wine from Monday night and decided another glass was in order. So she prepped her meal, drank some wine, and did her best not to picture a sweaty, sexy, shirtless drummer.

It made for a very long night.

—∿∿—

"You did a great job with this, Dylan. Seriously, this is impressive. I'm a little envious," Riley said as they finished touring the small guesthouse Dylan had converted into a personal studio. There were divided spaces to allow for isolation of instruments, recording equipment, an assortment of guitars, and the entire place was soundproofed. "I love my house and my studio, but compared to this it's tiny and almost unusable."

"Yeah, right," Dylan said sarcastically. "Your studio is awesome, and we've all jammed down there more than enough times to know that, so cut the crap."

"I'm expanding the space I've got back east," Matt said, accepting a beer Dylan pulled from the fully stocked kitchen. He took a drink and looked over at Julian. "What about you? When you start looking for a new place, are you going to want a separate building for a studio?"

All eyes were on him—Riley's, Matt's, and Mick's—and they were all obviously interested. Only Dylan opted to look away. Grabbing a bottle of beer for himself, Julian drank some of it down before answering. Might as well get it out of the way early in the day.

"No."

For a minute, no one spoke.

"You want to do something like what I have?" Riley asked. "The basement? I'll admit, it makes soundproofing a little trickier since you don't want anyone on the main floor to hear anything, but you can potentially have a lot more square footage on one level than you can with a guesthouse."

"That's not what I meant," Julian forced himself to say as he turned to pull up one of the barstools and sat down. "I'm not looking for any personal studio space because..." He paused and sighed, hating how hopeful they'd all been a minute ago and how he was going to be the one to ruin it all for them. "I'm not playing anymore. I'm retiring."

You could have heard a pin drop.

"Why don't we go back over to the house and talk," Dylan suggested even as he began to walk toward the door.

"I don't think that's necessary," Mick said, his eyes never leaving Julian's. "How long have you known about this?"

He shrugged. "It's been on my mind since the wedding. The more time I had to think about it, the more it made sense. I can't work around people who would stab me in the back like that."

"He was a studio tech!" Mick yelled. "In the grand scheme of things, he was a nobody. Trust me, he won't be working anywhere near us ever again!"

"All right, we need to calm down," Riley said levelly. "I think we all figured something like this might happen, and we need to sit down and listen to what Julian has to say."

So many times Julian had hated the way Riley always seemed to know exactly what to say and how to say it. It was annoying how the guy just had his shit together—always had—even when he was in the midst of his own crisis.

Wordlessly, everyone found a place to sit—except Mick—and waited him out.

"I don't know where to begin."

"Jules," Matt said cautiously, "you know we've all felt like this. It almost seems crazy that we're still together at all, because it's been a ridiculous few years for us. Riley having writer's block and wanting to call it quits, my Broadway flop that had me second-guessing my ability to play music at all, Dylan's rehab. Dude, seriously, you are among friends here. Literally. We've all been there."

It didn't matter how many people made that statement to him, it wasn't true. No one had dealt with the level of betrayal and embarrassment Julian had—no matter what they thought.

"I said it to Dylan and I'll say it again," Julian began, "it's not the same. I'm not doubting my musical ability. I love to play the drums and I've loved making a living at it, but at what cost? For years I was in denial about what was happening. I thought by not acknowledging it that it would all just…right itself. And time after time I thought it had. But in the end, look what happened. If I stay in this industry, I'm never going to be able to trust another living soul again, and that's not how I want to live."

"I get it, Julian, I do," Dylan chimed in. "The first event I went to after rehab, all I could think of was how I had to be on my guard constantly so I didn't find myself back with the people I used to party with. It was stressful, and even though I was approached and the opportunity was there for me to go back to my old ways, I resisted. Every day is still a struggle on some level. It doesn't matter how long I've been clean and sober, it's still hard. Right now, I'm sitting here drinking water while you guys are having beers.

"Six months ago, I wouldn't have been able to handle it. Even stocking the fridge for all of you had me sweating a bit, but I'm here and I'm handling it."

"That's just it," Julian countered, "I don't want to have to keep handling it. It's no way to live. At least not for me. I just want to have some peace in my life. For five freaking years I haven't had any peace!"

"And whose fault is that?" Mick snapped. "We all tried talking to you, Julian. You were convinced Dena was going to get her shit together and settle down. And that stunt at the wedding? That was all on you. No one asked you to make a public spectacle of the whole damn thing. I begged you not to do it, but you wouldn't be swayed!"

"You gave me the car and had everything waiting for me back at your house!" Julian snapped back.

"Because you gave me no choice! You were going to go through with publicly humiliating Dena no matter what I said, so I did what I could to make sure that at least you escaped the hotel before anyone could leak what happened to the paparazzi!"

Julian jumped to his feet, slamming the beer down on the table. "It was the only way to break the cycle! All along, everything she did was kept quiet. I knew how much she hated to look bad, and if I was really going to end this, it had to be in front of everyone she knew!"

"It didn't have to be at your wedding, Julian," Riley said, and for the first time, Julian heard disappointment in his voice. "I get what you were trying to do—at least now I finally do—but there had to be some other options."

"The end result would have been the same," Julian said dejectedly. "It still would have been devastating and humiliating and…and…"

"You can't be pissed at everyone for a situation you created," Mick stated, his frustration clear. "If you had given me even another day or two, we could have dealt with her without the public spectacle and having you essentially giving up the life you worked so hard for!"

Raking a hand through his hair, Julian sighed with frustration. "Look, I get that you're disappointed, all right? I get it! But there was always going to come a day when the band wasn't going to be the band anymore! And I'm not telling any of you that you can't keep playing. All I'm saying is that I'm not. So…go ahead and be upset with me and try to tell me how I'm wrong. I don't care. All I do care about right now is my sanity and just…getting out of the spotlight."

"Julian—" Riley began but Matt interrupted him.

"Jules, you may think this is going to last forever, but it will pass. I swear."

He shook his head. "It's not the press, man. I wish that was the only hang-up. I don't trust anyone. I *can't* trust anyone."

This time Riley stood and made sure he was heard. "Do you trust me?"

"What?"

"You heard me, do you trust me? Do you think I'm lying to you or betraying you?"

"Of course not."

"Do you think I'm going to hit on Charlotte?" Dylan asked with a smirk. "I mean, you know my history. Do you think I'm going to look her up and go and check her out, or maybe fix her up with one of my friends and—"

Julian stood and swung at Dylan, connecting with his friend's jaw.

It was chaos after that. Dylan stumbled back, Riley caught him, Matt grabbed Julian, and Mick stepped in between them all. "What the hell is going on here?" he yelled. "And who's Charlotte?"

Dylan straightened, and damn him, he still had a smirk on his face. He leaned in close to Julian. "You can be sure none of us would ever betray you. Ever. And you can stand here and play the victim, but in the last five years—even when you *knew* Dena was messing around—you never took a swing at anyone because of it. Think about that."

He didn't want to. Swinging at Dylan was out of frustration for the entire situation, not about Charlotte—it couldn't be. No way. She didn't mean anything to him other than a nice distraction since he'd returned home.

It had been a week since he'd seen her, and he hadn't even thought about her since she drove away after their kiss in the parking lot.

Okay, he had, but just a little.

Every night and pretty much every time he closed his eyes, but…it didn't mean anything.

"Are we all ready to sit down and talk like grown-ups or do we need a time out?" Mick asked sarcastically.

There were a few murmurs, but everyone sat back down.

"You're not quitting Shaughnessy," Mick finally said, his voice firm. "You need a little more time to adjust to the idea, fine. Take until after the label's anniversary party in January before setting up time to go back into the studio. Your appearance there isn't optional."

"You can't force me to play, Mick," Julian replied obstinately. "If I don't want to, there isn't a damn thing you can do about it."

"I manage this band and you have contracts and commitments. For the last three years I've had to deal with all of you having crap to work through. I stood by and helped with all of it. We've missed out on some pretty big things. Well, I'm here to tell you that I'm done standing by and waiting. If you don't start doing something—and soon—the fans will forget about you and you're not going to get them back." He paused and paced the room. "You're a great band and you can have the staying power of the Stones or Aerosmith, but not if this sabbatical doesn't come to an end soon."

"You never mentioned us missing anything," Riley said, confused. "Why haven't you brought it up before?"

"What good would it have done?" Mick yelled with exasperation. "You couldn't write, Matty was hiding, Dylan was in rehab… I mean, why would I add more pressure to any of you?" Then he turned to Julian. "But you?" He shook a finger at him. "You put yourself in this position, and you're going to pull yourself out of it."

Julian stood and shook his head. "Not gonna happen, Mick. There was a time when you could intimidate me and I'd cave. Not anymore. My mind is made up."

"Jules," Dylan spoke up. "This is a knee-jerk reaction. Just…give it some time. We can just put everything on hold until the New Year. Seriously. I think you need some time to settle back in and see that things aren't as bad as you think."

"I agree," Matt added. "We don't have to make any long-term decisions right now. We're all here together, so why don't we push the business stuff aside and just hang out and jam? That's really what I'm here for anyway." He grinned at the group and it seemed to ease some of the tension in the room.

And as much as Julian wanted to just leave, he had to admit that part of him was itching to get behind a set of drums. It had been so long since he'd played and…what harm could a couple of songs do, right? Looking across the room, he noticed the drums Dylan had purchased were Julian's signature set—Tama Artstar. His fingers twitched with the need to pick up a set of sticks and just play.

Not wanting to seem too anxious and get anyone's hopes up, Julian gave a careless shrug as he moved across the room toward the set. "Got nothing else to do today…"

And just like that, everyone took his place, picked up his gear, and began to play.

And damn if it didn't feel great.

The sky was clear and the stars were bigger and brighter than Charlotte could ever remember seeing.

There was a great breeze coming off the water as she walked along the nearly deserted beach.

She was happy from listening to a great jazz trio while enjoying some amazing wine and appetizers.

With a relaxed and happy grin, she thought the only thing that would have made this the perfect night was if her date had actually shown up.

Stood up.

Um…yeah. That was kind of a buzzkill on the evening and yet…it was hard to care when everything else around her was exactly to her liking.

After sitting at the bar for more than two hours, she'd given up. The thought of something happening to Oliver had crossed her mind, so she'd texted him to see if he was all right and he'd responded with: Sorry. Maybe we can try again next week. No explanation, no advance warning that he wasn't coming, so… *Sorry, Oliver. We won't be trying this again.*

In spite of what had just happened, she wasn't upset.

Was that what she wanted? The kind of guy who could be *called* dependable, but wasn't? A man who others made sound as though he was a safe choice rather than someone who made her heart pound with excitement?

"Nope," she whispered softly as she looked out at the ocean. She was far enough back that she could sit in the sand without getting wet and that's exactly what she decided to do. Pulling her knees to her chest—and thankful for the maxi dress so she could drape it over her legs—Charlotte sighed and closed her eyes and let her senses take over.

In her purse, her phone beeped with an incoming text. She knew it was going to be Tami or one of the girls asking how her date went, and when she pulled the phone out, she smiled at being right.

She let Tami know that she'd been stood up. Her

friend invited her to come over to talk, shocked to hear Charlotte was walking the beach alone at night.

While she appreciated her friend's concern, Tami had no idea just how often Charlotte indulged in this kind of activity and there was no way she was going to admit to that right now.

> **Charlotte**: I promise to text you when I get home—which should be soon.
> **Tami**: Don't make me get in the car, CC. Because if I don't hear from you in 1 hour...
> **Charlotte**: I promise! Geez. Relax.

She signed off with a heart emoji before sliding her phone back into her purse and laughing again. It would have been easy to be annoyed with her friend for fixing her up with a no-show, but she couldn't. The whole Oliver thing wasn't really Tami's fault, and as for her being concerned...well, it was nice that someone cared about her.

She was beginning to feel like no one else did.

"Okay, dramatic much?" she murmured with a sigh.

Unfortunately, now that Tami had put the thought in her head about her safety, Charlotte no longer felt particularly relaxed. Slowly she came to her feet and brushed the sand from her dress. Inhaling deeply, she looked out at the waves one more time before reaching down for her purse. When she turned around, she nearly screamed.

Julian.

He stood ten feet away from her and his expression was unreadable.

Charlotte normally believed in coincidences, but

she was having a hard time accepting this situation was just that. The hopeless romantic side of her—which didn't come out very often—really wanted to think he'd been hoping to find her here or that he'd specifically been looking for her. But from everything she knew about Julian, he was too stubborn and strong-willed for such things.

They stood like that—facing one another, silently assessing—for a few minutes.

"Hi," she said finally, but didn't make a move toward him. The breeze off the water kicked up and her hair was blowing wildly; her long skirt whipped against her legs. She groaned at what a mess she must look like but she still couldn't make herself move.

It took all her self-control not to sag with relief when he finally took a step toward her. "What are you doing out here alone so late?"

And her foolish heart kicked hard in her chest at his gruff question.

"Just getting my daily beach fix in."

But Julian shook his head even as he kept advancing. "You were out here this morning before you went to work," he said, his voice low and almost tortured. "Every morning this week you've been out here. I can see you from my deck. Try again."

He knew she'd been here earlier? How…? Why…?

Swallowing hard, she said, "I was heading home and wanted to come out here for a bit. I enjoy watching the sunset. A girl can get two daily beach fixes, you know." She meant to sound defiant, but she had a feeling it didn't come out quite that way.

Julian's gaze roamed over her from head to toe.

And Charlotte cursed how unsexy the windblown look was on her.

They were almost toe to toe and she studied him with equal interest. His jeans were faded and hung low on his hips, his T-shirt was of the threadbare variety and looked like he'd owned it for years. And his hair was a wreck, just as hers was.

And then there was the five-o'clock shadow.

It should have been a full-grown beard by now and yet it wasn't.

But that didn't mean she didn't want to feel it scratching her sensitive skin.

Everywhere.

Charlotte held her breath while she waited for Julian to call her out on the admission, but he didn't. Instead, he reached up and stroked one strong finger along her cheek right before his hand cupped it. Her lips parted on a sigh and—unable to help herself—she leaned into his hand.

"What are you doing out here?" she asked softly.

"Waiting for you," he replied, so quietly she almost didn't hear him. And before she could respond, Julian closed the distance between them. He felt so warm and solid and wonderful that she forgot what she was going to say.

Not that it would have mattered, because Julian lowered his head and gently touched his lips to hers. There was an uncertainty to him—a vulnerability—and it was quite possibly the sexiest thing about him. She loved the fact that he was comfortable enough around her to be like this.

One soft kiss turned to two and Charlotte slowly ran her hands up his arms.

Julian's tongue gently teased at her lips as her hands raked up into his hair.

And then she was lost.

They went from slow and sweet to nothing but need in the blink of an eye. Charlotte knew this was why she wasn't disappointed about being stood up—no one made her feel needy and out of control the way Julian Grayson did. Her date wouldn't have been like this.

It couldn't.

They kissed until they were breathless, and when Julian lifted his head, he began a trail of kisses along her cheek and nipped at her earlobe before shifting and resting his forehead against hers.

"Why can't I stay away from you?" he asked, but Charlotte had a feeling the question was more to himself than her. Reaching up, he caressed her cheek. "I should be able to stay away, but I just can't."

Trembling, she mimicked his pose and savored the scratchiness of his jaw. "Right now, I'm kind of glad you didn't stay away." It was good that she was looking down and couldn't see his reaction to her words. She knew how cagey he could be and the last thing she wanted to do was have him take off on her—not after the second-hottest kiss of her life.

"Come home with me, Charlotte," he begged quietly. "Please."

No words had ever sounded sweeter to her.

"We don't have to do anything but talk, if that's what you want." He paused. "I've missed seeing you, talking to you."

Pulling back, this time she did meet his gaze. "I've missed seeing you too."

If it were possible, Charlotte would say he looked relieved and almost…grateful.

Julian reached for her hand and they walked up the beach toward his house. Neither said a word, and Charlotte was thankful for these few minutes to get her emotions under control. Maybe it was the same for him.

At the foot of the stairs that led to his deck, she stopped and took her hand from his, pulling her phone from her purse. Julian looked at her quizzically.

"I promised my friend Tami I'd text her when I got home." As soon as she said the words, she realized how it sounded. "I mean—"

"She wants to know you're safe," he finished for her and then caressed her cheek again. "You are, Charlotte. I promise."

There were so many ways she could take that statement, but rather than analyze it, she quickly typed a message to her friend and slid her phone back into her purse. With a smile, she held out her hand to him. "Thank you."

He kissed her hand and gave it a gentle squeeze before turning and leading them up the stairs. At the top, Julian made to keep walking, but Charlotte stopped and turned to look at the view. She gasped softly.

"Breathtaking."

Julian stepped up behind her and wrapped his arms around her waist. "Yes, you are."

Charlotte knew she was blushing, thankful the moonlight was the only light on her. She leaned back against him and relished how good he felt, how perfect the view was, and how happy she was to be exactly where she was.

"I bet you get an amazing view of the sunset up here."

"There's no better view than the one I have right now," he said quietly.

And if their night ended right here—if for some reason Julian decided to take her back to her car and wish her a good night—she'd be okay with it.

But then he began nuzzling her neck and her head fell slightly to the side as she purred with pleasure at his lips on her skin.

Okay, maybe she wouldn't be all right with leaving, because she wanted so much more of this—of what he was offering—that she was almost frantic with need.

"Julian," she said breathlessly.

"Come inside, Charlotte," he whispered against her throat.

Slowly, she turned in his arms and nodded.

And as Julian led the way into the house, she knew nothing was ever going to be the same.

Chapter 5

IT WAS ALMOST AS IF JULIAN HAD CONJURED HER UP IN his mind.

That had been his first thought when he'd walked out onto the back deck earlier and spotted Charlotte. He wasn't normally someone who sat outside alone at night, but he'd been restless and it was as if something was drawing him there. And that something was now stepping tentatively into his temporary home.

She looked around with wide eyes as she took in the space. The house was rather impressive and had an incredible view, but that wasn't what he wanted to talk about right now. Instead, he pulled her in close and kissed her again—not with the urgency he'd felt a few minutes ago, but just because he could. And because they seemed so in sync with one another, she melted against him and he felt her begin to relax.

His hands went to her waist and all he could think of was what was she wearing under her dress. There were tiny straps on her shoulders and he could tell she didn't have on a bra, but what else was she wearing—or not wearing—under there? His hands slowly slid around to cup her bottom and he gently squeezed, confirming there were panties.

Good to know.

Except now he wanted to find out what kind they

were—silk or lace? What color?—and whether he was going to remove them with his hands or teeth.

Yeah, his mind went there.

"Come sit down," he said as he reluctantly ended the kiss. Honestly, he would be perfectly content kissing her all night long, but it wasn't particularly realistic and he wanted to honor his promise for them to sit and talk.

Charlotte nodded and followed him. He chose the sofa in the living room that faced the beach, and while she sat, he opened the sliding doors to let the ocean air in.

"Can I get you something to drink?"

"Some water. Please."

Nodding, Julian went to the kitchen and grabbed each of them a bottle, and then joined her on the sofa.

"It's an amazing view," she said, looking straight ahead and not at him. "You're lucky to have a place like this."

"It's temporary, but I'm enjoying it." As soon as he said it, he knew there was a chance Charlotte would want to know more. Honestly, it wasn't what he wanted to talk about right now.

Or ever.

"I know I would," she said, giving him a shy smile. "I've always lived in Malibu, but never close to the beach. I've looked at other cities to see if I could afford a house on the beach anywhere else, but…I can't. Not on a social worker's salary."

He nodded. "I grew up on the East Coast near Myrtle Beach, and the beach was only two blocks away. My mom used to complain we weren't close enough. I can definitely see the appeal—especially after being here—but it's not nearly private enough."

"You could always look into buying your own island," she teased and then laughed softly.

"Right," he said, laughing with her. "Because that's not completely overreacting to the need for privacy."

She shrugged. "I don't know, I hear about people doing that sort of thing all the time. I watch a lot of HGTV. There's even a show about it."

"About people who buy islands?"

"Uh-huh. And sometimes it's only a couple of acres— you know, big enough for a house or two—and sometimes they're a little bigger. I'm not talking about buying an island that's big enough for a small city or anything."

"Well, that really would be excessive…"

She laughed and it was like music to his ears. "Just a bit."

"I think I appreciate modern conveniences too much to live on my own island. Getting takeout would be a bitch."

That kept Charlotte laughing, and Julian found he wanted to keep doing it.

"Can you imagine the delivery fee for a pizza?" he joked.

"Or the wait time?" she said.

Her cheeks were a little rosy and her eyes were bright, and she just…she was beautiful. Charlotte Clark was quite possibly the most beautiful woman he'd ever seen and she wasn't even trying. Julian had dated models and actresses before, and all of them had been the kind of women who never had a hair out of place and wore designer clothes. In the short time he'd known Charlotte, he'd seen her looking anything but glamorous and she rarely seemed to wear makeup, yet she took his breath away.

Reaching out, he carefully ran a hand over her hair and took one long, loose curl and wrapped it around his finger. It was just as soft as he'd imagined it would be. Self-consciously, she pulled back and tried running her own hands over her hair to try to tame it, but he stopped her.

"Don't," he said. "I think it's very sexy like this."

Charlotte gave him a look of disbelief. "It's a wind-blown mess," she said quietly, glancing away. "I probably should have tied it back in a ponytail or something before heading down on the sand."

But Julian shook his head. "No. I was watching you while you were standing down there and was a little fascinated by your hair. You wear it up more than you wear it down and…" He paused and took that one curl around his finger again. "I really like it when you wear it like this."

She blushed and looked like she was about to argue with him, then thought better of it.

"Can I ask you something?" he said, still playing with her hair.

"Of course."

"Why social work? I mean, I know it's an admirable career and what you do to help people is amazing…"

"But…?"

He grinned. "How do you deal with it? It never ends—there are always people needing something from you. How can you possibly not end every day feeling a little defeated?"

"There are plenty of days where I do feel like that, believe me," she began. "Some days there don't seem to be any winners, and there's nothing I can do to make things right for anyone." With a shake of the head, she continued. "But then there are days when everything goes right and…you have no idea how gratifying it is to know that I've helped someone—I've made a difference in their lives and given them hope."

Julian released her hair and took her hand in his, feeling how soft her skin was too. "How do you make yourself go back after a bad day?" he asked gruffly. "On those days when no one gets the help they need or you just feel overwhelmed by it all, how do you find the strength to go back the next day and try again?"

For a long moment, Charlotte didn't respond. She looked at their linked hands and sighed quietly. "Because I have to," she finally said. "I can't let one bad day—or a hundred of them—defeat me. I know there are going to be times when I just want to throw in the towel and find a job that isn't quite so emotionally draining. Then I remember the days that leave me feeling so happy and hopeful, and I cling to those. And somewhere in between the highs and lows are days that just…are. Things go okay, nothing major happens, and it's all kind of textbook." Then she shrugged. "That's sort of what life's about, right?"

"What do you mean?"

She considered him. "There was a movie I remember seeing a long time ago—I can't even remember the name—but this one scene stood out to me. A man was arguing with his wife about their lives. He wanted everything to stay the same and for things to be what he considered normal. Well, they had three kids and were suddenly expecting a fourth, and the three they had were each having trouble in their own way, and on top of it, his elderly grandmother came to live with them."

"That doesn't sound familiar…"

Charlotte held up her finger to tell him there was more. "Anyway, they're arguing about what's normal and what's not and their expectations about how life is supposed to be when the grandmother comes in and starts to talk about carnival rides—the merry-go-round versus the roller coaster. And basically, she was saying how some people prefer the merry-go-round because there are no surprises, it just goes around and around. But some people prefer the roller coaster because of all the twists and turns and surprises. And that's how she looked at life. Are you someone who loves the merry-go-round or the roller coaster?"

Julian knew she wasn't specifically asking him that question, but…it certainly had him thinking. A few years ago, he would have said roller coaster, hands down. But now? Now he was telling himself he wanted—*needed*—the merry-go-round. And in the last few weeks he would have said he couldn't be swayed from that thinking. But as he sat here with Charlotte and knew there were possibly some twists and turns and surprises—at least where the two of them were concerned—he found himself looking forward to them.

All of them.

"Personally," Charlotte said, interrupting his thoughts, "I'm a roller coaster person who sometimes wishes for the merry-go-round."

Tilting his head, he asked, "How come?"

"There are times when I'm working on a case and I know it's going to get bumpy and complicated and rough for everyone. Sometimes I'd like to be able to step away and let someone else take my place when there's bad news to share. I hate disappointing anyone, and I hate when the system doesn't work." She paused. "I have some coworkers who don't have any one-on-one with our applicants. Their job is to process the paperwork, so to them, these people are just a name or a number on a page. But I look at them. I see them. I see the hope or the desperation on their faces and it's sometimes so hard to do that." Then she smiled ruefully. "Roller coaster."

He nodded in understanding. "I get it. With the band, every day was a roller coaster no matter how much we had things planned out and scheduled. We had rankings to worry about constantly and the need to stay on the charts and be relevant. There was always a line of people between us and all of that, but it trickles down and ultimately, it was up to us to make the music and put in appearances and do what we could to charm the public."

"That's a lot of pressure."

"Yeah, it is. For a long time, we kept crazy schedules, and I was always the kind of guy who didn't want to sit still. I needed something creative to do. So I wrote music. I taught myself how to play other instruments, I learned how to work the recording equipment and produce music."

"Wow!"

"My brain has a hard time shutting down sometimes and I love the thrill of learning something new or creating something new."

"Now, that's something I envy," she said with a bit of wonder.

"What is?"

"Your creativity. I'm just not. Like I've told you before, I'm very analytical. A problem solver. I haven't done anything artistic or creative since…I don't know when."

"It's not all it's cracked up to be," he said seriously. "It's a lot of pressure, and it opens the door for people to come in and use you and—"

Charlotte reached out and put a finger over his lips, effectively stunning him into silence. She shook her head. "No. Not tonight. We're not going there."

And if he hadn't already been prepared to get on this roller coaster with her—he was seriously loving that metaphor!—he would be now. She was the first person in he didn't know how long who wasn't anxious to talk about his music, his career, any of it. Charlotte just wanted to talk to him—Julian. Just the man. It was a little unsettling and yet it filled him with hope.

It was something he'd thought was long gone from his vocabulary.

But here it was.

Here *she* was.

Reaching over, he gently clasped her wrist. "Where are we going?"

And then Charlotte did something that probably wasn't intended to be sexy but it totally pushed him to his limit: she licked her lips.

Not even in a slow or seductive manner, just…licked her lips.

And he was done.

Tugging her to him, she spilled into his lap, and having her there was what he'd been waiting for since forever.

"Charlotte Clark, do you have any idea what you do to me?" he asked hoarsely, his eyes scanning her face.

Shaking her head, Charlotte held his gaze. "No, but I'm hoping it's the same thing you do to me."

"And what's that?" he whispered, leaning in to hope-fully kiss her again.

"You make me want," she admitted softly, breathlessly.

They were so close that when he licked his own lips, he almost touched hers. "That's good, because that's exactly how you make me feel too."

"What are we going to do about it?"

The things he wanted to do with her…

"Whatever you want," he said, letting her set their pace. "If what you want is to sit here and talk until the sun comes up, then that's what we'll do."

Her lips twitched with the need to smile as she asked, "Or?"

And he couldn't help but grin. "Or you can let me take you inside and lay you down on my bed and spend the night not talking."

She pouted slightly.

"What? What did I say to put that look on your face?"

Then she blushed. "I just… I guess…" Her eyes met his as she admitted, "I guess I envisioned us doing all those things—spending the night in bed together but talking. And not about life, but…"

It hit him what she was saying and it was like throw-ing gasoline on a flame. "Baby, I'll talk to you all night long while we do all kinds of things. I want to touch every inch of you, Charlotte. And kiss every inch of you and hear you cry out my name."

Her smile grew and it was a beautiful mixture of sweet and sexy and so completely Charlotte. "I think I'd like all of that," she said. "Very much."

Standing, Julian pulled her slowly to her feet and banded an arm around her waist to bring her body flush to his, and once more he was hit with how much he loved the feel of her curves pressed up against him.

And how much he couldn't wait to explore them all.

In bed.

Together, they shut the sliding glass doors and Julian turned out the lights, leading her to the bedroom.

"Oh," she gasped softly when she stepped into the room. She had kicked off her sandals while they'd been sitting on the sofa. When her feet went from the cool hardwoods to the plush carpeting, she obviously enjoyed the transition.

"It only gets better," Julian promised as he led her across the room until they were beside the bed. They stood facing one another, and he was suddenly nervous and unsure. The primal part of him wanted to strip her bare and take her—to ease the ache he'd been feeling since they first met. But there was another part of him, one that he'd never known existed, that wanted to go slow and savor and—

Without warning, Charlotte reached out and wound her arms around his neck, initiating the kiss.

And Julian was one hundred percent on board.

He anchored his hands in her hair to keep himself from ripping those tiny straps of her dress in his haste to get her naked. Tongues dueled and need built as every bit of him was consumed by her. On and on it went, and he couldn't believe what a turn-on kissing could be. It was always enjoyable, but kissing Charlotte was on a whole other level. She tasted like an exotic drink and smelled even better.

And he couldn't wait to see and taste and smell the rest of her.

Slowly, he lowered his hands to her shoulders and began to peel down the tiny straps resting there. His hands trembled. The last time he'd felt this nervous taking a woman to bed was—well, it was probably when he was a teenager.

He hoped it all went better than it had back then.

As if sensing his wayward thoughts, Charlotte broke their kiss and looked up at him with those impossibly blue eyes. Even in the dim lighting of the room, they stood out to him. She took a step back and smiled shyly at him.

"I wanted to go slow with you," he said. "But I think I'm failing miserably."

She laughed softly, slid her arms out of the straps, and placed her hands over her breasts. "It's the same for me. I keep thinking that slow is good, but right now all I can think of is doing this."

Wordlessly, she shimmied out of the dress until it was pooled around her feet. Julian felt his heart kick hard in his chest.

Hot pink.

Her panties were hot-pink silk.

Reverently, he dropped to his knees and placed his hands on her hips as he leaned forward and kissed her belly. She sighed his name and raked her hands through his hair.

"I was kind of hoping that would motivate you to lose your shirt," Charlotte said, looking down at him with a smile that was sexy and very pleased with herself.

Julian whipped the shirt off and tossed it over his shoulder. "Seeing you like this makes me want to lose more than my shirt, sweetheart."

This time her laugh was throaty, and for a minute,

Julian wasn't sure if he should stay on his knees or jump to his feet and kiss her sassy mouth.

Her nails scraped against his scalp and she tugged on his hair to make him look up at her, and the heat Julian saw in her eyes made the decision for him.

Mouth.

Always her mouth.

One minute they were standing by the bed, the next they were on it. When Charlotte's legs wrapped around him, he knew slow was off the table. For now. They had all night, and he promised himself they'd go slow the next time.

Bracing his hands on either side of her head, Julian stared down at her face, knowing his expression was fierce. "The next time I feel your nails on me, I want them to be on my back."

She licked her lips and quirked one perfect brow at him. "Why do you think I wanted your shirt off so badly?"

Sexy banter. Who knew?

One of Charlotte's hands came up and wrapped around his nape, pulling him down close until their lips were a breath apart. "Bring it," she whispered.

And Julian was a goner.

———— ᴡᴡ ————

"Hey, beautiful girl," Julian murmured against her ear. "C'mon. You need to get up."

Charlotte groaned. They hadn't slept for more than an hour—if that—and if he was seriously waking her up to ask her to leave, she was going to be pissed.

Majorly, majorly pissed.

On any given day, she was a morning person. But today all she wanted was just a little more sleep in this magnificent bed. She only had a full-size one at home, and if she had more space, she'd definitely invest in a king-size after this.

Julian was pressed snugly against her back, kissing her shoulder. Okay, so maybe he wasn't asking her to leave, and they certainly didn't have to get up to do more of what they'd been doing all night.

"Charlotte," he whispered softly, now kissing her cheek. "If you don't get up, you're gonna miss it."

Miss it? Okay, *that* piqued her curiosity.

Slowly, she turned in his arms and placed a kiss on his chest. "Any chance you can bring whatever this is that I need to see here?"

He chuckled. "Unfortunately, no. But trust me, you're going to want to see it."

"Julian…"

But he wasn't listening. He kissed her one last time and then rolled away. Even with her eyes closed, she knew he was putting on his jeans.

And that was really a shame.

Rolling onto her back, she yawned and then felt something soft land next to her. Turning her head, she saw it was Julian's shirt from last night.

"You can wear that," he said with a grin. "Now come on. Hurry."

Wasn't a girl at least entitled to a few minutes to fix herself so no one saw her with bedhead and morning breath? When Julian said her name again, she huffed in frustration. "Okay, okay, sheesh."

She slid the shirt on and it awakened her senses. It

smelled of Julian, and all she wanted was to drag him back into the bed and—

"Oh no, you don't," he said with a laugh. He reached for her hand and tugged her from the bed. "I could tell by the look on your face what you were thinking, and in a few minutes, I promise to give you whatever you want. But right now, humor me."

Hand in hand, he led her from the bedroom, down the hall, and to the living room. Everything was still dark—the house, the sky. For the life of her, she couldn't figure out why he wanted her here.

As they walked past the sofa, he reached for the afghan that was draped over it, and led her out the back door onto the deck. The air was cool and Charlotte immediately gasped and shivered, but Julian didn't stop until they were down the steps and on the sand. Then he sat and pulled her down into his lap, wrapping the blanket around them.

"Julian?" she asked in confusion.

"Shh." With his arms and the blanket keeping her warm, she followed his motion and looked out toward the water. "I know the sunsets are better here, but...I thought you might want to watch the sun come up too."

Everything in her melted. There were so many things she'd come to learn about Julian: On the surface, he looked like this big, tough badass. But what she was finding was another layer to him—a softer side—that made her heart race. She'd never known a man who thought about her on the level he did and she didn't think she ever would.

Quietly, they sat and watched the sun come up. It was something she'd never done before and knew she'd never forget. Snuggling against him with her head on his shoulder, Charlotte wished the moment would never end. If she could, she'd be perfectly content to stay like this forever.

As the sky grew brighter, she began to wonder what would happen now. There was no way they could stay like this—and part of her wanted to pout about it—but she wasn't sure if she was supposed to get dressed and go or just assume she was going to stay. If she had to base her decision on Julian's previous behavior, she'd say it was a safe bet that she'd be leaving soon.

But the way his hand was slowly creeping under her shirt, she'd wait and reserve judgment on that.

Lifting her head, she sighed.

"What'd you think?" he asked quietly, his lips warm against her throat.

Right now, she could hardly remember her own name, let alone think. She tilted her head to give him better access and purred with pleasure. His hands were doing some pretty wicked things to her.

"Think?" she asked breathlessly.

"Uh-huh," he murmured between kisses. "About the sunrise."

She moaned when his touch grew bolder, more intimate. "Amazing."

He chuckled softly. "What do you say we take this back inside and see what other kinds of amazing things we can see?"

Charlotte was ready to say "yes, please" when Julian simply stood with her in his arms and carried her back up the stairs and into the house. There were so many questions racing through her mind that it took an act of iron will to keep quiet and not ruin the moment. For now, she was learning to let Julian lead when he wanted something.

And she knew—at least in this instance—she was going to benefit from it.

Soon they were back in the bedroom and Julian was placing her gently on the bed, throwing the afghan over his shoulder.

No doubt she looked like a hot mess—hair tangled from sleep and the wind on the beach, a wrinkled T-shirt that was twisted and barely covered her—and she was sprawled across the mattress.

But the way Julian was looking at her told her that wasn't how he saw her. No. The heat in his eyes and the way his gaze held hers as he took off his jeans told her he liked what he saw.

It was both empowering and a little terrifying.

No man had ever looked at her like that or wanted her like that.

When Julian crawled over her and stretched out on top of her, she welcomed his weight, his warmth. Wrapping her arms around him, Charlotte hugged him close.

"Thank you," she said softly.

He didn't ask what she was referring to—he knew. "After our conversation last night, I thought you might enjoy it."

Slowly she slid her legs along his until they wrapped around him. "I'm enjoying this too."

He smiled, and man, did she wish he'd do that more. His entire face transformed. It was amazing how relaxed he could look when he wasn't brooding about something.

"I know I should suggest that we get some sleep, but…"

Charlotte grinned knowingly at him. "But?"

"But you're all soft and sexy right now and so damn beautiful." He paused and reached up to caress her face. "You completely take my breath away."

And then her heart just stopped and squeezed hard. This man—this normally gruff and closed-off man—was making it very hard not to fall head over heels for him.

"I don't even know what to say to that," she admitted.

Julian shook his head. "I don't want you to say anything. I just want you to stay right where you are and let me look at you." He kissed her cheek. "And let me touch you." He kissed her throat. He lifted up slightly and helped her slip the T-shirt over her head. His hands skimmed along her rib cage and cupped her breast right before he lowered his head and kissed her there.

Sighing his name, Charlotte gripped his hair and held him to her.

Then he lifted his head and gave her a sexy grin. "And let me have you."

"I'm yours."

—◦◦—

"So, what did you do?"

"What do you think? I grabbed an apron and a note-pad and started taking orders!"

They were sitting on the sofa, eating pizza and laughing. It was midafternoon and honestly, Julian thought he'd be feeling restless and ready for Charlotte to leave, but…he wasn't. If anything, he was enjoying her stories about growing up in Malibu and some of her crazier cases helping people find jobs. Apparently, it had started out as a hobby but had ended up taking her to places she hadn't expected.

And not always by choice.

"Did your friend ever show up?" he asked.

She shook her head as she took a bite of her slice of pepperoni pizza. "I thought I was doing a good thing by offering to work her shift, but after I dropped three trays of food, the manager asked me to leave."

"Asked?" he said with a grin.

"Okay, maybe he told me while shoving me out the door," she replied. "Oh gosh. I had chocolate milk shake down my shirt, fries in my hair, and coleslaw in my shoe! I didn't even want to get in my car!" She laughed. "When I got home, my dad was out front washing his car. He took one look at me and just hosed me off right there in the driveway!"

"No!" By this point, Julian could picture exactly how she must have looked and was laughing hard. "Did you tell him to stop?"

She shook her head again and almost couldn't speak. "I yelled out for my mom to grab me some shampoo!"

And it hit him—again—as she sat there laughing at herself, just how different she was from any other woman he'd ever known.

Especially Dena.

How many hours in a day had Dena talked about herself and exaggerated how good she was at everything? And heaven forbid she would ever admit to doing anything wrong! In their years together, he never remembered her owning up to anything. Even when he'd caught her in a lie or cheating, she'd somehow managed to turn it around so it wasn't her fault and he'd end up apologizing!

And before her, the women he'd dated—even casually—never wanted to be seen in an unflattering way. He couldn't remember a time when he'd sat with a woman who looked as tousled as Charlotte, who didn't have on any makeup, and wasn't freaking out about it. Yet here she was—with a little sauce on her chin and some cheese on her shirt—and she was just laughing it off.

Now he had to wonder if she was the norm or those other women were.

Man, he hoped it was her. That would give him hope for the future.

Hope? Geez, when was the last time he'd had any of that?

"Julian? Are you okay?" Charlotte had stopped laughing and was looking at him with concern, her hand reaching out and resting on his knee.

He shook his head and cleared this throat. "Um… yeah. Sorry. I guess my mind wandered for a minute."

"That's probably my fault," she said with a self-deprecating laugh. "I'm sure you're used to talking about way more exciting things than me being a klutz at eighteen. Sorry."

Tossing his pizza slice back into the box, he straightened. "You want to know what I was thinking?" He didn't give her a chance to respond. "I was sitting here thinking how freaking refreshing it is to have a conversation with someone who is genuine. I love hearing you talk about the things you did growing up and how it all adds up to make you the woman you are right now."

"Julian—"

"I'm serious," he interrupted. "Do you know how long it's been since—"

His words were cut off by the sound of his phone ringing. Excusing himself, he went to grab it from the kitchen counter. It was Mick.

"Hey, Mick. What's up?"

"Julian, hey," Mick said, sounding unusually cheerful. "There's an offer on the house. It's not quite what we were asking, but…"

"Accept it."

Mick was quiet for a minute. "It's only the first offer, and I thought you might want to counter it and try to get at least a little closer to the asking price."

"Then why didn't you just do it?" Julian asked, hating how this part of his life was interrupting his time with Charlotte.

On the other end of the phone, Mick sighed loudly and lost a little of his chipper tone. "Because this isn't my house and I thought you'd want a say in it."

"And I do. I said to accept the offer."

"Jules, can you just take a minute and think about this?" He gave Julian the number the potential buyers were offering, and while it wasn't the price he had wanted, it was pretty close. Did he really want to haggle and drag this out? Which was what he said to Mick.

"How about I go back with another twenty-five grand?" his manager replied.

"Mick, seriously, why are you asking me, if this is what you want to do? I already told you I don't care about this. I just want it gone. I don't want to have to look at the house or think about it again. Just—do what you think is best and get it done, okay?"

Another round of silence. "You can't just keep putting off dealing with things, Julian. Sooner or later, you're going to have to come to grips with it all and actually deal with it. Avoidance isn't the answer."

"Thanks, Dr. Phil. I'll take that into consideration," he said.

"Fine. I'll get it sold and we'll never talk about it again."

"That's all I want, man. Told you that weeks ago."

"Okay, fine. Excuse me for making sure you make a little money," Mick said flatly. "So what's going on with you today? You going to see the guys again this week? Matty's only here until next weekend, and you all sounded great when you played the other day. You should try to do it again before he heads back east."

Julian looked over at Charlotte as she rose and walked out on the deck. She had been cleaning up her pizza mess and was trying to give him some privacy. Maybe he should have been the one to leave the room.

"I don't know," he finally said. "Maybe. We didn't make any plans."

"You got something better to do?" Mick asked sarcastically. "Aren't you tired of your own company by now?"

"I'm doing okay. I've got no complaints."

Mick laughed quietly. "You hanging out with the social worker?"

Tension started a slow build. "That's none of your business."

"So that's a yes," Mick said, clearly unfazed by Julian's terse tone. "Trust me, I'm not complaining. I think it's great. You need a good shrink in my opinion, but I'm sure she's got a background in that too. Might as well get a little help while you're having some fun."

Tension turned to rage. "What is wrong with you?" he snapped. "What kind of person do you think I am, first of all? I'm not hanging out with Charlotte for freaking therapy! What she does for a living has nothing to do with anything!"

"Fine, consider me put in my place," Mick said. "Whatever. Look, I really was just calling about the house. Don't let me put you in a mood and ruin your day. It was good to see you looking so relaxed at Dylan's. You need to focus on feeling like that and not being all…you know…*you*."

"There's nothing wrong with me," he said defensively.

"You keep telling yourself that, Julian. Maybe someday you'll get everyone else to believe it."

He wanted to growl with frustration. "Are we done here?"

"Yeah, we are," Mick said. "I'll call you when there's a contract."

"Good." And Julian hung up before Mick could say another word.

He hated this. Hated how defensive he got and how easily riled up he became at the mention of just about anything. The only time he truly didn't feel like that was when he was with Charlotte. Why? Because she didn't ask him anything about his life. Well, she had and he'd cut her down and she hadn't asked again.

Looking out toward the deck, he saw her leaning on the railing with her head tilted back as the sun shone down on her, a serene smile on her face. What he wouldn't give to feel like that.

Seeing her like that, the last thing he wanted to do was go out there and talk about himself and bring her down—which he definitely would. His life was such a mess, and she would probably run the gamut from shocked to horrified to disapproving. Did he really want to ruin what they had and what they'd been feeling all day by bringing up the crap he just wanted to forget?

As if sensing his stare, Charlotte looked over her shoulder at him and smiled.

And just like that, she drew him to her. He couldn't have stayed away even if he tried. Julian wanted to be near her and simply…hope that some of her goodness would rub off on him.

How pathetic was that?

When he got close enough, he wrapped his arms around her waist and gazed out at the water with her. "Not too crowded out there today," he said conversationally. "Sundays are usually a busy beach day."

She shrugged. "I think by this time of day most of them are heading home. Probably been out here since earlier and now it's time to get dinner ready and all that. Plus, tomorrow's Monday, which means it's time to transition back into work mode." She paused. "Which I probably should do too."

Damn. He wasn't ready for the real world to interfere just yet. Especially not after his conversation with Mick. Right now, he wanted to be selfish and ask her to stay so he could go on feeling better and—not that he'd admit it—wouldn't have to be alone.

Yeah, he was pretty tired of his own company.

Rather than respond to her statement, he held her a little closer and rested his chin on her shoulder. He had to admit, he was beginning to understand her obsession with listening to the sound of the waves. It really was relaxing, and the anxiety he felt moments ago while talking to Mick seemed to slowly disappear.

Or maybe it was just having Charlotte in his arms.

"Don't go," he said softly, unable to keep from saying the words. "Not yet."

To her credit, she didn't react in any obvious way, but simply said, "Okay."

And then the weirdest thing happened.

He started to talk.

"That was my manager on the phone. He was calling to tell me there was an offer on my house in LA."

She nodded. "Was it a good offer?"

"It wasn't bad."

"Okay."

"It pissed me off that he called because I really don't care about the negotiations. I just want it gone so I can be done with it."

"I can understand that. I've never owned my own house, but I know how it feels to be ready to move on from a place."

"There was a time when I really liked that house," he admitted. "I never loved the place, but it met all of my needs."

"What kind of place would you love?"

He shrugged. "Honestly? I don't even know. For so long I've been listening to other people telling me what I need and what I should want that I haven't given any thought to what I really do want."

Turning her head, she gave him one of those smiles that he loved. "Well, it looks like now you have the chance."

It couldn't possibly be that easy, could it?

"What about you, Charlotte? What kind of place would you love?" he asked, turning the tables on her.

"Oh no," she said with a small laugh. "You're not

getting out of it that easily. You said you never had the chance to think about it for yourself, so I want to hear your thoughts."

"I wouldn't know where to begin…"

"Ranch style or multistory?" she asked, turning in his arms to face him. Her hair was whipping around, so she stepped to the side, took him by the hand, and led him back into the house. "Sorry, that was going to be distracting."

He found everything about her distracting.

But in a good way.

Once they were back on the sofa, Charlotte sat between his legs with her back against his chest. His arms immediately wrapped around her as she asked her question again. "So, ranch or multistory?" She paused. "No thinking—what's your first thought."

"Ranch style," he said automatically and then had to stop from laughing because the house he was selling was two stories.

"Okay, that's a good start," she said and he knew she was smiling. "Now, Craftsman or modern?"

"Craftsman."

"New or fixer-upper?"

Huh, he'd never given any thought to doing his own remodeling. That definitely sounded intriguing.

"I wouldn't mind a fixer-upper. I think it could offer a lot of possibilities."

"So could building from scratch. Either way, the place would have your own personal stamp on it."

"Okay, my turn," he said. "Which would you do—new or fixer-upper?"

"Ooo, a fixer-upper. Definitely."

"Tell me why," he encouraged, curious to know her thoughts.

"So many older houses have cool design features, and even though most of them could be replicated, it just wouldn't feel the same. Plus, I love the thought of rehabbing a house and taking something old and making it look new again."

Why was he not surprised? Basically, it's what she did for a living—but instead of homes, she did that for people. She took people who were down and out and helped fix them up and make them feel like new.

He hugged her a little tighter.

"Back to you," she said. "City or suburbs?"

"It would depend."

"On?"

"The house. I'm open to both. I've always lived near a city because I like the conveniences, but I thought I'd want some more privacy this time around. You know, have a lot of property, that sort of thing."

"That's a good plan."

"But…now, after living here on the beach, I'm beginning to see the appeal in that, too."

"You could always just have a vacation home on the beach somewhere and have your full-time residence somewhere more private."

And he'd never thought of that either. Dena had never wanted him to invest in a vacation home because she wanted to stay places that had room service and spas she could access around the clock. Personally, he hated staying in hotels—even though it was a large part of his life when the band was on tour. And when they weren't touring and he just wanted to go away someplace and relax after having people around him 24-7, he wanted a home away from home. But Dena had bitched so much that he always caved, and he'd hated it.

It was looking as if he suddenly had so many options in front of him and he was the one in control of them.

"Do you want to stay in California or move someplace else?" she asked.

There was a time when he'd considered moving back to the East Coast. He'd grown up near Myrtle Beach, Matt and Riley each had places along the North Carolina coast, and his parents were still there as well. California hadn't been his dream, but—

Dammit. He needed to stop going there in his mind. All it did was piss him off at how he'd given up for far too long on the things that made him happy.

"East Coast," he said, a little more harshly than he realized.

"O-kay," Charlotte responded slowly.

"Sorry. I'm just...every time I answer one of these questions, I get mad at myself over and over again, because it makes me realize how I haven't been living the way I've wanted to."

And now that can of worms was open.

"It shouldn't make you mad, Julian. It should make you happy that now you *can* live the way you want with nothing holding you back. Some people go their entire lives living in circumstances they don't like and they can't change. You can. Don't look at this as a negative thing. You're lucky."

Right. There were many words Julian could think of to describe himself, but lucky wasn't one of them.

As if reading his mind, Charlotte said, "It's true."

Then she twisted in his arms so she could look up at him. "You were in a crappy relationship. I see that sort of thing a lot in my line of work. I have women come in who have been abused and abandoned and have nowhere to turn. They all cry because they stayed in those relationships for too long, and they talk of how they escaped." She paused and went contemplative. "I always thought it was such a strong word for their situation—escaped—but that's really how it is. It takes time for them to transition and realize they're now in control of their own lives. Then they flourish. They blossom into the person they always wanted to be. I love when that happens."

He thought about those words. "Are you saying you think I'm ready to blossom?" he asked with a hint of a smile—amazed to be poking fun at himself.

Charlotte playfully swatted at his arm as she giggled. "I didn't mean you," she clarified. "I was just saying it's similar to the situations I've seen. You're just looking at things in a negative way rather than seeing all the ways that it's positive."

That was true—no matter how much he wanted to deny it. He'd been living in such a negative state of mind for so long that he wasn't sure he'd know how to go about changing it.

"I—I don't know how to do that," he admitted, painfully.

And in a move he didn't see coming, Charlotte turned to straddle him. She wasn't smiling. She wasn't serene. If anything, her expression had gone completely neutral and it made him instantly regret saying anything. He wanted her lightness, her playfulness. Because right now, he knew she was in social worker-slash-helper mode and the last thing he wanted was to be some sort of pity case for her.

You need a good shrink in my opinion, but I'm sure she's got a background in that too.

Mick's words came back to him, and he firmly placed his hands on Charlotte's hips to move her aside. She must have guessed his intentions, because she grabbed his wrists to stop him.

"There's no time limit on how long you're supposed to grieve, Julian," she said seriously. "If you had just walked away without feeling anything and simply moved on, I'd be concerned. But the fact that you're still struggling—that you're unable to focus on the good because you're still feeling bad—tells me that you're not as heartless as you seem to want everyone to think."

She placed her hand over his heart and he swore he felt it all the way through his chest.

"You're angry, and you are entitled to feel that way. I'm not here to tell you that it's time to get on with your life. Only you will know when that time is." She paused.

"But…?"

She didn't even crack a smile.

"But eventually you will. If you allow yourself to."

He frowned. "What does that mean?"

Her expression softened and he knew it was the kind she'd give to anyone who came to her for help.

He wanted to be annoyed by it, but he was too curious about what she had to say.

"It means that sometimes we're our own worst enemy. We go through something traumatic and we put up walls around ourselves thinking it's for our own good. It's a defense mechanism to keep from getting hurt again. And in theory it sounds great, but the reality is that it keeps us locked in the pain. It keeps us in that negative mind-set because we're refusing to move forward."

Holy crap—that actually made sense.

"Every day we wake up and we have to remember why it is that we've got these walls in place. And all it does is give the person who hurt us the victory. Not only did they hurt us, but they have permanent residency in our minds with the daily reminder of the pain they created. So they win and we miss out on having the life we so desperately want."

His heart was hammering hard in his chest because every word she was saying was true. He was waking up every day thinking of all the ways Dena had screwed him over and he was forcing himself to stay in isolation—something he had always hated—because of her. And he knew he would remember it every day even though he longed to break free!

Could he possibly do it? Could he—in time—not think about it? And be happy?

Slowly, Charlotte climbed off of his lap and looked down at him. "You may not believe this, but you have all the power here, Julian. No one else. You have the power to grow or to stay in this place." She took the drinks they had put on the coffee table earlier and handed Julian his.

He thought about how great it had felt to jam with the guys on Friday—how amazing to sit behind a drum set and just let the music take over. Then he thought about how incredible it had felt to walk out on the beach last night and take Charlotte in his arms and kiss her and make love to her all night long.

And even right now—on the edge of a damn anxiety attack—he felt hopeful at her words.

Three days of not letting the negative memories win.

Three days of not letting himself stay locked up in the house.

Three days of not letting someone else dictate how he was supposed to live.

Swallowing hard, he reached for her hand. "It's not enough," he said gruffly, desperately.

Confusion covered her face. "What's not enough?"

"Three days," he said, coming to his feet. "For the last three days…I've been happy. Happier than I've been in years. I want that, Charlotte. I swear I do. I just don't know how to make it happen."

She smiled.

She was serene.

She was beautiful.

Stepping in close, she pulled her hand from his and cupped his jaw. "One day at a time," she said softly. "It happens one day at a time, and you have to decide to do something every day that brings you joy rather than anger or sadness."

"That's what you do for me," he said and hoped he wasn't scaring her or coming off sounding too needy.

She closed the distance between them and melted against him. "Then together we're going to find ways to make that happen for you."

He believed her. Why? Because everything he'd learned about Charlotte in the last few weeks told him that she was someone he could trust. She was sweet and pure and represented everything that was good in this world. Somehow, he had been lucky enough to meet her.

Julian rested his forehead against hers and felt all the tension leave his body. "Don't go. I know you have work tomorrow, but I really want you to stay tonight." He swallowed hard. "And not because I want to talk or even stay on this topic, but because I want you. I'm not ready for this day to end. I'll take you home in the morning so you can get to work on time—I'll even pick up your coffee while you get ready. Just—don't go."

She didn't answer right away, and then he really did think he was coming off as too needy and almost began to backpedal.

"My car is probably either sitting with a ticket on it or was towed. I parked at a meter last night and didn't think to go back," she said and then laughed softly. "So how about we go and find out where it is, and then we'll compromise."

He immediately lifted his head. "Compromise?"

Nodding, she explained. "We check on my car, and if it's still there, I drive it home and you follow, and we spend the night at my place."

Not a bad option, but he had a better one.

"Or…we check on your car, I follow you home so you can get a change of clothes and whatever you need for the morning to get ready for work, and then we come back here and have dinner out on the deck and watch the sunset." Her smile was a little hesitant and he could tell she was considering it.

"And maybe tonight," he said, hoping to sweeten the deal, "after dinner, we can open these doors and listen to the waves crash on the shore as I make love to you." Lowering his head, he claimed her lips and kissed her with everything he had, everything he felt, and knew from her response that they weren't going to check on her car just yet.

They weren't waiting until after dinner to make love as they listened to the sound of the waves.

Chapter 6

IT WASN'T AS IF SHE NEEDED TO PINCH HERSELF TO believe that this was her life, but as Charlotte sat beside Julian while they drove to Riley Shaughnessy's home, she really did.

Dinner with a group of rock stars. I'm having dinner with a group of rock stars.

That's what she had been saying to herself all day. Julian had casually mentioned the dinner invitation to her that morning, and at the time, she had been pretty darn proud of herself for not acting like a complete dork and squealing with excitement.

She'd waited until she was driving to work to do that.

It was weird, because she was dating a rock star. Sleeping with a rock star. But invite her to a dinner with the three guys he happened to be in a band with, and suddenly she was a bundle of nerves and insecurity.

The psychologist in her told herself it was only natural to be excited and a little nervous about meeting Julian's friends. That—in and of itself—was a big step in a relationship. The fact that Julian's friends happened to be famous only added to it. So really, she knew her nerves were normal. What she didn't know was how to calm them down before they got to Riley's house.

"You okay?" Julian asked. "You've been very quiet since I picked you up."

Even though she had insisted she would just drive

over to his place and leave her car there, Julian was adamant about picking her up. He was such a gentleman that—at times—it reminded her of how few men were these days.

She could just be vague about why she was quiet or blame it on work, but…why lie?

"I guess I'm a little nervous about meeting your friends."

He smirked a little and glanced over at her. "Because they're my friends or because of who they are?"

"Both. I mean, if you were just a group of normal guys, I'd be a little nervous. Having dinner with one of the biggest rock bands in the world takes that up a couple of notches." She paused. "I may need you to pull over so I can throw up."

Clearly, he didn't take her seriously, because he just laughed and kept driving. She knew she should be at least a little offended, but she couldn't be. It was so good to see this side of him. The entire week had been like watching a giant transformation. Every day she'd seen him become a little more comfortable in his own skin, and he'd smiled, relaxed, and talked more about what he wanted to do with his life.

Unfortunately, none of it had to do with having a future in the band.

It was a constant struggle for her not to slip into social-worker mode and try to get him to talk about what his big hang-up was where the band was concerned. Maybe tonight over dinner she'd get a little more of a clue by watching the way he interacted with Dylan, Matt, and Riley.

Or maybe she'd get a little background from their wives.

The idea instantly didn't feel right to her, like she was sneaking around behind his back to get information. If there was something Julian wanted her to know, she would prefer that it come from him. That was better than asking any of the girls for specific details.

Now, if they were the ones to bring it up…

No! Bad Charlotte! Don't think about this!

"Personally, I think you're making more of this than you need to," Julian said, and for a minute, she thought he was hearing her inner dialogue.

"You do?"

He nodded. "We're all just regular people, and you don't strike me as the type to get starstruck."

"How do you know?" she asked sassily. "I'll have you know that I met John Stamos at a Starbucks and turned into a complete babbling idiot. How can we be sure that won't happen over dinner?"

Chuckling, he kept his eyes on the road. "You're too level-headed for that sort of thing. And running into a celebrity on the street? You're not expecting it. We're going to Riley's home, and you've been warned far in advance, so you've had time to come to grips with it. And trust me, it's not that big a deal. His house is great but not overwhelming, his wife, Savannah, used to write for *Rock the World* magazine—it's how they met—and they have two great kids."

"Okay, so I can just look at them as a normal married couple with kids. Got it."

"Matt and Vivienne are normal too. She's a food blogger and she used to be an editor for an online style magazine. Now she works as a photographer—she's had exhibits at galleries around the country. Very cool, if you ask me. I introduced her to my mom and she really encouraged her with her work."

"It's not the wives I'm worried about meeting, Julian. I meet people all the time for work. While none of them are celebrity wives, it's still easier to talk to someone who isn't…you know…famous."

He rolled his eyes. "Okay, so it's the guys you're worried about."

She nodded.

"Here's the deal—and remember this when you start to get overwhelmed."

"Okay."

"Riley is one of six kids. He's always been musical. He's got a twin brother—fraternal—who is scary smart. But basically, Riley is just a normal guy who would rather have a backyard barbecue with family and friends than be out getting his photo taken and appearing in the tabloids. He met Savannah while he was dealing with writer's block on his solo album and was forced to do an interview with her."

"There's nothing to that story that makes me feel better about meeting him."

"I'm pointing out how normal he is. He just happens to have a great singing voice. It's not that big a deal." Then he turned to look at her. "Do you like to sing?"

"Love to."

"Are you any good?"

She laughed. "Not even a little bit."

"Duly noted. Do you have any friends or family who sing well?"

"Sure. My mom has a great voice. She sings in the church choir."

"Does she intimidate you?"

"She sings at the First Presbyterian Church, Julian, not Madison Square Garden."

He grinned. "Point taken."

"Good."

"Matt, who hates to be called Matty—"

"But that's how the press refers to him all the time," she argued lightly.

"And he hates it all the time. Trust me."

"Good to know."

"Matt had a really bad childhood—his mom left, his dad was an abusive alcoholic who took out his frustration on him."

"Oh no."

"I know, right? He pretty much escaped and ran away when he was eighteen."

"How did he survive? Did he have a safe place to go?" Immediately, her mind went to all the bad things that happened to teens living on the street.

"His best friend, Aaron, took him home and his family took him in. He stayed with them until graduation and then he went out on his own." He chuckled. "Vivienne is Aaron's little sister."

Her eyes went wide. "Were they in love all that time?"

"Nah, they didn't reconnect until years later."

"Now that's quite a story," she commented. "And I kind of love it. Not the fact that he had such a rough childhood, but how he and Vivienne met up again." She paused. "What ever happened with his father?"

"They ran into each other a couple of years ago—by accident. Matt had a failed Broadway show and he sort of went into hiding back at Aaron's place in North

Carolina, which is where he met up with Vivienne again. Anyway, he was out in town one day and wanted to buy her flowers, and it turns out his father owns the place—along with his new wife and their little girl."

"No!" she gasped. "And he just happened to walk in there?"

"Yup. It was a major shock to him."

"I can't even imagine!"

"Good news is they're working on their relationship. He loves having a little sister—something Aaron teases him about—and it's not easy, but they go to family counseling and they're trying to make it work."

She felt herself relax on Matt's behalf. "Good for them. I know that sort of thing is really tough, but it's nice when everyone tries to work together to heal." She paused. "Do he and Vivienne have any kids?"

He shook his head. "They both felt it was important for Matt to have some time to get in a better place with his father and deal with some things from his childhood before they did."

"That's understandable."

"Then there's Dylan."

"Oh, I remember reading about him more times than I care to admit. It seems like he was the poster boy for bad behavior for a while."

"That he was. And really, he had no reason for it. He had a good childhood, he's an only child, normal parents… He just wanted attention. I think it was a case of not caring what kind of attention he got. Then he struggled with addiction and it magnified everything. He's come a long way and now he's married, clean and sober, and expecting a baby."

"Addiction can ruin lives, end them. I love hearing about someone overcoming it."

"And when you meet the woman who keeps him on the straight and narrow, you'll love it even more."

"Why?"

"Paige is a tiny little thing and doesn't look like she could hurt a fly, but she is one serious kick-ass chick. I've never seen Dylan with anyone the way he is with Paige."

"Good for them," she said, smiling.

"Basically, what all this rambling was meant to do was put your mind at ease. At the end of the day, we're just a bunch of guys who have normal lives."

That made her laugh. "Except you're all rich too, right?"

Reaching over, Julian took one of her hands in his and kissed it. "Don't be such a snob. I know there are people in this industry who live very extravagant and ostentatious lifestyles. That's not us. Never has been, never will be. We're just four people who like playing music for the masses. It's not a crime."

"I didn't think it was," she said, feeling like she was being judgmental. "It's still a lifestyle most people will never know."

"Doesn't make it any better than anyone else's."

And that, she knew, was true.

When she stayed quiet, Julian squeezed her hand and glanced at her. "So? Do you feel a little better about this? Because we can totally turn around and go home."

"Julian! That would be horrible!"

He shrugged. "It's not a problem. They were actually surprised when I agreed to come."

"Wait—do they know I'm coming?" she asked, suddenly even more self-conscious than she was before.

"Yes, they know you're coming with me and they're all looking forward to meeting you."

"I think I'm even more nervous now."

Letting go of her hand, Julian pulled the car over to the right and then made a complete U-turn.

"Julian! What are you doing?" she cried. "Turn this car back around! This is ridiculous!"

But he wasn't listening, just kept on driving.

"I'm not kidding, Julian," she said more firmly. "I'm allowed to be nervous, but I don't run away from situations like this. I'll be nervous, but I'll be fine. Please! Turn the car around and let's go!"

And just as mildly, he executed another U-turn.

Five minutes later they pulled into Riley's driveway. When he shut the car off, he turned to her, his expression fierce. "If at any time you feel uncomfortable or overwhelmed, you just say the word and we're gone."

This time she rolled her eyes. "I'm a grown woman and I think I can handle staying through dessert. I'll be fine. I just—I needed a minute to let it all settle in. I never should have said anything." She reached for the door handle, but Julian stopped her.

"I don't want you to feel that way," he stated in that near growl she was so familiar with. "I know how much I hate being forced to stay in places or situations where I'm uncomfortable. I just want you to know you don't have to."

Her shoulders sagged and she leaned in to kiss him. "Thank you. I appreciate your concern, I really do. But I don't want you to spend the night worrying about me. I want you to go in there and enjoy your time with your friends, and if you spend the whole time worrying about me and what I'm thinking, you're not going to."

He kissed her softly on the lips. "Charlotte, I think about you all the time—it doesn't matter where we are or what we're doing or supposed to be doing. Tonight's no exception."

It was crazy, but all of her girly parts seemed to sigh and melt at that admission.

Maybe she should have let him turn the car around and head home.

A loud knock on her window made her jump. Julian chuckled.

"I know you're contemplating leaving, but it's too late!" Dylan said from the other side of the door. "We've all seen you, so now you have to get out of the car and come in!" He laughed and opened the door for Charlotte.

She looked over at Julian and smiled. "I guess we've been found out."

The smile he gave her in return showed her just how much he was looking forward to what was about to come.

The food was delicious. The conversation flowed and everyone was having a great time.

Including Julian.

They'd all been doing their own thing for far too long so they hadn't had a lot of time like this, and he realized now just how much he missed it. Missed them.

"So there I am, pulling into my driveway like I'm sneaking in after curfew, and who pulls in next to me but my dad!" Riley was saying, sharing a story about the first time he brought Savannah home to meet the family.

"No!" Charlotte said, laughing with everyone.

Riley nodded. "We both walked to the front door with our heads hung low and just sort of vowed never to tell anyone about it."

"And yet here you are blabbing about it," Savannah said, playfully smacking her husband's arm.

"We meant none of my siblings. There was no way I was going to tell any of my brothers or my sister about it."

"Speaking of your siblings, how is everyone?" Dylan asked. "Paige and I stayed at Hugh's resort in Napa last month for a long weekend. He wasn't in town, but you have to tell him how amazing that place is."

"It seriously is," Paige chimed in. "It was like being in our own little world."

Riley smiled and took a sip of his wine. "That resort is one of my favorites, too. I don't go often just because of time constraints, but I've stayed with him at some of his other resorts when I was in between tour dates."

"Does he spend a little time living at each place every year?" Dylan asked.

"Nah, after he and Aubrey got married, they made themselves a permanent home right outside of Wilmington." He paused and smiled. "Two months ago, they got word that their adoption paperwork was approved. Hopefully, they'll be leaving next week to pick up their new baby."

Beside him, Savannah nodded, her eyes bright with unshed tears. "It was such a long process for them and we were beginning to think it wouldn't happen, but…" She reached for Riley's hand and squeezed it. "We're all just so happy."

Charlotte looked at them with confusion. "Will this be their first baby?"

"They have a son, Connor," Riley explained. "But Aubrey had cancer when she was a child and had some complications with the pregnancy. They really wanted another baby, but her doctors strongly advised her not to put her body through another pregnancy."

"And they have three large dogs," Savannah said with a laugh. "Who they treat like babies too."

"Anyway, as I'm sure you've probably heard, I come from a large family. We all think having a lot of kids is the norm," Riley explained. "So Hugh and Aubrey are going to have two kids very soon, and my brother Aidan and his wife, Zoe, have two kids now—Lilly and Caroline. My middle brother, Quinn, and his wife, Anna, have two kids—Kaitlyn and Brian—and they're pregnant with their third."

"No way!" Vivienne said. "Didn't they just have Brian?"

Savannah laughed and nodded. "Those babies will be less than a year apart."

"Poor Anna," Vivienne said, laughing.

"Are you kidding?" Riley asked, laughing along with them. "Poor Quinn!"

"Tell them about Owen," Savannah encouraged.

Riley shook his head and his smile was wide enough and bright enough to light the room. "My twin brother, Owen, and his wife, Brooke, already have twins, and Brooke is ready to give birth any day now to another set of twins!"

There was a collective gasp around the table and then everyone seemed to be talking at once.

"Wait, wait, wait," Matt said, holding up a hand and talking over everyone. "Why are we just now hearing about this?"

"Well, there were some complications, and I think we've all been walking on eggshells and not wanting to do anything to jinx it. I know I was afraid to say anything, but at the last doctor appointment just two days ago, everyone was healthy and ready to go!"

"Isn't that rare?" Paige asked. "Two sets of twins can't be all that common, can it?"

"I'd like to quote my twin brother because he's the statistics king," Riley went on. "Let's just say it's pretty rare—like one in ten thousand for the first set. Then he threw a lot more numbers at me and I couldn't take it all in. So, um…we'll just stick with rare." He paused and then chuckled. "And we're strongly encouraging them to not try for a third set."

"Oh stop!" Savannah teased. "You know this family would be over the moon if that happened. Your father would burst with pride!"

"How is Ian?" Matt asked. "I saw him in passing not too long ago, but all we could do was wave and say a quick hello."

"Dad's great. He and Martha are doing well and starting to travel a bit now that he's semiretired. I don't think he loves not working as much as he thought he would. Luckily Martha's the same, so if nothing else, they find ways to keep busy. They're going out to visit Darcy and Ben next month. It was hard for them to find the right time to go to Washington—with Hugh and Aubrey's adoption news, Brooke and Owen expecting the twins, they hate to miss out on anything."

"And Darcy's the only girl in the family?" Charlotte asked, fascinated by the entire dynamic.

"Don't feel bad for her," Riley said quickly. "You'd

think you should feel sorry for her with five older brothers, but let me tell you, she holds her own pretty well and kind of scares the crap out of most of us."

Charlotte laughed. "And I'm sure her husband had to be at least a little intimidated by all of you."

"Please," Savannah said with a snort. "They grilled that poor man like he was public enemy number one and he held his ground and managed to put all the Shaughnessy men in their place."

"That's impressive," Charlotte replied.

"I saw Darcy at a gallery show in Seattle a few months ago," Vivienne said with a knowing smirk. "Do you have any news?"

"She and Ben are expecting a baby at the end of March," Riley confirmed. "I think it's going to be hard for my dad to be far away from her for that. It's actually weird for all of us, because we don't want to admit that she's grown up and married and old enough to have a baby of her own. She'll always be the baby of the family."

"That's so sweet," Charlotte said as Julian rested his hand on her thigh and squeezed.

This was good, he thought. They had been at Riley's for just over two hours and it was already like Charlotte had known everyone forever. Maybe her nerves were all in her head or maybe she was good at hiding them, because she'd been nothing but relaxed with everyone.

He studied her as she started talking with Savannah about writing, and if it were possible, he was even more enamored with her. Tonight, she was wearing a little more makeup than usual, with her hair long and loose. His fingers twitched with the need to play with those curls. She had on a pair of black skinny jeans and a sleeveless blue blouse that matched her eyes, and he couldn't seem to make himself look away.

Over the last week he'd seen her in every way possible: dressed for work, dressed for a date with him, first thing in the morning without a stitch of makeup on, and completely naked and sweaty from their lovemaking, and it didn't matter where they were or what they were doing, she was beautiful.

Like make-his-chest-hurt, squeeze-his-heart-at-the-sight-of-her beautiful.

So many times, he'd wanted to tell her how he was feeling. But no words came to him—which was ironic, considering how writing songs was something he normally did with ease.

He stiffened at the thought. Was that what he should do—write a song for her?

That almost made him groan out loud. How cliché would that be?

Oh, hey, Charlotte, I wrote this song for you…

What was he, twelve?

"Dude, you look like you're sucking on a lemon over there," Dylan called across the table. "Knock it off." Then he threw a dinner roll at Julian.

There's your twelve-year-old.

Rather than throw it back or even acknowledge the comment, Julian reached for his wine and took a sip. "Dinner was fantastic, Savannah."

She smiled at him. "I wish I could take the credit, but this was all Riley. My cooking skills don't hold a candle to his."

As if on cue, everyone began to rise and help clear

the table while talking about recipes and cooking and favorite meals. Julian knew it was right up Vivienne's alley, since she was a food blogger, which meant Matt would also enjoy the conversation.

"You okay?" Charlotte asked when they were alone in the dining room. She had a plate in her hands and Julian took it from her, placing it back on the table.

He nodded and wrapped his arms around her waist, pulling her in close. "I'm good. You? You seem like you're having a good time."

She smiled, and there was that squeeze to his heart again. "I am. Everyone has been wonderful and I feel silly for being such a mess in the car. I don't know what I was expecting."

"You have every right to feel how you feel." Then he leaned down and nuzzled her neck, inhaling her perfume and moaning with pleasure. "And right now, you feel and smell freaking amazing."

"Mmm…you feel pretty darn good too," she whispered. "But now is not the time to be thinking about that. I have a feeling everyone's going to come back in for another round of dishes any second."

While he knew she was right, he didn't care. Instead of worrying, he lifted his head and captured her lips for a searing kiss. Charlotte pressed against him as her arms draped over his shoulders.

"For the love of it," Riley teased as he walked into the room and picked up a couple of dishes. "We were gone for less than a minute. And that's no excuse for getting out of helping with the cleanup."

Charlotte giggled as she moved from his arms, and Julian tried to glare menacingly at their host.

"Save it," Riley said. "I have three older brothers and a dynamo of a little sister. I don't scare easily."

After that, both of them carried in the remainder of the dishes and hung out in the kitchen, lending a hand where needed. With so many helpers, it didn't take long for everything to be put away.

"Okay, Riley!" Savannah called out. "Take the boys down to the studio and show them the new soundboard you got so the girls and I can talk about all of you."

Everyone laughed, even Julian. He knew this was coming, and he glanced over at Charlotte to make sure she was okay being left alone with the girls. She gave him a discreet nod, and unable to help himself, he walked over and kissed her again.

"Call if you need me," he murmured for her ears only before following the guys out of the room.

As the last one down the stairs, Julian realized maybe he was the one who'd have to call for help. Riley, Dylan, and Matt were all standing at the bottom of the stairs, arms crossed and grinning like idiots.

He sighed and stepped into the room. "Is there even a new soundboard or was that a code word to get me away from Charlotte so the girls can grill her?"

"Actually, we wanted to grill you a bit," Dylan said, his grin getting bigger. "But I'm sure the girls can handle things on their end just fine."

Julian could have turned around and walked back up the stairs, but even he was getting tired of walking away when things got a little uncomfortable.

Deciding to surprise them all, Julian went over to one of the oversized chairs and sat down, resting an ankle on his knee and looking for all the world to be relaxed.

No one needed to know how hard his heart was racing.

"What do you want to know?" he asked casually.

It was like a scene out of a Three Stooges movie, with Riley, Matt, and Dylan all scrambling around, banging into one another and grabbing a place to sit. When they were all finally seated, Matt spoke first.

"So…um, it looks like things are going well with Charlotte."

Seriously? That's what they wanted to open with? That just made him relax more. He got comfortable in the chair and smiled serenely.

"They are. We've spent the entire week together and things are great." He shrugged. "She works long hours and it's mentally grueling for her some days, but I bring her lunch and we have dinner together every night."

"And what have you been doing while she's at work?" Riley asked. "Mick mentioned you had an offer on your place. Have you started house hunting yet?"

"Nah. I've been thinking about it. I'm trying to figure out what I want and where."

His friends all nodded and then looked at each other before looking at Julian again.

"Okay," he said with a weary sigh. "Spit it out. I can tell you've all got something on your minds, so just—say it."

"I think we sounded great on Friday," Riley stated, his tone and expression going serious. "I know we've jammed here and there over the last few years, but on Friday we just sounded better than I remembered."

"I agree," Dylan said, and Matt nodded.

Before Julian could comment, Riley started talking again. "There's the big anniversary thing for the label and we want to play it."

With a shrug, Julian said, "And you should. I'm sure it's going to be huge." But he wasn't an idiot. He knew exactly where this was leading. So, he straightened and leaned forward, elbows on his knees. "Look, I get it. I do. I had a lot more fun on Friday than I thought I would. And all week, I've had music in my head I want to get down somewhere."

Dylan jumped to his feet. "So, let's do it now! C'mon! We can do some of it right now! The girls are all hanging out and they'd totally understand if we stayed down here for a couple of hours. We've done it before."

"No," Julian said adamantly. "I wouldn't do that to Charlotte. She doesn't know the girls, and she was nervous enough about coming here. It would be ridiculously rude of me to leave her like that."

They stared at him as if he were crazy.

"Screw you," he said to them. "It's not my fault that I have manners and none of you do."

"Jules, you can't tell us you're ready to just walk away from all of this," Matt said evenly. "We were all there with you on Friday and you were loving it just as much as we were. And if you've got music that you're wanting to try out, why not do it?"

Where did he even begin? All week he'd thought about it but… He sighed. Might as well just get it out there.

"You want to know what I did all week while Charlotte was at work?" he said with a hint of frustration. "I spent most of that time trying to figure out what my future looks like. And you know what? The only thing right now that's tripping me up is the business."

Three pairs of eyes looked at him in confusion.

"Can I play music? Yes. Do I enjoy it? Definitely. Do

I want to step back into a studio or go to an event where I see anyone who I knew before?" He paused. "No."

"Julian…"

"Every time I think about it, it grabs me by the throat," he cried in frustration. Standing, he began to pace. "I've always been a confident guy. Always. And even when all this was going on, I managed to convince myself that I was okay with it. That no one looked at me like I was a sucker when she was cheating on me or that I was to blame. But I was kidding myself."

"What would it take, Jules?" Riley asked. "Do we change labels? Do we only record our music ourselves? Never tour again? Because I think I speak for all of us when I say we're willing to meet you on this if it means staying together!"

He stopped pacing and stared at Riley, not doubting the sincerity in his words. "I can't ask that of you. Of any of you."

"Why not?" Riley asked. "When we decided to take a break, didn't you reach out to me when I was struggling with my solo album?"

"Well, yeah. But…"

"Didn't you offer to send me some songs?"

Julian looked guiltily at Matt and Dylan before turning his attention back to Riley. "No one was supposed to know about that."

"And they didn't until right now," Riley said. "You reached out and were willing to do whatever it took to help me."

"How many games of chess did you play with me and listen to me talk endlessly about how messed up my life was?" Dylan asked. "I was so screwed up and doubting every single aspect of my life, and you sat and listened to me and helped me put everything into perspective."

He shrugged. "That's what friends do."

"You did the same for me, Jules," Matt added. "When I was hiding out, you were the first one to call me. The first one to offer to come and get me and take me wherever I needed to go."

"Not like you listened," Julian said with a smirk.

"And good thing I didn't," Matt said with a laugh. "If I had taken you up on your offer, I never would have found Vivienne again."

"We can go on and on with this," Riley said to Julian. "We're friends first, a band second. And we are willing to do whatever it is that you need to do to keep playing. Could we find another drummer? Yes. Do we want to? Hell no."

The thought of Shaughnessy playing with another drummer bothered him more than he was willing to admit.

"You know I'd walk through fire for any of you," Julian began solemnly, "but we all know there's no way to function as a band at our level by doing the things you're suggesting. It's just not practical, and I'd hate to be the reason we disappointed the fans."

"But they're going to be disappointed if we come back without you," Dylan said. "You know that. After all this time away from the circuit, it would mean so much more going back on stage with the four of us. We all know we can play with other people and the fans are okay with it, but the same thing keeps coming up— when is Shaughnessy getting back together. If it's not the four of us, then it's not Shaughnessy. End of story."

"All right, all right," Riley said. "Now it's coming off like a guilt trip and that's not what we're going for,

I swear. We just thought…you know, maybe you'd started to reconsider. That maybe having Charlotte around to talk to would help you come to grips with some things."

"And why would that happen, exactly?"

The look of panic on their faces would have been comical if the implication wasn't quite so insulting.

"You think I'm sleeping with Charlotte as some sort of—what, therapy? Is that what you're saying?" he snarled.

"No!" Riley said quickly, his hands going up defensively. "That's not it at all. I'm just saying I thought… well, just having someone else to talk to and going out and engaging in life again—that you're seeing that all is not doom and gloom."

"Dude, he's right," Matt said cautiously. "We took it as a good sign that you're getting out and looking so freaking happy. It was good to see you smile tonight. I'll be honest, I think it's been years since I've seen you look so happy. So it's no coincidence that we're attributing at least part of that to Charlotte."

He glared at Dylan, who simply shrugged and nodded.

"I didn't go looking for this," Julian admitted in a low voice. "She sort of took me by surprise. Once I stopped fighting it…I didn't want to fight it anymore. There's something about her that just makes me want to feel again."

"And there's nothing wrong with that," Dylan said. "Maybe in time you'll feel that way about the music again."

"I don't know."

"Look, just think about it. Again," Matt said. "I may not live close by like the rest of you, but I can get here in less than a day any time you're ready to play. Okay?"

Julian's throat was tight with emotion. He seriously

would walk through fire for any of them and it was humbling to know they'd do the same for him.

"Okay then," Riley said and grinned. "We'll set a timer and jam for maybe…an hour. How does that sound? You can even go up and make sure Charlotte's okay with it before we start."

Unable to help himself, he laughed. He glanced toward the stairs—if he went up there to check on her, she'd be embarrassed. He also knew she'd want him to have this time with the guys. And on top of that, Julian knew Charlotte could hold her own in any situation. She was amazing like that.

The drum kit set up in the corner was calling him.

Who was he to fight it?

"One hour," was all he said as he walked over to take his seat.

—◈—

"Oh my God, I swear I just wanted to bite him the first time I saw him without a shirt on!" Paige said, and they all laughed with her.

Charlotte knew within the first few minutes of meeting Savannah, Vivienne, and Paige that she was going to like them. She'd just had no idea how much she was going to love them and laugh with them!

As soon as the guys had gone downstairs, she'd been met with three curious looks, and then the grilling had begun. She'd shared how she and Julian met, when she first realized she was attracted to him, and their first kiss.

Luckily, they were sensitive enough not to ask for more details than that.

After she was done, they'd each shared their own

stories—most of which Julian had already told her—but it was nice to hear it from their point of view. And the stories were way more romantic than Julian had described them; Charlotte caught herself sighing more than once at just *how* romantic.

She had to stop herself from trying to imagine if hers and Julian's would be too.

"I never really thought I was the kind of girl who would be attracted to a rock star," Paige went on. "But after meeting Dylan, I was hooked."

"The feeling is clearly mutual," Charlotte said as she accepted a refill on her wine from Savannah. "And you're having a baby! That's so exciting!"

Talk moved to pregnancy, babies, and nurseries, and she was more than happy to simply sit back and listen. The fact that the guys hadn't come back up had her wondering if they were playing. She hoped so. Like, seriously hoped so. When Julian had talked about jamming with the guys last week, he became so animated that she wished he'd be like that all the time. It was the only time he'd mentioned his music. After her one failed attempt at asking him if he was going to play again, she'd kept her curiosity to herself. Maybe tonight after they left he'd be willing to open up about it.

Savannah stood and walked over to the basement doorway, carefully opened it, and smiled.

Music.

There was music.

She closed the door and sat back down. "God bless the creator of soundproofing material. I love music and I love listening to Riley play, but sometimes it's a little too much."

"I'm so glad they're playing," Vivienne said with relief. "Matt was disappointed they only had that one day to do it. He was hoping to spend the bulk of our time here with the guys planning for a return to the studio."

"Do you think that's going to happen?" Paige asked no one in particular.

Then they all looked at Charlotte.

Crap.

"Don't look at me," she said with a nervous laugh. "The last time I asked Julian about it, he stormed off. Lesson learned."

"He didn't say anything after playing on Friday?" Vivienne asked.

"He's been talking about it all week. Not a lot," she quickly corrected, "but he's brought up a couple of times how much he enjoyed it." Then she paused. "And he's humming."

"Humming?" Savannah repeated.

"Uh-huh. Humming. You know, music. A lot," Charlotte explained. "I can't say with any certainty that it's something he usually does, considering this is only the first week we've spent any real time together. But it was something I noticed."

"I don't ever remember Julian humming," Savannah said. "And out of the four of us, I've known him the longest—even though we never spent a lot of time together. Dena always made sure—Ow!" She stopped and glared at Vivienne.

"I don't remember hearing him hum whenever we were around him either," Vivienne said and glared at Savannah. "I'd take it as a good sign."

It didn't take a genius to figure out what had just

happened, and Charlotte thought she'd make everything easier on all of them if she just said it first.

"Look, I'm aware of Julian's relationship with Dena and what went wrong. We only talked about it once, and I'm not going to lie to you, I went home that night and did a little internet sleuthing to find out what I could." She took a sip of her wine. "My heart breaks for all he's gone through and how much it's still messing with him."

"Don't you think he needs to talk to someone?" Paige asked. "Like a therapist or something?"

Sighing, she stared into her glass. "As a professional, yes, I do. I think it would help him immensely if he talked about his feelings. But therapy doesn't work for everyone, especially if they're not ready for it. I don't think Julian is."

"Surely he's talked to you about some of it—not Dena specifically, but how he's feeling," Vivienne commented. "It would be hard to avoid that topic considering he's just so…you know…angry."

"We have, and I think it's going to take time. And it's okay for him to take as much time as he needs. It's not like there's a clock ticking, right?"

Savannah, Vivienne, and Paige looked at one another and then anywhere else but at Charlotte.

That can't be a coincidence.

"Wait, is there? Is there something the guys are waiting on Julian for?" Charlotte asked, hating herself for wanting to know.

Savannah went to grab a couple of bottles of water and put them on the table. Vivienne excused herself to use the bathroom and Paige sat there and cursed.

"Let's talk about something else," Savannah said

when she returned. "You mentioned growing up in Malibu. Are your parents still there?"

It would have been easy just to go with the new topic, but Charlotte's curiosity won out. "C'mon. Tell me. It probably won't make any difference because I can't guarantee Julian will mention it to me, but at least I can be on the lookout for any signs that he's thinking about it. Whatever it is."

Vivienne came back in, noticed how awkward everything still was, and threw her head back and exhaled loudly. "Okay, fine," she said. "Shaughnessy is supposed to play at a big twenty-fifth anniversary for the record label. Julian told the guys he was retiring and to play without him. But the guys don't want to." She slouched down onto her chair. "Whew. I'm so glad it's out there now."

Paige and Savannah shook their heads as they looked at her. "Good thing we weren't dealing with government secrets or anything. You caved pretty fast."

"Can't help it. Matt and I are all the way on the other side of the country and we feel disconnected from everything that's going on with Julian. So, if Charlotte can help convince him to play—"

"Wait, wait, wait," Charlotte quickly interrupted. "I'm not going to convince Julian of anything. That's not my place. If he wants to play, then it has to be his decision and it has to come from him. Not me or anyone else trying to force him to do it."

"I didn't mean for you to force him to," Vivienne clarified. "It's just that right now you're the only one close to him. You can maybe try to—"

"Viv, no," Savannah said. "It's not fair to ask that

of Charlotte, and it's certainly not fair to Julian. You remember how hard things were for Matt when you first met up with him again. He didn't exactly appreciate you pushing him to go out in public."

"But eventually he did," Vivienne countered. "And then he saw how he'd been overreacting for most of the time he was in hiding."

"It wasn't overreacting," Savannah said with a weary sigh. "The press was relentless with him, and the situation just needed to settle down and time had to pass. I'm sure Julian's going to feel the same way, but like Charlotte said, it has to be his decision."

"Maybe," Vivienne said with a small pout.

"I love how concerned you all are," Charlotte said, "but your concern for your husbands is obviously most important. Put yourself in Julian's shoes. Can any of you honestly say you'd be handling it any differently or better?" When no one commented, Charlotte knew she'd made her point.

They sat in companionable silence until Paige spoke up. "Any chance we can move on to dessert? I know I'm not that far along in this pregnancy, but the baby is craving sweets. Preferably something gooey with chocolate."

"Ooo—you're in luck," Savannah said as she made her way over to the kitchen island. "I got salted caramel brownies for us today. I've been fighting the urge to eat one all day!"

Charlotte stood and went to see if there was anything she could do to help. In no time, they were making coffee and putting all kinds of desserts on the table—brownies, pies, and cookies. Not more than fifteen minutes later, the guys came up, looking a little sweaty but with big smiles on their faces.

Julian made a beeline for her and kissed her soundly on the lips and then immediately asked what was for dessert.

—⁓—

Breathless and sated, Julian stared up at the ceiling as he tried to catch his breath. Beside him, Charlotte was lying on her belly doing the same. It had taken every ounce of self-control just to get home before having his way with her. The entire night he'd been thinking about all the things he wanted to do with her when they returned to his place, but after playing with the guys, one look at her had given him an overwhelming need to take her home and claim her.

They'd barely made it inside before he'd reached for her and begun stripping her.

Round one had been against the front door.

Round two had been on the kitchen counter.

After a quick, cool drink, he'd carried her to bed for round three.

He reached out and skimmed a finger down her spine and watched her shiver. Turning her head toward him, she peered through her wild mane of hair and said, "Sleep. I need sleep before we do that again."

Julian couldn't help but grin. Good to know she wasn't completely shutting him down.

It was late and he knew he should be exhausted, but he wasn't. He was invigorated. Between the music, his friends, and Charlotte, Julian felt more alive than he had in years.

Years.

And that was a damn shame.

Charlotte moved closer and snuggled up against his side. Wrapping an arm around her, he held her close and kissed the top of her head. She hummed her approval.

"Aren't you tired?" she asked sleepily.

"A little," he lied, knowing if he admitted how he felt, she'd feel obligated to stay awake with him. He knew she'd worked a long day and then they'd had a long night, and she needed her sleep. Tomorrow they could sleep in and he'd make her breakfast in bed. Maybe they'd even go to the farmer's market that she'd mentioned to him earlier in the week.

She relaxed against him and her breathing was starting to even out as he kissed her again and began to hum. The melody had been in his head all week—a ballad. For almost a year, Julian had blocked music from his mind. Long before the wedding. He'd been so consumed with what was happening in his personal life that it had been impossible to think of anything other than what was going on around him.

But now the music was back, demanding to be heard.

Back at the house he was selling sat a magnificent baby grand piano. If he were there right now, he'd be sitting at it and working through the song in his head.

Instead, he hummed softly. It was so loud and strong in his head that he was surprised Charlotte couldn't hear it with him. When he was certain she was asleep, he slid from the bed and gently covered her with the blankets before putting on a pair of sweatpants and heading out to the living room.

Grabbing a notebook, he walked out onto the deck and breathed in the beach air. He sat down on one of the lounge chairs and began to write down as much as he could about what he was hearing—he wrote out the melody, made notes on how he would like to see it orchestrated, and then played around with some lyrics. Those were always the hardest for him, but when the four of them were together, the lyrics always seemed to come.

That was why Riley couldn't write.

That was why Matt couldn't perform.

They were a unit, and no matter how much Julian tried to convince himself it wouldn't bother him to retire from music, he was discovering it was a lie. He wanted to play. He wanted to write and create and record and perform for the fans.

There were so many obstacles to overcome, however. And although most of them were his own mental issues, it didn't make it any easier to work through.

Tonight had left him feeling what he hadn't felt in far too long—happiness and hope. Could he really keep that going? Keep the momentum and work toward getting back to that place where he had been when he was maybe twenty or twenty-five? That was when Shaughnessy was new and everything they did gave him a sense of accomplishment. Wouldn't going back to that time be as counterproductive to him as focusing on the past five wasted years with Dena?

No. It took him less than a second to realize that. In one instance he was focusing on positive, where the other was purely negative.

Only…sometimes it wasn't.

Tossing the notebook down, Julian leaned back in the chair and sighed. The reality was that in the beginning, things with Dena were good and the two of them were happy. At least…he was. With nothing but calmness around him and his mood better than it had been in a while, he could look back on those years with more of an open mind.

Yes, some of the time together had been good, but he knew now the exact point when he should have walked away.

And it was certainly before he was standing at the front of a church for his own wedding.

Why had he stayed with her? Why had he been so adamant to save a relationship that was so obviously toxic? Where had that overwhelming need that made him think he could fix something that should have been let go come from? His entire life, Julian had been taught to work for what he wanted, and he had. Especially with his music. He had been relentless in that pursuit to climb the ladder of success, and there had been rewards. Why had he been that relentless where Dena was concerned, when there had never been any rewards with her?

Raking a hand through his hair, he stared up at the sky. It was cloudy and dark with not a star to be seen. How could he have been so blind for so long? How could he have given up so many years to something that left him feeling nothing but rage and emptiness? Because of his own stubbornness, he lost everything. Okay, not everything. He still had his friends, his health, and most of his finances—damn Dena for that payoff he'd made to get rid of her—but there was still a large part of himself that was missing.

"Julian?"

Charlotte's soft voice called from behind him. He turned and saw her standing in the doorway, wrapped in the afghan from the sofa. Holding out a hand, he silently beckoned her to him. She seemed to float like an ethereal vision toward him. When she was next to the lounge chair, he carefully guided her down until she was cradled in his arms.

"What are you doing awake?" he asked softly, combing the hair that was blowing in the ocean breeze away from her face.

She kissed his jaw. "I woke up and you weren't there."

Everything negative that he'd been thinking was gone. This woman—this amazing woman in his arms—was all he wanted to think of. He kissed her forehead. "My brain wouldn't be quiet, so I came out here to write a bit and then I was enjoying the peacefulness of the night."

"Mmm... It's good, isn't it?" she asked. "That's why you found me on the beach that night. Sometimes it just helps quiet my soul."

He shifted to get them more comfortable, and when the afghan slipped, he noticed she was naked beneath it. His eyes met hers and she gave him a shy yet mischievous grin. "Had I known what was going on underneath this blanket, I would have come back inside. You must be cold."

But Charlotte shook her head. "Not when I'm near you. You always keep me warm."

Holding her closer, he felt so many emotions that he had no idea how to put into words. Did she have any idea how the things she said made him feel? Affected him? Did she know that every day with her had him this much closer to falling in love with her?

And even saying it in his mind didn't scare him.

Reaching up, he cupped her cheek and kissed her lips.

They were soft kisses. Gentle kisses. Shy kisses. Charlotte was warm and sleepy in his arms and with nothing but the moonlight over them, she was beyond lovely.

She moved over him until she was straddling him. The blanket fell open, and her breasts pressed against his bare chest and it felt so good, so perfect, it had him taking those soft, sleepy kisses a little deeper. His tongue licked at her lower lip and she sighed as she opened for him, her own tongue easily meeting his.

With his hands moving up to anchor in her hair, Julian held her close, devouring her mouth and moving against her, cursing the fact that he had on sweatpants. If he could, he'd—

But Charlotte was one step ahead of him. With nimble fingers, she pulled his waistband down and together they worked to slide the garment off him. He broke the kiss and looked at her. Making love outside hadn't been on his agenda when he'd asked her to join him. The feel of her silky skin, her warm breath dancing across his own, and the things her hands were doing to him were more than enough incentive to convince him.

"Please," she whispered breathlessly against his lips, her hips moving against him, seeking what she wanted.

What they both wanted.

She kissed his throat, his shoulder, and down to his chest. Her tongue circled his nipple and he hissed out a breath—he was harder than a man should be who had already come three times. And yet…he was more than ready to go a fourth time.

"Charlotte," he said, gripping her hair and bringing her mouth back to his. Their kiss was wild and untamed, bordering on brutal. Gone was the sleepy woman, and in her place was his every fantasy come to life.

It was easily three in the morning and there wasn't a soul around, and they were sheltered by the deck so no one would see them, and yet it felt a little decadent, a little naughty to be outside like this—naked except for a thin afghan to cover them.

But when Charlotte straightened and the afghan draped around her hips, Julian looked at those perfect breasts in the moonlight and he was lost.

Again.

Only this time, he would be more than happy if he was never found.

Chapter 7

IT WAS A GOOD THING THEY'D HAD THAT PERFECT night, because for the two weeks after it, things were less than idyllic.

As Charlotte shut down her laptop and slid it into her briefcase, she yawned loudly. Two of her coworkers had quit, and she'd had to take on more cases than she could comfortably handle. On top of that, Hank had called because they had two families come to the shelter with a combined ten kids and he wanted her advice on developing some sort of children's program for them.

Her eight-to-five workdays had morphed into seven-to-seven workdays—and that was if she was lucky.

Julian had been wonderful through it all—when she stayed at his place, he always had her coffee ready and then sat out on the deck with her so she could still get a beach fix in the morning. He'd brought lunch to her almost every day and managed to have dinner either ready or delivered every night whether they stayed at his place or hers.

And that was an experience.

The first night she had called to say she was working late and was just going home, he had met her there with a bag of Chinese takeout. Her nerves had been more than a little frazzled at the thought of him seeing her tiny apartment. Her entire place could fit in the living room of his place. But Julian being Julian, he never commented on it.

He had, however, commented on how small her bed was and all the reasons why they should just stay at his place.

After three nights in her full-size bed with him, she agreed.

Her phone beeped with an incoming text and she smiled when she saw Julian's name.

> **Julian**: Lighting the grill. How do you like your burger?
> **Charlotte**: I'll have to take a rain check. Problem at the shelter. Heading there now.
> **Julian**: Anything I can do?

She wished. Unfortunately, there was no way for him to find jobs and homes for all the people currently crowding the shelter and also develop a children's program. It was bad enough that she had the resources at her fingertips and couldn't get it done.

> **Charlotte**: Thanks but I need to go and see what we're dealing with.
> I'll talk to you tomorrow
> **Julian**: Call me tonight. I want to make sure you get home safely

That made her smile. She wished she could just tell him she'd see him later, but it was already after seven and she had at least a forty-five-minute drive and then who knew what she was going to find when she got to the shelter? It would be a late night and then she'd have to get up early and start all over again.

She was already ready for a nap tomorrow.

Charlotte: I will. I promise.

Julian: Make sure you stop and get something to eat.

Charlotte: Yes sir ☺

Slipping the phone into her purse, she pulled out her keys and made her way out to the car. It was funny how well Julian knew her. In all the planning for tonight, not once had she thought about herself or stopping to get something for dinner. When she got in her car, she realized she wasn't particularly hungry and decided to get to Santa Monica first and see what she was dealing with, and then think about dinner.

At least, that was the idea.

Two hours later, she was sitting with her head on Hank's desk, feeling ready to cry.

Another family had arrived with three more kids. Their food truck had shown up late, and had a lot less on board than they were expecting. On top of that, she was starving and now she had a headache.

She hated days like this.

Out in the common area, people were talking and milling about, kids were screeching, and somewhere in the distance she heard something crash to the floor. At that moment, it took everything she had not to grab her purse and sneak out. No one would have to know, and if Hank should call her out on it the next time she came in, Charlotte would say she thought she'd said goodbye to everyone when she left.

"You are many things, Charlotte Clark, but you're no liar," she murmured and then gently banged her head on the desk. "Dammit."

With a sigh, she sat up and tried to focus. Pulling out her laptop, she started a document for all the things the shelter was in need of: more food, more volunteers, and something for the kids. Normally that wasn't her area of expertise. Creating something to entertain children just wasn't in her job description.

That made her stop and think, because she loved kids. Somewhere down the line, she wanted to have some. Why hadn't she felt inclined to work on something for children until now?

That still didn't make any magical lightbulb go off. Leaning forward, she banged her head on the desk again.

"Uh-oh. That's not a good sign."

Julian.

As much as she wanted to sit up and smile, she was too exhausted to pull that off. Instead, she sat up and exhaled slowly. Then she smelled something wonderful and noticed the cooler bag in his hand.

And she smiled.

Walking toward her, he gave her a sympathetic smile. "Rough night, huh?"

"You have no idea."

Placing the bag on the desk, he sat on the corner and looked at her. "I have an idea." He paused. "What's going on?"

"Is there food in this bag?" she asked instead.

Julian nodded. "A burger, pasta salad, and a Coke. It's not gourmet, but I thought you could probably use it." And before Charlotte could even get to the bag herself, Julian opened it and set the food out for her. "Eat. Then tell me what's happening here."

She was too hungry to argue, and the first bite of the

burger was almost orgasmic. She took two more in rapid succession—unmindful of Julian watching her and how unladylike she was eating. Putting the burger down, she opened the cola and took a long drink, sighing happily.

Leaning back in her chair, she looked up at him appreciatively. "Thank you."

"My pleasure."

Then she told him about her day and what had transpired here at the shelter. "Honestly, Julian, my brain is just mush at this point. I have no idea what to do to help these kids."

"How old are they?"

"They range from around six to sixteen, I think. There're two infants in the group so I'm not worried about them, but the other kids definitely need something to do."

He nodded once and then stood up. "Finish eating. I'll be right back."

Charlotte was about to call him back, but her stomach had other ideas. As soon as he was out of sight, she picked up her burger and wolfed it down happily. Then the pasta salad. And then the rest of the cola. With her hand on her pleasantly full belly, she leaned back in the chair and was almost asleep when Julian walked back in.

"You ready to go?" he asked casually, cleaning up her dinner mess.

She looked at him oddly. "Go? Julian, I still haven't figured out what I'm going to do. I need to talk to Hank and see what he's thinking and—"

One finger covered her lips as he leaned in and kissed her on the nose. "You're done for the day. I spoke to Hank and everything's under control." He took one of her hands in his and gently tugged her to her feet.

"But…but… I still need to…"

"You need to come home and sleep," he said firmly but softly. "C'mon."

She couldn't speak because she yawned broadly, loudly. "Sorry."

Julian laughed and picked up her purse and briefcase, carrying them along with the cooler bag in one hand while keeping her hand in the other. He nodded toward Hank and wished him good night, and Charlotte waved because she was yawning again and couldn't speak.

How the heck was she supposed to drive home like this?

They stepped outside and she looked for Julian's car. "Did you park in the lot around the corner again?"

He shook his head and walked over to her car, opening the passenger side and helping her get in.

"But… I need to… How are you going to…?"

He placed the bags in the back seat and climbed in the driver's side. "I took an Uber to get here because I was worried about you driving home late."

If she wasn't so tired, she'd be…well, she'd be incredibly thankful, because as much as she didn't like him—or anyone—thinking she couldn't handle herself, she also appreciated how he was so concerned for her, how he came all this way to take care of her. Julian pulled away from the curb, and her eyes felt so heavy that she swore she'd close them just for a minute.

"Come on, sleepy girl. Let's get you inside."

Charlotte blinked several times and tried to understand where they were. It wasn't until Julian got out of the car and came around to open her door that she saw they were in his driveway. "How…?"

Instead of answering, he lifted her in his arms.

"I can walk," she protested, followed by another yawn.

"Humor me."

So she did. Resting her head on his shoulder, she let him carry her into the bedroom, where he placed her on the bed. Her limbs felt like they were filled with lead, and as much as she wanted to sit and talk to him, she was just too tired. With her eyes closed, she felt Julian remove her shoes, then move up to unbutton her slacks and slowly slide them down her legs. He placed a light kiss on her belly as he worked.

Part of her perked up.

With her pants gone, his hands slid up and took her shirt with them.

He placed a kiss between her breasts.

Okay, maybe she wasn't completely tired. She'd had a nap on the way home, after all.

Those big, talented hands of his moved around to her back and unhooked her bra. As he pulled it away, he stopped and caressed her breasts and damn if that didn't feel great. She must have purred or moaned, because she heard him chuckle softly.

"You like that?" he asked, his voice low and husky right next to her ear.

"Mm-hmm."

Julian stretched out beside her and began to suckle one breast as he gently kneaded the other.

Yeah, every day should end like this, she thought.

Her back arched, and little by little, she became more awake. "Julian," she cried breathlessly.

"I'm right here with you, sweetheart. Right here."

His tone was both soothing and arousing, and as he

continued to tease and pleasure her, sleep became the very last thing on her mind.

"I need you."

She didn't think she'd ever seen someone move so fast. One minute he was beside her and seemingly very relaxed, the next he was straddling her and whipping his shirt off. "You have me."

And she knew she did. She also knew it was becoming more than just a physical need. The more time they spent together, the more time Charlotte wanted with him. She loved their talks, she loved sharing meals with him, and more than anything, she loved wrapping herself around him at the end of every day and sleeping in Julian's arms every night.

Lost in her own thoughts, she didn't notice how he'd moved away and finished undressing until he was stretched out on top of her, kissing her cheek, her shoulder, her throat. His body was warm and hard, and lazily her limbs wrapped around him. As he moved over her, with her, she vowed she was going to tell him very soon just how much he meant to her.

Being a fairly private person, Julian had no problem keeping his plans to himself. He'd kissed Charlotte goodbye that morning and watched her drive away before heading into the house.

Then he'd set about putting his plans in motion. It took about seventeen phone calls, but he finally had everything in place.

Charlotte had called to tell him she was leaving the office early and heading over to the center to try to work out some things with Hank. He knew she worked through lunch so she could leave early. He hoped it wouldn't be long before she could go back to her normal hours.

He admired her for her work ethic and for all the things she did for the community. What he was struggling with was how little she got back. And he wasn't referring to her pay or all of the unpaid overtime she put in, but the overall lack of reward for all of her hard work. In the last week he'd watched her grow a little wearier, a little less optimistic, and he just couldn't allow it to continue.

Hence tonight's plan.

Standing on the street, Julian grinned as he saw all of his calls and efforts had paid off.

"I'm not gonna lie to you," Dylan said as he approached, "I am freaking giddy like you can't believe about this."

Riley stepped up beside him. "This is brilliant. I'm seriously impressed."

Julian's chest swelled with pride. There were no guarantees that this was going to work, but he hoped it would at least work for tonight. Then maybe it would ease a little of Charlotte's—and the shelter's—burden.

"Thanks for being willing to come," he said and smiled when Paige walked over along with Savannah. "I know this was all last minute and meant you had to get a sitter for the kids."

"My parents are still in town," Savannah said easily. "And they love having the kids to themselves."

"Be sure to thank them for me," Julian said and then looked around as more people came walking toward them.

Soon there were about a dozen people standing around him, and he carefully laid out his plan to them all. Once everyone was in agreement, Julian took out his phone and texted Hank to let him know they were ready to come inside. After Hank texted him back, he looked out at his group of volunteers.

"Hank is our go-to person. He'll meet us at the door and show you all where to set up. You're not punching a clock here, but I would appreciate if you could give us at least two hours tonight." Everyone nodded in agreement. "On top of that, this place is always looking for volunteers. If any of you find that's your thing, talk to Hank. He'll more than appreciate it."

After taking another look at the group, Julian realized he was nervous. What if this whole thing failed? What if it was just a huge clusterfuck and he only succeeded in making things worse?

"Stop worrying," Riley said as if reading his mind. "This is gonna be great."

With a nod, Julian motioned to the door and held it open for everyone. They filed inside, and he heard Hank instructing them where to go. By the time he stepped inside, Charlotte was standing beside him in confusion.

"What's going on?" she asked.

Rather than answer, Julian took her hand and walked over to where they were setting up. Then he explained.

"We're here tonight to do a little music therapy," he said. "We've got instruments for everyone to try. We're going to teach the kids some songs and do a couple of sing-alongs, and Paige is going to set up a library. Savannah brought snacks and drinks for everyone."

When he looked at Charlotte, tears were in her eyes. "I… I can't believe you did all this."

With his arm draped around her shoulders, Julian

hugged her in close and placed a kiss on her temple. "Help me get everyone set up and then you can thank me properly later," he teased.

And then she hugged him—full-on, full-body hugged him. "You are an amazing man, Julian Grayson, and I love that you did this."

He held her with equal fervor and knew that if he didn't let go of her now, he wasn't going to get anything accomplished.

And certainly he wouldn't be thanked properly later.

It was a great incentive.

"Come on," he said, taking one of her hands. "Let's do this."

In his mind, Julian knew what he hoped to do here tonight, but the reality was even better. For two hours, there was music and laughter and one of the craziest jam sessions he'd ever witnessed. Every kid was playing something—drums, guitars, tambourines, triangles—some of them danced, and everybody sang. A lot of the parents and staff joined in, too. At one point he spotted Charlotte on the far side of the room smiling broadly even as her eyes were shining with unshed tears.

Yeah, he'd done this for his girl.

Seeing how happy she was made all the phone calls and all the stress of pulling this together worth it.

"Okay, everyone!" Hank called out. "It's after eight and we need to let our guests get packed up!"

It took more than an hour to make that happen, and Julian lost track of how many people had thanked him and how many had asked if they'd be back. If it were up to him, they would, but he wasn't ready to make that commitment for everyone. They'd talk about it after they left and he heard how they felt.

By the time he was ready to go, Charlotte was standing by the door waiting for him. They waved to Hank and the staff and made their way out to the sidewalk, where Riley, Dylan, and the others were waiting for them.

"What do you say we meet up for coffee and talk about how the night went?" Julian asked.

"Opposite directions, dude," Riley said as he pulled Savannah in close. "You're heading west to Malibu, and we're all heading back toward LA."

"There's a great rooftop restaurant not far from here—it's at the Marriott," Charlotte suggested. "They have a dessert menu, or we can just order some appetizers or something. It has amazing ocean views."

Julian chuckled, and when she looked at him in confusion, he said, "Leave it to you to throw that last part in."

She shrugged. "It's true." Then she called out the name and general directions and they all agreed to meet up there. Julian walked her to her car and she handed him the keys.

"Uh-uh. I drove this time because of my equipment, but I wanted to make sure you got to your car okay."

"That's very sweet of you." She leaned in and kissed him softly on the lips. "I'll see you over at the hotel."

He stood back and watched her start up the car and drive away, hating that they weren't riding together. It just made more sense for them to drive separately for now.

On his way to the hotel, he thought about how well the night had gone. This was something they could do again—maybe not with this exact combination of people, but certainly with another group of musicians and volunteers to keep it going. He knew he'd be down for doing it whenever he could—especially on the nights when Charlotte was volunteering. Then he remembered that this was a temporary shelter for these families. With any luck, they wouldn't be there for long and their kids wouldn't need a little fun to keep them busy.

Something else they'd need to talk about.

Within minutes, the valet had parked and Julian was joining his friends at the hotel entrance. He took Charlotte by the hand and let her lead them inside and up to the restaurant.

Luckily, they were seated quickly—of course Riley had charmed the hostess into doing that right away—and soon they were ordering drinks.

"So?" he called out once the waitress walked away. "What did everyone think about tonight?"

"Wait!" Charlotte said before anyone could respond. "I just want to take a minute to thank all of you for volunteering your time tonight. Maybe it didn't seem like that much to you, but to those kids and their families, it meant the world. I never would have thought of anything so creative and wonderful that had everyone wanting to join in, and…" She stopped and Julian could hear in her voice how emotional she was feeling about it all. "And I just want to say that it meant the world to me too. So…thank you."

Everyone was talking at once but Julian wasn't fully listening. He reached over and squeezed Charlotte's hand, bringing it to his lips to kiss it. "You okay?"

She nodded. "I'm just blown away by this, Julian. I don't think I've ever seen anything like what you did tonight. I…I don't even have words."

"You said plenty," he replied, pleased that she was so happy with what they'd done. All around them, discussions were being had on what they could do the next time and who else they could call upon to help out.

Drinks were served, food came out, and from his other side, Riley nudged him.

"You did good tonight, Jules. Seriously. This was a great idea and you seemed to have a lot of fun doing it."

He nodded. "I really did. It made me remember the first time I held a pair of drumsticks in my hands and how bad I sounded but how enthusiastic I was."

"It was the same for me with the guitar," Riley admitted. "I always knew I could sing, but I didn't think I'd be able to play an instrument, too. When I got my first guitar, everyone in the house used to beg me to go and play it outside or in the garage because I sounded so bad, but in my head, I was onstage in front of millions of people."

Julian chuckled at the image. "Millions, huh? That's ambitious."

"Math never was my thing."

"I don't expect you to come out here every week, but I'd like to see this thing keep going with other combinations of people. Or maybe we can get someone to help organize it based on the needs of who is staying at the shelter."

Taking a sip of his drink, Riley nodded. "I don't think it will be a problem to get volunteers. We can put out the call for help and I'm sure Paige can assist. Don't forget she's organized campaigns for all kinds of things. Getting volunteers or figuring out how to put this all together should be a breeze for her."

"Good call." Rising, Julian walked over and pulled up a chair between Dylan and Paige and began talking to her about what he was thinking. She was incredibly enthusiastic about it and was telling him all about her contacts and who she'd start making calls to in the morning, when Julian glanced back to where Charlotte was sitting and talking to Randy—a studio bass player who had helped out that night. He didn't know anything about the guy other than what instrument he played and that he was good at it, but the way he was looking at Charlotte and the way she was smiling at him made Julian's gut clench.

Dylan elbowed him. Hard.

"Dude, what the hell?" Julian snapped.

With an easy grin, Dylan leaned back in his chair. "Quit scowling at Charlotte and Randy."

"I wasn't," he lied.

"Please. Don't even. You were, and you need to stop."

Fine. Consider him warned.

Maybe. But just in case…

Julian smiled—or at least tried to smile—at Paige. "Call me tomorrow and let me know what I can do to help."

Paige reached for Julian's hand. "Don't go over there with a head full of steam."

Warning number two.

So maybe he moved the chair with a little too much force, but that wasn't his intention. He needed to get back to his seat and see what Randy and Charlotte were talking about so intimately.

"Julian—" Dylan said, but all he did was flip him off before he walked away.

Randy was talking about some show he did—bragging was more like it. Julian didn't care if the guy was midsentence; he sat down, placed a possessive arm around Charlotte, and kissed her cheek.

"Paige is going to make some calls tomorrow to see about getting more volunteers to help out with nights like this. What do you think?"

Her eyes went wide and she looked at him, then Randy, and back again. "Oh, um…yeah. That's great! Randy was just telling me about—"

"I think we can get a rotation of people who can come in here, and we'll coordinate it all with Hank, and who knows, maybe we can start doing this sort of thing at other shelters or as after-school programs."

After an awkward glance at Randy, Charlotte turned to Julian. "Wow, I wasn't even thinking of something that far-reaching. That sounds wonderful. Although it does seem like a lot for Paige to be taking on. It's not like we can afford to pay her for this or anything, but…"

"I'll pay her if she needs to be paid," Julian said confidently, shooting a glare at Randy.

Moving away slightly, Charlotte looked at him oddly and nodded. "So, Randy was telling me about the time he played—"

"Have you ever played Madison Square Garden, Randy?" Julian asked cockily.

"Um…no," he replied, this time giving Charlotte a nervous look.

"Really? Oh, well, how about the Hollywood Bowl? Ever play there?"

"Julian," Charlotte whispered, her eyes narrowing.

"No, can't say that I have," Randy replied, reaching for his glass. "If you guys will excuse me, I'm going to see if Nigel's ready to head out. He's my ride."

"Don't have a car of your own, Randy?" Julian asked smugly.

"Julian!" Charlotte gasped, before she quickly said good night to Randy. Once he was out of sight, she faced Julian. "What in the world was that all about?"

"What?" Feigning ignorance seemed like the way to go when he realized how angry she appeared.

"Want to explain why you were practically having a pissing match with Randy?"

"*Randy?*" he repeated with annoyance. "What difference does it make? And I wasn't. I was just curious about his career, that's all. I don't see what the big deal is."

"The big deal is that you were a colossal jackass. I mean really."

Unfazed, Julian shrugged and reached for a piece of the bruschetta they'd ordered. He took a bite and hummed appreciatively before holding it up for Charlotte. "You should taste this, it's delicious."

Declining, she crossed her arms and simply sat quietly beside him. For the life of him, Julian had no idea what she was so upset about. Why would she think it was okay for him just to let some random guy hit on her? All he was doing was showing how much he cared about her by making sure Randy didn't get any ideas. Nothing wrong with that.

Except—there was.

And that was blazingly obvious by the way she continued to give him the cold shoulder for the rest of the time they were with everyone, and how the only words she spoke were to tell him she was going back to her place. Alone.

They walked out to the parking lot. Julian offered to drive her home and deal with getting his car tomorrow, but Charlotte said, "Don't bother."

He sighed with frustration. "I still don't see what the big deal is here, Charlotte."

Without looking at him, she pulled out her keys. "The big deal is that you were incredibly rude tonight. You walked over and…and…it was like you were staking your claim, and it was ridiculous. Everyone knows we're together. You didn't have to behave the way you did."

Now he growled with frustration. "That guy was hitting on you!"

"That guy was telling me about how he plays guitar once a week at his daughter's preschool!" she shouted. "If you had shut up long enough to let him answer a question or hadn't interrupted the story he was telling me, you would have known that!"

Okay, yeah. He was a colossal jackass.

Raking a hand through his hair, he looked up at the sky and almost growled. "Fine. I get it. I overreacted."

"Ya think?" Sarcasm lacing her words, she stormed over to her car and opened the driver's side door, tossing her purse inside.

Julian immediately followed her over. "I'm sorry, okay?" he asked when she made to move around him and get behind the wheel. "I was wrong."

"Whatever," she murmured, still trying to get around him.

Grasping her by the shoulders, he waited until she would look at him. "Don't go home tonight. Please. This was a great night and I hate that I ruined it. I got feedback from everyone else tonight except you, and you're the only one I wanted to talk to about this. Please come back to the house."

She eyed him warily. "I'm really tired, Julian, and I

think it would be better for me to go home and get some sleep. I'll call you tomorrow, okay?"

It wasn't okay. He wanted to haul her over his shoulder and take her home. But he figured he'd already acted like a Neanderthal once tonight and clearly that wasn't a good thing.

Rather than argue or plead his case, he simply leaned in and kissed her on the forehead and said, "Okay."

He stood in the parking lot long after Charlotte drove away, and realized that he'd done all of this tonight to help her, yet somehow all he'd managed to do was hurt her. Well, not where the actual volunteering was concerned, but on a personal level, and he hated himself for that.

And now he was left trying to figure out how to make it right.

―⁓―

"I'm sorry."

Charlotte looked at the beautifully wrapped box and then back at Julian. He'd been almost relentless all day about earning her forgiveness. He'd sent coffee and muffins to her office. Then flowers. Then he'd personally delivered lunch—a fantastic gourmet salad from one of her favorite restaurants. Unfortunately, she'd been too busy to take a real lunch break with him and had to eat at her desk.

While he watched.

Now it was after eight and they were having dinner out on his deck. He'd grilled steaks and made a big salad and baked potatoes, and even had her favorite wine.

The box was served as if it were dessert.

"What's this?"

He smiled warmly at her. "Open it."

Something about this bothered her. There was no mistake that it was some sort of jewelry; the small, slim box couldn't possibly fit anything else. She'd never gotten jewelry from a man before. Well, there was a puka shell necklace she'd gotten from Billy Miller in the tenth grade, but she had a feeling this was nothing like that.

And she was right.

Gasping softly, she pulled the tennis bracelet from the box. "Julian, what in the world…?"

Without answering, he took the bracelet from her trembling hand and put it on her wrist, securing the clasp. Then he brought her hand to his lips and kissed it. "A beautiful gift for a beautiful woman."

It was hard not to melt a little at his words, and she had forgiven him earlier—multiple times. She hated how he was still trying to earn it somehow. "You didn't have to do this," she said, but couldn't help but love the way the diamonds looked on her. "It's too much."

With her hand still in his, he shook his head. "No, it's not. I want you to know how much I regret my behavior last night. I hated sleeping by myself. I missed you."

She laughed softly. "Julian, we've already been over this. I accepted your apology and you already did so much today for me. I don't expect you to lavish me with gifts. It's not necessary. And we're fine. I think a night apart was a good thing—for both of us."

He didn't look convinced. "You deserve to be lavished. It occurred to me last night how we really haven't gone out a whole lot or done much together except hang around here. I want to change that. I don't want to stay holed up at home anymore."

That perked her up. "Does this mean you're thinking of going back with the band?" she asked carefully.

"Um…no," he responded. "This has nothing to do with the band and everything to do with us. We went out last night and nothing happened." He paused at her furrowed brows and then laughed. "I mean, something happened and I hate it, but what I meant was, no one bothered me. We were at a nice restaurant with a big crowd, and I was even there with most of the band, and no one bothered me."

Well, someone had bothered him, but she wasn't going to mention that. "So, what are you saying?"

"I'm saying I no longer feel the need to live like a hermit," he explained. "Although it's not like I want to do anything that draws attention to myself, but I want to take you places and do things. What do you say we go to Hawaii next week? I can make a call and we can have a place with a private beach and—"

She held up a hand to stop him. "Julian, I can't just take off like that. I have a job," she reminded him. "I'll have some vacation time after the first of the year, but for now I can't just pack up and go. And besides, we're short-handed at the office. I couldn't do that to my coworkers."

By the look on his face, he wasn't quite comprehending what she was saying.

"But…it's Hawaii," he said slowly. "I'm paying for everything. You wouldn't have to worry about a thing."

And that was like a slap in the face.

For some reason, his high-handedness rubbed her the wrong way. As if the fact that she didn't have to pay for the trip herself made everything else just work out.

"Again," she began and slowly pulled her hand from

his, "I'm not asking you to buy me anything, Julian. That's not the problem. The problem is that I have a job and responsibilities and I can't just take off on a moment's notice."

And still he looked a little befuddled.

"How about this—we start small," she began cautiously. "Why don't we go to San Francisco next weekend? I love walking around Fisherman's Wharf, and there are some great restaurants. We can ride the cable cars and just be tourists for the day. What do you say?"

He was quiet for a moment and she thought for sure he was going to counter with Hawaii again, but he didn't. Instead, he reached for her hand and kissed it. "Sounds like a plan. I'll see if I can find us a place to rent."

"Why? We can just stay at a hotel. Nothing fancy, just—"

"I hate hotels," he said a little roughly, and she had a feeling she'd struck a nerve.

"Okay. No worries," she said soothingly. "Honestly, I don't care where we stay just as long as we're there together."

That seemed to work. Julian visibly relaxed and smiled at her.

"How about dessert?" he asked, his tone going smooth and a little seductive. She smiled shyly at him.

"What did you have in mind?"

That *definitely* worked. His grin was wicked and she realized how much she had missed him last night too.

"There's a death by chocolate cake inside I planned to serve, but—"

Feeling bold, Charlotte rose to her feet and tugged him to his. "It can wait until later, right?"

In a flash, she was in his arms and he was kissing her. She felt all of his pent-up anger, frustration, and all of the emotions she'd been watching him deal with tonight. It was a heady feeling, and as she wrapped herself around him, she knew she was struggling with them, too. But when they were like this, everything else faded away. All she could focus on was the feel of Julian—the warmth of his body, the way his hands felt as they moved over her—and she wanted more.

As if he sensed her thoughts, he lifted her. Charlotte wrapped her legs around his waist, more than happy to let him take her wherever it was he wanted to have her. They'd made love in just about every room of the house, and it really wasn't about where they were, but how fast they could get there.

Now.

She really was hoping for right now.

"Julian," she murmured against his lips.

"I know, baby," he said and placed her on the sofa. The sliding doors were open and the night air was cool and salty and just served to heighten her senses.

There was no finesse.

There was little foreplay.

It had only been one night apart and yet she was equally frantic for him.

Warning bells should have been going off in her head—this was too soon, too intense, too…everything—yet they weren't. And if they were, they were drowned out by the sounds they were making along with the noise of the outside world drifting in.

She was naked before she even realized he'd been undressing her. When he stood and stripped, she licked

her lips in anticipation. His body was like a work of art—
it didn't matter how many times she'd seen it, touched it,
kissed it, it still made her go weak. No man should be so
sculpted and sexy and perfect, and she had to keep from
pinching herself to make sure this wasn't a dream.

He was hers.

And she was his.

And if this was a dream, she hoped she'd never wake
up.

"So, what's your favorite place to travel to?" Charlotte
asked later that night as Julian fed her a piece of chocolate cake while they were snuggled under a blanket on
the couch.

He thought about it for a minute and took a forkful of
cake for himself. "On our second world tour we had a
couple of dates in London and had a week off before we
moved on. Riley went home to visit his family, Dylan
partied his way around London, and Matt went to Paris
for a week to visit some friends. I just wanted a little
peace and quiet and didn't want to go far because it felt
like we were constantly on the move. The day of our last
performance, I was hanging out at the arena and there
was this older guy sweeping up around the place. I asked
him where he'd go if he only wanted to travel an hour
from home and just wanted a little down time."

"And what did he say?"

"East Sussex," he said. "More specifically, the town
of Rye." He fed her another bite of cake. "I had nothing
to lose, so I made some calls and rented a place for a
week, and it was one of the greatest weeks ever."

She smiled as she listened to him, because even if he didn't give her any other details, she could hear in his voice how much he loved it.

"It was a two-hour train ride out of London, but I didn't care. It was an incredibly scenic ride and it was the perfect choice after all the noise and chaos of the tour."

"What kind of things were there to do in town?"

He shrugged. "It's not really a tourist place—which was perfect for me—but the architecture and the town itself was really beautiful. It's a shipping town and used to be completely surrounded by water." He sighed and took another bite of cake for himself. "I just enjoyed walking around and learning the history."

"Have you ever gone back?"

"No." He shook his head. "Never had the time."

"You haven't been back to London since?"

"We have, but..." He paused. "It's not important. What about you? What's your favorite place to travel to?"

She knew a diversion when she heard one, but right now she didn't want to be diverted. Turning, she faced him head on. "I find it hard to believe that with all the time off since touring that you haven't made the time to go back to a place you loved."

He shrugged again. "It wasn't meant to be. Been there, saw that...you know the rest."

"Julian," Charlotte began patiently, "I really wish you wouldn't shut down when we're talking. I could tell you had more to say and then you just stopped. What were you going to say? Please."

For a solid minute he didn't say anything. Hell, he barely blinked. She saw the instant he resigned himself to it.

"When the band first started touring, I did stuff like that a lot when we had a couple of days off. I don't mind staying in hotels, but I like my privacy, and believe it or not, I'm kind of a homebody. So even if I couldn't be home…"

"You wanted it at least to feel like a home," she finished for him.

"Exactly." He paused. "Anyway, when Dena and I started dating, she begged to come on tour. I didn't have a problem with it and as long as we were going from city to city, we were fine. But the first break in the action, when I had rented a place in advance and told her where we were going, she got pissed. She ruined the entire week for me with her complaining and bitching about being away from everything and how she hated having to cook for herself and do her own laundry. I shrugged it off that first time and figured she was just enjoying life on the road. But it wasn't that at all—she just liked having people waiting on her and always wanted to be where the party was. So I stopped renting places after a while."

"That hardly seems fair. She got to be happy and have her way and you didn't?"

"Pretty much."

"Wow."

He fed her the last piece of cake and placed the empty plate on the coffee table in front of them. "I got used to it."

"But it makes you angry to think about."

"Well, yeah," he said with a humorless laugh. "I was paying for everything and never got to do what I wanted."

Now they were getting somewhere.

Finally.

Charlotte took a minute to think about her next words

carefully. She adjusted the blanket and put a little space between them. "How long into the relationship before you realized there were issues?"

Then she held her breath and hoped he wasn't going to shut her down and walk away.

"Six months," he admitted as he looked down at his hands, the blanket...pretty much anywhere that wasn't directly at Charlotte.

And to her surprise, he kept talking.

"It was after that tour when I knew there were problems. Enough that I seriously was ready to throw in the towel. The problem was—at first—Dena put on a good show for everyone. She was a freaking delight to everyone we met—including my parents. So, when I mentioned how I wanted to break up with her, both of my folks got on me about it. They always told me that you have to work hard for the things you want, how all relationships have their ups and downs, and how I needed to try to exhaust every option before calling it quits."

Charlotte nodded, thinking it was admirable of him.

Then he looked at her. "My parents weren't particularly close. Never have been, never will be. I can't ever remember seeing them show affection for one another, although they were always very respectful to each other. I thought that's how relationships were supposed to be. Except—for me—they never were. I'm not like that. When I'm with someone, I enjoy laughing and kissing and touching..." He gave her a lopsided grin. "As I'm sure you've noticed."

"I have, and I've enjoyed it very much," she said lightly, hoping he would continue.

"The first time I found out Dena had cheated, my

parents were visiting. I was mortified. Like, seriously mortified. It wasn't until later on that I realized I was more upset about my parents witnessing it than I was about her cheating."

Yikes.

"We fought, with my parents in the next room, and Dena stormed out. My dad never said a word to me about it, but my mom came out and we talked through the night."

"And what did she say?"

At this point, Julian reclined and let his head fall back against the cushions as he sighed. "She told me how when I was little, she'd had an affair. She took full responsibility for it, even though she said it was because she was lonely and she wished my dad was more… affectionate, caring, emotional. It wasn't that she was in love with this other man, she just wanted to feel something from someone."

"Oh, Julian. I'm so sorry," she said softly, but he wasn't really listening. He seemed to be lost in his memory.

"The guilt of what she'd done was killing her, so she confessed to my dad and he forgave her. But he also told her that if she wanted to leave him for this other man, she could do that too."

Charlotte could only stare in wide-eyed shock.

Julian lifted his head and looked at her and let out another mirthless laugh. "Yeah. That was pretty much my reaction too."

"I…I don't even know what to say to that."

"I asked her why she decided to stay if she wasn't happy, and after she gave all the usual answers—there was me, and she still loved my dad—but the craziest thing about it all was how she kept waiting for him to fight for her. She never left, so it wasn't as if he had to beg her to come home. She wanted him to fight for her and let her know that she meant something to him." He scoffed. "She's still waiting."

"And you heard that and thought…"

He rose and stretched, reaching for his jeans and sliding them on before facing her. "I thought if I just kept fighting for Dena, she'd change. Joke was on me though, right?"

Her heart broke for him all over again. Carefully, she stood and wrapped the blanket around herself as she stepped in close. "No, the joke's not on you. I think what you did just shows the kind of person you are, and it makes me angry for you that Dena didn't appreciate all that you sacrificed for her and the relationship. She didn't deserve you."

She saw him swallow hard. "My life was a freaking joke for those years, Charlotte. Everyone knew I was making a mistake, but I was trying to prove a point." He shook his head. "And it wasn't even a point I wanted to prove! I didn't want my parents to be disappointed, and I didn't want to lose, and in the end, both those things happened!"

"Your parents can't possibly be disappointed in you, Julian."

But he nodded and looked a bit arrogant as he did. "But they are. After the whole wedding fiasco, I took a few days and then called them to let them know I was all right, and I got lectured on making a scene. A scene! There was no real concern about my feelings or how devastated I was. It was all about how my actions made them look!"

"Okay, but you have to admit, from everything you've told me about the wedding, that had to be a bit of a shock for everyone. Maybe you could have given them a warning about what you were planning."

"They would have talked me out of it. Or my mother would have. I was finally ready to take back control of my life, and maybe that wasn't the best way to do it, but it's done and I can't change it!"

He stormed away from her and went to look out the windows toward the beach, while Charlotte took a moment to wrap her brain around what Julian had just confessed. It was no wonder he had such a strong will and ironclad control now—for far too long he'd felt like he was being told how to live his life, and now…now he'd taken it to the extreme.

She walked over and stood beside him. "I think you're very brave," she said quietly, and although she kept her gaze forward, she felt him staring at her. "You were in a bad situation and you needed to get out of it. Most people would have stayed in the cycle and resigned themselves to being miserable. There was never going to be a winner where you and Dena were concerned. I'm just sorry that not everyone saw it that way."

Together they stood silently and watched the waves until Julian said, "Thank you." His voice was gruff—almost raw.

"Thank you for sharing that with me." And she meant it. It helped her to understand him so much more than she'd ever thought she would. He was still struggling with this and he probably would for a long time, but at least now she could understand.

"It doesn't mean I'm weak," he said, this time his voice so low she almost didn't hear him.

"I know that." And that just shattered her heart. For someone as strong and proud as Julian to think anyone would view him as weak, and to admit it, had to be one of the hardest things he'd ever done.

There were still dozens of questions she had for him, but not now. They'd talked enough.

Without a word, she reached for his hand and led him to the bedroom. Beside the bed she dropped the blanket she'd been clutching to her and let it pool at her feet. The heat in his gaze battled with gratitude that she hadn't pushed him for more.

And as she wrapped her hand around his nape and pulled his lips to hers, Charlotte knew that she was the one who was thankful because she had earned his trust.

And she'd do everything in her power never to betray it.

Chapter 8

THEY DIDN'T MAKE IT TO SAN FRANCISCO.

The day before they were supposed to leave, Charlotte's car died and she was too upset about repairs and having lost half a day of work to go. To say he was disappointed was an understatement, but Julian knew when to push and when to let her be. It would have been easy for him to step in and take care of the car repairs and have them be on their way, but he knew she wouldn't want or appreciate that.

Luckily Charlotte was a little easier to figure out than most women he knew.

Monday morning while she was getting ready for work, Julian walked into the bedroom with her coffee. "You want me to drive you to work, or do you want to take my car?"

She was shimmying into a dress and he had to hide a smile as he watched her move. There was a small selection of her clothes here at his place and an equally small selection of his over at hers. When her car died on Friday, he'd brought her back here and they hadn't left since. He'd tried to reason that they could as easily be in San Francisco as they were in his house, but he could tell she was too distracted to enjoy herself. There were a ton of reasons why it made sense for her to keep her own place, and it wasn't like this house was his, either, but he was finding there had only been a handful of nights that they'd spent apart in weeks.

"If you don't mind driving me in, that would be great," Charlotte responded as she took the coffee from his hands. "Thank you."

He watched in fascination as she got ready. It was the shortest routine he'd ever seen: Charlotte could shower, do her hair and makeup, and get dressed in thirty minutes.

That was a record in his book.

She took a sip of her coffee before securing her hair in a ponytail. Smiling at him, she said, "On a positive note, we have three new people starting today. Two are transferring from other human services offices, so they won't require training."

"And that means…?"

"It means my days are going back to normal. I'll be done at five, and I have nothing scheduled at the shelter this week." With a sassy grin she added, "That's practically like a vacation for me and I plan on taking advantage of this schedule."

The pure joy on her face and in her words was infectious, and Julian found himself smiling with her. "We should do something to celebrate tonight. Maybe go out for a nice dinner, a little dancing? What do you think?"

"Ooo, I like the sound of that. Yes, please!"

Leaning in, he kissed her. "Then leave it to me. I'll make reservations, but I'll make them late enough so you can do whatever you need to do to freshen up before we go."

"And I greatly appreciate it," she said and took another sip of her coffee. "I need to check with the mechanic today after lunch and see what the deal is with my car."

"You know he's thinking transmission. That's not a small job."

"I know," she said with a small pout. "The car is getting old and I'm not the greatest about maintenance, but I was really hoping it would last me a little longer before anything major happened. I'd love to get something new, but I'm not loving the idea of a car payment right now."

"Maybe it will be something a little less major. You never know." He was hoping he sounded optimistic, but he'd driven her car enough to know she really was bad about maintenance and it had a lot of miles on it. It was a wonder the transmission was the only thing to go.

"Maybe," she said with a sigh, finishing her coffee. "You ready?"

Nodding, he followed her out of the bedroom and out to the car. He didn't mind driving her to work. He kind of enjoyed it. By the time she walked through the front doors of the office building, however, Julian's mind was already working on what he was going to do that day.

Once he was back home, he looked around and realized that as much as he liked this house, it wasn't his and he was ready to start looking for one of his own.

Milestone number one, he thought.

It was time, and while it would have been easy to call on Mick to help him start looking, this was something he wanted to do on his own. Although…he hadn't heard from Mick again about the sale of his house, so no doubt he was going to have to talk to him about it anyway.

Not the worst thing in the world. They hadn't spoken in more than a week and that was usually the longest they'd go—even while Julian had been on the road searching for himself, Mick had forced him to check in once a week just so he'd know Julian was alive.

And those were his exact words about it too.

"No time like the present," he murmured as he picked up his tablet and began scrolling real estate sites while his second cup of coffee brewed.

He stalled after only five minutes, because he realized he wasn't glued to LA anymore. He could live anywhere he wanted to. The conversation he and Charlotte had weeks ago came to mind and he still didn't have an answer. California had been his home base for so long that it seemed strange to consider anyplace else. The East Coast still held a lot of appeal for him. Between Riley having a vacation home there and Matt living there full time, he'd be close enough to them to—

Oh, right.

The band.

Probably something else he needed to resolve.

Suddenly, everything felt daunting. There were so many decisions and he had no idea where to begin.

His phone rang, and it was a number he didn't recognize but he decided to answer anyway. "Hello?" he asked with a bit of snap in his tone.

"Um…hello. I'm looking for Charlotte Clark. This is Jake from Precision Auto Care. I'm calling about her car."

Julian relaxed a little and remembered they had given his number as a backup in case they couldn't reach Charlotte. "She's at work right now. Did you try her cell number?"

"Yes, sir. We did, and we left a message, but we figured we'd try this number, too."

"No problem. Have you had a chance to look at the car?"

For the next few minutes, Jake explained all that was wrong with it—the biggest issue being the transmission.

Unfortunately, it wasn't the only one and by the time the mechanic had recited all the problems, Julian's head was pounding.

There was no way Charlotte could afford everything that needed to be done, and did it really make sense pouring all that money into an older car? Which was what he asked Jake.

"It depends on who's asking. Some people prefer to invest the money because it's a one-time expense and it saves them from having to go out and look for a new car. If it were me and replacing the car wasn't an issue, I'd get another car."

He sighed. "Thanks, Jake. Let me talk to Charlotte and one of us will get back to you, okay?"

"No problem. We'll hold off on doing anything until we hear from you. Thanks."

Julian hung up and immediately changed his search from houses to cars. Car shopping was way more appealing than house shopping. Julian already knew the kind of car he enjoyed driving, and really—all he wanted was the new model of the one he already had. He called the dealership, told them what he wanted and when he wanted it, and was pleasantly surprised to find they had one he could have today.

He offered a bonus if they could deliver it to him by lunchtime.

By the time he hung up, he was a little impressed with himself and couldn't wait to see Charlotte. Deciding to call her and offer to take her to lunch, he picked up the phone again, glad she was able to answer.

"Hey," she said and Julian could hear the smile in her voice. "You caught me at a quiet moment."

"That's good. I was hoping I'd be able to come and take you to lunch today—no sitting at your desk, but actually going out and grabbing something to eat. What do you say? Would one o'clock work?"

"Oh, that's perfect! We were just talking about lunch breaks."

He found himself smiling just because he loved hearing her happy.

"I missed a call from the mechanic," she said. "I haven't even listened to the message yet."

"He called here, too, and I talked to him." He was cautious because he didn't want her telling Jake to go ahead with the work.

"And?"

"And it's what he suspected. And then some."

"Oh no."

"I told him I'd talk to you about it and we'd call him later on. So don't worry about him right now. Go and take care of your clients and we'll talk car stuff over lunch, okay? How about Italian?" he said as a diversion. "I don't know about you, but I could really go for some pizza."

"Ooo…that does sound good. There's a place around the corner from the office that has really great pizza."

"Perfect. Then that's where we'll go!" Then his mind began to wander with a new plan. "Listen, I have to run. I've got some calls to make too, so I'll see you at one, okay?"

When they hung up, Julian quickly called the dealership back and made new delivery plans.

He couldn't wait to surprise Charlotte.

Feeling pretty good about his plans so far, he opted to call Mick next and get a status update on the house.

"Julian Grayson," Mick said as he answered the phone. "I was beginning to think I was going to have to check on you."

Julian laughed quietly. "Yeah, yeah, yeah. I'm sure if you've talked to Riley or Dylan in the last few days, then you know I'm alive and well."

"Maybe. Still, it's nice to be able to confirm it myself. So what's up? You ready to let me start making deals for Shaughnessy yet?"

While he knew it was bound to come up, he wasn't quite ready to get into it yet. "I'm calling to see if you have any updates on the house. I've been here about a month and I know I'm on a time limit here, so I figured I should start the process of house hunting."

"Funny you should call, because I'm expecting an offer later today—same buyers, just a better offer. Hopefully list price."

"No matter what it is, take it. I just want to be done."

"Excellent. That's what I like to hear. So, what neighborhood are you looking in for the new place? Back in LA? Or are you wanting to see some places near Dylan? The area is fantastic and there are a couple of new builds there we can get you in to see."

"I haven't given it much thought. I figured selling the house was the most important thing to start with. Today was the first day I even started looking at listings."

Mick made a noncommittal sound. "Still, you have to have some kind of idea where you'd like to be."

The beach.

That was the first time he'd felt so strongly about the subject, but he couldn't be sure if it was coming from within or if he was influenced by Charlotte. How much would she love living on the beach and being able to walk out her door and onto the sand every day, whenever she wanted?

And that had him sitting up straight and his heart flying to his throat. Wasn't it a little soon to be thinking of a permanent home and Charlotte in the same thought? He was aware of his feelings for her growing stronger every day, but that didn't mean he was ready to start planning his life around her. Hadn't he learned the lesson that making decisions based on someone else— and only someone else—didn't work out well for him?

Okay. Scratch the beach.

"I don't. For now, I plan to scan the real estate sites to see if anything grabs my attention. But I'm open to anyplace. I might even give Matt a call and visit him to see what North Carolina has to offer."

"Oh, please. That's not anything new to you. You grew up not far from him, so it's not like anything he tells you is going to be a surprise."

"True, but back then I wasn't looking at it as a place to invest in and build a home."

Mick sighed. Loudly. "I swear I don't understand the appeal, but all of you keep doing it, so who am I to say no."

"Dylan hasn't."

"That's because he's a city boy and Paige is a city girl. Living here made sense for them. But you've got nothing tying you to any one place, so I say…take your time and do your research."

"I've only got two months left on this place."

"I'll get you two months more if you need. Trust me. It won't be a problem."

"Let's see if it comes to that. I just wanted you to know I'm looking and I'm trying to be productive."

"You'd be a lot more productive in the studio along with Riley, Dylan, and Matty."

Well, he'd walked right into that one.

"Mick, come on. Give me a break here."

"Julian, I've done nothing but give you breaks. It's time you gave the rest of us one."

"What the hell does that mean?"

"It means we've all been waiting patiently for you. Even before the band went on hiatus, you were distracted by Dena. We all tried real hard just to give you some time. That was our mistake. Maybe if we had nipped this thing in the bud years ago, we wouldn't be here right now like this."

Rage began to build. "This isn't a group thing we're dealing with, Mick. This is about me and my life and—"

"No," Mick interrupted firmly. "This stopped being about you and your life when you made it a public spectacle. Do you have any idea of the mess we all had to deal with after you left town? Did you even once consider how the guys were going to be harassed for interviews or a sound bite? We had to hire extra people and all kinds of spin doctors for damage control! So, while you were off trying to get your head on straight, the rest of us held down the fort. And now when we need your help, where are you? Bailing again. Looking to run again."

"No one's running anywhere!" Julian cried, jumping to his feet. Pacing seemed like the only thing to do. "All I'm doing is looking for a house! I didn't say I was looking for a house in another country, for crying out loud!"

"Not yet," Mick countered, and then he took a long

pause. "What I am trying to tell you is you need to start living your life again, and you owe it to your friends to make things right. You know if the tables were turned, they'd do it for you."

Yeah, he did. But right now, it didn't make him feel any better.

"Guilt isn't gonna work on me, so you can forget it."

His statement was met with silence before Mick changed the subject. "Okay, fine. I hear the music thing at the shelter was a big success. I've got a list of people who are interested in joining in."

"Seriously? That's great!"

"I sent two of them to see your friend Charlotte."

And rage had him by the throat again. "Why? Why bother her with that stuff when I said I was handling it?"

"Actually, you said you were handling it *that* night. Then I talked to Paige and she referred me to some guy named Hank, who put me back to Charlotte. I have to tell you, Jules, I was almost dizzy from the way things kept going round and round. Either way, Ty messaged me that he was going with Rex to see Charlotte today, I think." He paused and then confirmed. "Yeah. Today."

"Who the hell are Ty and Rex?" he demanded.

"Two more guys you didn't want to know, remember? Trust me, they've never been anywhere near anything Shaughnessy-related. They're new to LA and looking for some studio work. I happened to mention this to them and they were more than happy to volunteer their time."

"I'll bet."

Mick chuckled and it rubbed Julian the wrong way.

"What's so funny?"

"I heard you got a little…shall we say…territorial the other night. You know you need to stop that, right?"

Huffing with annoyance, Julian made an excuse to get him off the phone. "I gotta go. I bought a car today and I've got paperwork to deal with."

"Wait, wait, wait—you bought a car? Why? Yours is only two years old and you rarely drive it."

"Just wanted something new."

"So, you're trading yours in?"

"Not exactly," he said and then realized he really needed to get off the phone. "Look, I have to go."

"What do you mean, 'not exactly'? Either you're trading in or you're not. What's up?"

Raking a hand through his hair and tugging on it, he told Mick his plans. "It's nothing. It's not a big deal, okay? I really need to go, because I need to take care of some things here and then get over to Charlotte's office and meet the salesman with the car."

"You're doing it again, Julian," Mick said, his voice somber.

"Doing what?"

"This is how it started with Dena. Don't do this crap again. It's okay to be involved with this girl, but you're buying her cars, jewelry, taking on her causes… Man, you need to start thinking about yourself!"

"The new car is mine. I'm giving her my old one."

"Old," Mick said derisively. "It's practically new."

"I'm not looking for your approval here, okay? I'm going."

"Yeah, yeah, yeah. Fine. Go. I'll take care of the offer on the house and get back to you later today."

"Great. Thanks." And Julian hung up before they could say anything else.

Tossing the phone aside, he couldn't help but think about what Mick had said. Was he? Was he doing it again? Was he making the same mistakes with Charlotte?

"Hell no," he said adamantly and immediately pushed the thought aside and focused on surprising her at lunch.

———

Saying a prayer of thanks for her new coworkers today, Charlotte was able to have a little breathing room to handle her surprise visitors. Ty Martin and Rex Reynolds were both extremely polite and very enthusiastic about creating songs and games for the kids at the shelter. She was excited about what they had in mind, and she couldn't wait to see it all in action.

"This all sounds amazing," Charlotte said, almost gushing. "I had no idea anyone was coming here today, and to see how you already have ideas and are ready to go just makes it all the better!"

Ty—young, blond, and this side of angsty—grinned at her. "Back home I was involved with my church youth group for years. When I started playing music, some friends and I used music to get the teens to engage with one another rather than with their phones. My pastor caught on to what we were doing and asked us to do something similar with the younger kids on Sunday mornings." He laughed and looked a little sheepish. "I know my appearance doesn't quite say Sunday school, but I was raised in the church and I'm comfortable working with kids."

"As for me, I wasn't involved in any youth groups,"

Rex said, "but I have four younger siblings and I used to play guitar to calm them down. I'm eight years older than the next one after me, so I used to help my mom a lot by babysitting and just sort of doing what I could to help watch them."

Charlotte was so pleased that her face almost hurt from smiling. "I really love what you've laid out for me here and I think it would be great for you to go and talk with Hank if you have the time. I can give you the address and I'll call to let him know when you think you might be going in. Then he'll work with you from there."

"I thought you were in charge of the project," Ty commented. "At least, that's the way Mick made it sound."

"I'm sort of the liaison," she explained. "I'm the social worker assigned to the shelter, and I try to help them in whatever way I can."

"Awesome," Rex said. "We can probably head over there this afternoon if you think that would work."

Charlotte quickly made the call and wrote down the address before standing to thank them. Unable to hide her giddiness, she hugged them and thanked them both again. When she stepped back, Julian was standing next to her cubicle and not looking at all amused.

"Holy crap! You're Julian Grayson!" Rex cried. "Oh, man! I am such a fan! Dude, it's so awesome to meet you!"

To his credit, Julian pasted a stiff smile on his face and shook Rex's and Ty's hands before looking at Charlotte. "Are you ready for lunch?"

Nodding, she reached for her purse and explained to him what the guys were doing.

"I spoke to Mick," he said curtly. "I know all about it."

"Oh," she said and did her best to put herself between

Julian and the two younger musicians. "Hank's expecting you guys, so thank you again for your willingness to help out."

"Our pleasure, Charlotte," Ty said and with a quick wave, he and Rex walked out the door.

Bracing herself, she turned to Julian and almost dared him to make any kind of snarky comment. The look on his face told her everything he was thinking, but luckily he opted to stay quiet.

Smart man.

"The restaurant is just a couple of blocks and it's a beautiful day out, so I thought we'd walk," she said, choosing to ignore his black mood.

But he completely surprised her when he leaned in and kissed her. "Actually, I was hoping you wouldn't mind driving."

She looked at him oddly and figured he meant he'd be driving them. Shrugging, she agreed and led the way out of the office. When she stepped outside and walked around to the parking lot, she spotted his car and walked over. She went to open the passenger side door, but Julian stopped her and handed her the keys.

"It's not hard to find," she said lightly. "You can drive there."

Julian shook his head and placed the keys in the palm of her hand, closing her fingers around them. "You drive us."

It seemed odd, but she was starving, so with a shrug, Charlotte walked around to the driver's side and climbed in. They were parked at the restaurant minutes later and seated five minutes after that. They'd made small talk and she was nervously waiting for Julian to question her about Ty and Rex.

"So, I spoke to the mechanic," he said instead as they looked over the menu. "There's a lot wrong with the car and—in his opinion—it's almost not worth fixing."

Placing her menu down, she sighed. Her appetite was gone. "Well, damn."

He continued to scan the menu for a minute, then put it down and looked at her thoughtfully. "I agree. The car had a lot of mileage on it, and you need something newer and more reliable."

"I know, Julian, but it's not really in my budget right now. I like not having a car payment and being able to put money in savings every week. I needed that car to last me at least another year and a half."

When they'd been seated moments ago, Charlotte had put the car keys on the table beside her place setting. Julian reached for them and jingled them in front of her. "Now you don't have to worry. These…are yours."

Maybe she was delirious from hunger, because she thought he said he was giving her his car.

His like-new Mercedes SUV.

"You mean to borrow until I get something, right?"

He shook his head. "Nope. I've signed the title over to you and we'll find time to get it registered in your name in the next day or two, but it's yours, Charlotte."

Just to be sure she wasn't hearing things—or crazy— she reached for the bread their waitress had brought, wolfed down a slab of it, and then drank some of her water. She took a steadying breath and looked at him— his expression was amused.

"Julian, you can't just give me your car. That's insane. I'll admit I don't mind borrowing it for a couple of days, but then how are you going to get around?"

"I bought a car today. It's back in the parking lot by your office."

"Wait…what?"

He explained what he had done, and still Charlotte couldn't quite wrap her brain around it. Nothing like this had ever happened to her before and she had no idea how she was supposed to respond other than—

"I can't accept it, Julian."

His amusement quickly turned to confusion. "Why not?"

Where did she even begin?

"It's…it's too much. I appreciate the sentiment behind it, I really do, but we've only been dating for a month. You don't just…give someone a car like that."

He shrugged. "I don't see it that way. I think it makes perfect sense. I considered giving you the car I bought today, but I knew that would definitely freak you out. This is a used car. It's not a big deal."

"A used car isn't usually worth more than a year's rent, Julian! And it may not be a big deal to you, but it is to me!" she cried, frustration making her want to scream. "It's like the bracelet and Hawaii and—you just don't get it, do you?"

His confusion quickly turned to annoyance. "You're making a bigger deal out of this than it needs to be. I'm just trying to do something nice for you."

"I appreciate it, but…can't I just borrow the car and not have it be a gift?" she asked.

His eyes went wide. "Charlotte, I just bought myself a new car. I don't need two."

"Then you should have talked to me about this first," she stated and was relieved when the waitress came over to take their orders.

Conversation was stilted and awkward after that and as much as it pained her, she had no choice but to accept the keys and the car for the time being. There was no way she was going to register it in her name so Julian could forget it, but for now, she just wanted to try to enjoy the rest of their lunch.

Unfortunately, the only other thing she wanted to talk about was the musicians Mick had referred to her and she knew that was going to be a sore subject, too.

"What else do you have planned for today?" she asked casually.

"I started house hunting," he said flatly, obviously feeling as uncomfortable as she did.

Pushing aside her current mood, Charlotte tried to remember how this was a big step for him. "That's great! See anything you like?"

But he shook his head, obviously unwilling to try to lighten the mood.

So, lunch essentially sucked. The food was great, and it felt good to get out of the office for a change, but the tension was too thick for either of them to enjoy anything.

When they got back to her office, Julian kissed her on the cheek and said he'd talk to her later. As Charlotte watched him walk away, she realized it was the first time he hadn't asked her when she was coming over, and considering he had mentioned them going out on a real date that night, it seemed odd. And a little unnerving. Part of her wanted to call him back and remind him of those plans, but then it hit her how a night away from each other had helped the last time they'd had a disagreement.

She just hoped this wasn't going to become a pattern of behavior for them. It was petty and a little childish, and it wasn't as if she was mad at him. She just hated that he felt like he had to take care of her or buy her expensive gifts—something she knew was a big part of his relationship with his ex. Not that Julian had shared anything that deep, but from the things he had shared— and the things Savannah, Vivienne, and Paige had shared when they'd had dinner a few weeks back—she knew that was the way their relationship worked. Dena got mad and Julian would buy her stuff.

And clearly Dena got mad a lot.

Now it was Charlotte who was mad. There was no way she wanted to be compared to Dena. She was her own woman, and from everything she had heard and even researched online, Charlotte knew they were nothing alike. It was a little insulting to be put in the same box. Their relationship had been toxic, and she hoped Julian wouldn't want to repeat those mistakes.

And yet…here they were.

The only difference was that she wasn't expecting anything from him. It was plain to anyone who could see that they lived in such vastly different worlds—he was a millionaire rock star and she was a social worker who lived in a two-room apartment. Most people would probably assume she'd *want* Julian to buy her things and take care of her, but that didn't make Charlotte comfortable. Not that she didn't enjoy nice things or didn't appreciate a gift. Flowers were fine and even the bracelet was beautiful, but a car was way too over the top for her—especially at this stage of their relationship.

She never wanted there to be a time where Julian—or anyone for that matter—looked at her as a gold digger. Having lived in a nice middle-class home her entire life, it was what she was used to. Staying in Julian's beach house had been like a decadent treat, but she wasn't looking to move in! That was why it was so important to her that they sometimes stay at her place even though she knew how much he hated it.

Sometimes Mr. Rock Star couldn't get his own way.

Bottom line, they needed to talk about this—about their relationship, and who they were as individuals. By now, Charlotte would have thought Julian would know enough about her to realize she was attracted to who he was as a person—not his fame or wealth.

Something she probably should have shared with him sooner.

Either way, this was the type of thing that ruined relationships, and that was the last thing she wanted to happen here. What she felt for Julian ran deep and she wasn't ready for it to end. Saying she was in love with him scared her a little, but only because it was so soon. Her feelings for him overwhelmed her at times, and he was normally so closed off that she had a hard time getting a read on how he felt. So, unless his love language was buying gifts, she was clueless as to how he was feeling.

But for today, she was willing to let things be. After work, she'd go home to her own place, have a quiet dinner, and read. Maybe they'd take the rest of the week to let the dust settle and make plans for the weekend.

Yes. That seemed like a nice compromise.

Feeling a little more in control of her emotions, Charlotte realized she was late heading back to work. With one last look at Julian's car—and her temporary one—she sighed. Calling the mechanic was probably something she needed to do sometime this afternoon too. Oddly, it didn't give her nearly as much anxiety as she'd thought it would.

"You're a problem-solver by nature, Charlotte," she murmured as she turned to walk back into her office. "You're just not used to those problems being your own."

Best laid plans and all…

Her afternoon had been too busy to call the mechanic, so Charlotte figured she'd do it the following day. Only…she didn't.

And while she had spent the one night alone at her own place, Julian had surprised her the next night by waiting for her at her apartment when she'd gotten home and…well, he really was hard to resist. So…she didn't.

The only thing she had stuck to was her plan not to register Julian's car to herself.

Baby steps.

For several weeks things had gone really well. There was a steady rotation of musicians coming to volunteer at the shelter, and on one of those nights, Charlotte and Julian went along, too, with Riley, Dylan, Savannah, and Paige, and then to dinner afterward. She was finding she really enjoyed her time with his friends and felt silly for how intimidated she had been the first time she'd met them. They invited the other musicians to go with them, and she wasn't surprised when Julian stayed particularly close to her.

He was jealous and she supposed she understood it, and hopefully in time he'd see he had nothing to be jealous of.

Unfortunately, that night it was her own jealousy that took her by surprise.

"Oh no," Savannah hissed from beside her at the table.

"What? What's the matter?" Charlotte asked. It was obvious Savannah hadn't meant to comment out loud because she quickly elbowed Riley, who in turn motioned to Dylan. Julian was talking to Paige when he noticed something was up.

Under the table, Charlotte nudged Savannah to get her attention.

"What the—?" Julian's curse was fierce and colorful.

"Why don't we go?" Riley said as he went to stand, but no one was paying attention. All eyes were on Julian.

A beautiful blond was walking toward the table, and she had eyes only for Julian. Charlotte had done enough snooping online to know this was the infamous Dena, and the desire to jump up and claw the woman's eyes out was strong. It wasn't until she was beside them that Charlotte noticed the uncertainty and, if she was guessing correctly, nervousness on Dena's face.

Meanwhile, Julian's was completely closed off and his body was stiff like granite.

This can't be good.

"Hey, Julian," Dena said quietly. "How are you?"

All Dena did was say his name and Charlotte could feel him bristling with barely restrained rage. She looked nervously to Dylan and then Riley in hopes of someone stepping in.

At first Charlotte didn't think Julian was going to respond, but with clenched teeth he said, "What are you doing here, Dena?"

Charlotte felt kind of bad for the woman because she looked so uncomfortable and it seemed like everyone in the restaurant was staring. She saw so many phones up taking pictures, and it was the first time she caught a first-hand experience of how little privacy celebrities had.

"I—I wanted to talk to you, if I could. Please."

"No."

With a huff and a nervous look around, Dena stepped in closer. "Julian, please. Five minutes. That's all I'm asking for."

He let out a snort of derision. "I gave you five years, Dena. I think that was more than enough." Then he glared up at her. "Now leave."

Holding her breath, Charlotte had no idea how this was going to play out. Part of her wanted Julian to talk to Dena and get it over with, then she realized this wasn't the proper venue for that to happen. If Julian was going to have his say and get everything off his chest, it couldn't be in the middle of a crowded restaurant with a hundred witnesses.

Witnesses who were still taking pictures, and no doubt video was being broadcast all over social media.

Great.

Dena gave a small nod before she turned and walked away. There was a collective sigh of relief around the table. Both Riley and Dylan leaned forward, while Charlotte pulled back. These were his friends, and right now, she was definitely not the person to speak up and ask if he was all right.

"What the hell?" Dylan said quietly. "I thought she wasn't supposed to come around you anymore."

Riley nodded. "Yeah, that's what I thought too. Mick said part of paying her off was having her agree not to come near you again."

It was obvious his friends and their wives were concerned, and while Charlotte was too, this wasn't about her. Not really. So for now she'd sit back and observe. When they got home later, she hoped she'd have a better idea what to do or say.

"I'm calling Mick," Dylan stated as he pulled out his phone, and before anyone could stop him, he was.

"Why don't we leave?" Riley asked a little more calmly. "We can go back to our place. I know it's in the opposite direction of yours, but it's the closest right now."

Both Paige and Savannah were in agreement and were gathering their things when Julian said loudly, "No."

Everyone seemed to stop and stare.

"Jules, come on," Riley said. "We don't need to stay here."

"I don't need to leave. She did. End of story." Then he motioned for the waitress to come over and ordered another round of drinks and the desserts they had been discussing before Dena showed up.

If it were anyone else, Charlotte would chalk it up to growth. Unfortunately, knowing Julian the way she did, she'd say it was avoidance. If they left and went to Riley's, they'd be talking about this. She knew how much he hated talking about this particular situation.

Avoidance. Definitely.

Dylan put down his phone and looked around the table before addressing Julian. "Mick's on it."

Shrugging, Julian reached for his drink. "Obviously it won't matter. The rules don't apply where Dena's concerned." He took a sip and placed it back on the table, and Charlotte was sure she wasn't the only one to notice the slight tremble of his hand. "So where do we stand for next week? Do we have a schedule in place for who's going to the shelter?"

And just like that, everyone changed the subject. Charlotte was dumbfounded. How could everyone just…not say anything?

Excusing herself, she stood and walked to the ladies room. It wasn't a surprise when Savannah walked in a minute later.

"You okay?"

Charlotte nodded and checked her reflection in the mirror. "That was…different."

"Sadly, it wasn't. That was…" Savannah paused and shook her head. "You know what? It doesn't matter. I'm sorry you had to see it."

Clearly there was more to the story, but there was no way she could just change the subject like the rest of them.

Facing Savannah, Charlotte crossed her arms as she rested her hip against the vanity. "'That was…' what?"

"Come on, Charlotte. It doesn't matter. It was awkward as hell and it sucked, that's all."

"Nuh-uh. You said it wasn't different. That means you've seen this little scenario play out before, right?"

They stood in silence for a moment but Charlotte refused to back down.

With a sigh of resignation, Savannah leaned against the vanity as well. "It was sort of their thing—they'd fight, Julian would leave, Dena would show up and act contrite and he'd tell her to leave. It was almost comical how predictable it became. I thought after everything that happened it would be different, but…"

"What do you think is going to happen now?"

"I wish I knew. I really do. It seemed like Julian was finally getting back to his old, pre-Dena self. At least, that's what Riley's been calling it. And we have all been so happy about that. We know you're the reason and we're all so thankful."

But Charlotte shook her head. "No, no, no. It's not me. I don't want that kind of responsibility and it makes me sound like I've been a therapist—and believe me, I haven't. The amount of time we've spent talking about… you know…has been minuscule. Any time we've talked about it, it's either been a very short conversation or Julian's shut me down. This is all his journey, Savannah. I'm just along for the ride right now."

"Oh, please," Savannah replied with a light snort. "Don't sell yourself short. You are like a breath of fresh air, Charlotte. You are so good for him, and it has nothing to do with anything therapy-related. It's who you are as a person."

As much as she wanted to believe that, things were a little too intense at the moment.

The door swung open and Paige poked her head in. "Um…the guys are starting to wonder what's taking so long." Then she gave a sheepish grin. "Sorry."

Together, the three of them walked back to the table and Charlotte was feeling mildly better, except that Julian wouldn't look directly at her.

Not a great sign.

Almost on principle, they stayed for another hour, enjoying their desserts and talking more about volunteering at the shelter and the possibility of branching out to other facilities. Paige talked about possible campaigns her PR firm could help with to raise both awareness and money for the cause, and they all agreed to talk more about it in a couple of weeks after she had time to do a little research.

Julian took Charlotte's hand in his as they walked out of the restaurant to a lot of continued curious stares. It was all she could do to keep from crying out for everyone to mind their own business and go back to their meals. How did Julian stand it? How did any of the guys stand it?

It was after midnight by the time they got to Julian's, and as much as she wanted to go back to her place—and give them both some time to regroup and recover from the night's awkwardness—she didn't. Julian walked in the front door and straight out to the back deck, where he leaned on the rail and stared out at the ocean.

"I don't know if I'm supposed to say something or let you stay out here alone," she said quietly as she came up beside him.

Rather than answer, he reached out a hand to her and then gently pulled her to his side. With an arm wrapped around her waist, he continued to stare straight ahead. "I'm sorry you had to see any of that."

"There wasn't anything to see, really," she said honestly. "I'm the one who's sorry."

Then he did face her with an odd look. "What are you sorry for?"

"That she still has the power to hurt you. I hate that. I hated to feel how tense you got or to hear in your voice how angry you were. You handled it well, but…I don't know, Julian, it upsets me to see you hurting."

Wrong. Thing. To. Say.

Pulling away, he took a few steps back. "I'm not hurting, Charlotte," he said defensively. "I was annoyed that she showed up where she wasn't welcome. Again. That's it. She doesn't have the power to hurt me anymore."

Oh, if only that were true.

She could argue the point or she could let him come to the realization on his own. Thinking of her conversation with Savannah earlier, she knew she didn't want to step in and play therapist. That wasn't who she was to him and it was the last way she wanted him—or anyone—to view their relationship.

"Okay," she said simply as she smiled at him. "I'm sorry. My mistake."

That seemed to soothe him because he visibly relaxed. "I don't want to talk about this any more tonight," he said as he stepped in closer and wrapped his arms around her. His gaze was intense as he studied her face. "I don't even want to think about it ever again. The only person I want to think about, the only person who means anything to me, is you. You know that, don't you?"

In that moment, she did. If she shut her brain off and did as Julian was suggesting and just forgot about their evening, then it was only the two of them.

And for right now, it worked.

It was enough.

Chapter 9

NORMALLY JULIAN LOVED THE MORNINGS WITH Charlotte. Even when she had to leave early for work, he loved waking up with her and having lazy conversations in bed before she had to get up and start her day.

Today? Not so much.

Last night had been a complete shit-show, and while he had done everything in his power to push all thoughts of it aside, he couldn't. And now he couldn't wait for Charlotte to leave for work so he could just be alone and...think.

So yeah, seeing Dena last night had freaked him out more than he'd thought it would. Why the hell was she in town and how had she found him? They were eating in a place Julian had never frequented, so...how? Why?

It would have been easy to call Mick and see if he had any information, but he was tired of having someone else handle his problems. While he wasn't ready to pick up the phone and call Dena himself right now, the bigger problem was figuring out why he was still reacting so strongly.

He was happy with Charlotte. Hell, he was in love with Charlotte. So why had it taken three minutes in Dena's presence for him to feel such blinding rage that he should have been over by now?

"Okay, I'm heading out!" Charlotte said cheerily as she walked into the kitchen to refill her travel coffee mug.

Julian walked over and kissed her until they were both breathless and then smiled down at her. "Have a good day, beautiful."

Her smile warmed as she leaned into him. "You're a dangerous man, Julian Grayson."

He arched a brow at her as he laughed softly. "Me? How come?"

"I normally love my job and I always look forward to the new workday. But when you kiss me like that, all I can think of is playing hooky, or better yet quitting so I can stay here all day like this with you."

The reality was she could. He knew that. Just like he knew he'd take care of her and her bills and whatever else she needed, because he would love to have her here with him all day, too. But he also knew her too well. She'd go crazy without something to do. Which she immediately confirmed before he could comment on it.

"But there are people who need help finding jobs and I'm just the girl to help them do it."

Hugging her close, he kissed her again. "Then you better fix your red cape and go help the masses."

They laughed and he walked her out to the car—which he knew she hadn't switched over to her name yet, but he wasn't going to harp on it—and they made plans to see each other after work. Waiting until the car was out of sight, Julian went back into the house and started on some of the things he wanted to do to make up for last night.

First was the florist.

He made arrangements to have a bouquet of wild-flowers sent to Charlotte's office at lunchtime. She had mentioned once how much she loved them and he wanted to surprise her with something pretty to look at while she worked.

Next was the jeweler.

Yeah, he knew she had issues with the last time he'd bought her jewelry, but he felt like he needed a bit of a grand gesture to make up for last night. No doubt she had been embarrassed and confused and maybe even a little angry at the entire situation, and he liked the idea of spoiling her a bit to make up for it.

An hour later he was on the couch staring at the ceiling and wondering what he was supposed to do next. The logical part of him said he needed to cave and call Mick, but he was fighting that for the time being. Or maybe he was supposed to call Dena and just let her say what she had to say and be done with her.

Right, like that was ever going to happen. He'd thought by paying her off she'd stay gone.

Wishful thinking.

And maybe…maybe that was the key right there. For months—years even—Julian had been simply wishing for things to change without doing anything to make it happen. Where his ex was concerned, he always caved and gave her what she wanted in hopes she'd change or their situation would get better. This time he wasn't going to give her what she wanted. He would stand his ground and maybe it would make a difference.

That's what he was going with as he got up and made himself something to drink, and then went in search of his tablet so he could do a little online house hunting.

He was in a good frame of mind while he searched and the day seemed to speed by. There had been a couple of times when he'd wanted to call Charlotte and see how

her day was going—or at least thought she'd call when
her gifts were delivered—but he decided that maybe she
was waiting to thank him in person.

There was also a random thought or two about why
none of the guys had called him. The phone had been
suspiciously quiet all day.

It was definitely odd and a little unnerving, but...

The front door slammed open and shut, and it took
him a minute to realize it was only three in the afternoon. Charlotte came storming across the room toward
him, carrying the flowers and what he guessed was the
jewelry box.

"What the hell, Julian?" she cried, tossing the flowers
on the coffee table.

And she did not look happy.

Slowly he came to his feet and eyed her warily.
Smiling in hopes of defusing the situation, he said,
"Hey! How'd you get out so early?"

Nope. Still not happy.

Stepping toward him, she shook the jewelry box.
"Seriously, what is this?"

When he'd talked to the jeweler earlier, Julian had
told him he was looking for a necklace with aquamarine
stones and diamonds. What they'd decided on was a
design with a two-carat stone surrounded by diamonds
and set in platinum. From the pictures he had received,
it was a beautiful piece. It was something he knew
Charlotte could wear every day if she wanted to rather
than just for special occasions—which was why he was
a little perplexed by her reaction.

"A gift," he replied simply.

"For what?" she demanded with exasperation.

Okay, now they both weren't happy. With a sigh of frustration, he raked a hand through his hair. "Look, I feel bad about everything that happened last night. I thought everything at the shelter went great and we were having a good time out with everyone and then… It got ruined and I kind of acted like an ass. So I wanted to get you something to make it up to you."

Her eyes—eyes that were as blue as the aquamarine in her necklace—went wide. "Make it up to me? How about by talking to me and just saying you're sorry?" Before he could respond, she spoke again. "And you realize what happened last night had nothing to do with you, right? You weren't the one to kill the mood."

"Not directly, but it was still about me," he argued.

She slowly let out a breath and seemed to calm down. "Julian, don't you get it?" Holding up the jewelry box, she went on. "This? This doesn't mean anything to me. I'm not with you because of the gifts—they're beautiful and it's a nice gesture, but this kind of thing isn't necessary. I would rather have you talk to me and let me know what you're thinking or how you're feeling than get flowers. I want to know what would make you happy because that's what makes me happy! Do you understand that?"

In a million years, he'd never thought a woman would argue with him for buying her a gift.

"Charlotte, I felt bad about what happened, okay? We covered that last night. If you're waiting for me to lie down on the couch so you can ask how it made me feel, you can forget it. That's not going to happen."

"Okay, wow," she said with a hint of disgust. "I can't even believe you went there."

"Look, all I'm saying is you tend to take a shrink approach to things and you're looking to counsel and advise, and I'm telling you I don't need or want that. As for this," he said, motioning to the box, "it's a gift and I don't see what the big deal is!"

"The big deal is you do this—you buy me stuff—rather than talk to me about whatever it is we're arguing about!"

"So now we're arguing about last night? Because I thought we'd moved on from that."

She let out a little scream of frustration and paced away and back again. When she faced him, she took another deep breath and let it out slowly. "You don't need to buy me things, Julian," she said carefully, enunciating each word precisely.

Maybe no one had ever felt the need to spoil her before, he thought. Maybe that's why this was such a foreign concept for her. Closing the distance between them, he wrapped his arms around her waist. "Charlotte, I know you don't need me to buy you things and you'd certainly never ask me to, that's why I enjoy doing it. If I could, I'd give you everything, don't you get that? I would give you the sun, the moon, and the stars if I could," he said earnestly, and he thought he had her. Thought she was finally understanding where he was coming from. Reaching up, he caressed her cheek. "You mean that much to me."

Her shoulders relaxed and her expression turned just a little sad. "I don't want the sun, the moon, or the stars. All I want is you, Julian. I want to be able to sit and talk to you about anything and everything without it leading to one of us getting upset and then you buying me a present to make it better."

"That's not what's happening," he countered.

But she nodded and deep down, he knew she was right. *Dammit.*

"It is. If this relationship is going to continue, then there has to be communication, Julian. And that's not because you think I'm trying to be a therapist or a counselor or anything, it's because that's what makes a healthy relationship. I can't keep going like this—where I have to walk on eggshells, afraid to talk about your life before I met you."

"But that life is over," he said earnestly. "I don't want to look back at it. I need to look forward. You're my future, Charlotte. Anything that happened before doesn't matter."

"Yes it does!" she cried softly. "The band, your music, that's all part of your past and you have to talk about it and deal with it."

"I am."

"No, you're walking away from it." Then she paused. "No, that's not right. You're stopping the guys with one hand and waving them on with the other."

"What the hell does that mean?" Taking a step back, he couldn't wait to hear this theory.

Her frustration was obvious. "You tell them you're finished, you're not playing anymore, and then you start up this program with the shelter where you get together with them and jam. Don't you think that's sending some mixed messages?"

"As a matter of fact, I don't. One has nothing to do with the other. Helping out for charity is one thing, committing to going into the recording studio, making an album, and touring the world is another. And I think the guys all understand that."

At least…he hoped they did.

They all knew each other so well that Julian just took for granted that Matt, Riley, and Dylan would get where he was coming from. One was charity, one was a job—two completely different things. And while he loved jamming with the guys, and there was still a lot of music in his head that he was jotting down whenever he got the chance, that didn't mean he would go back and open that door again. It was closed. Permanently. There was no way he was letting anyone take advantage of him again, and when you lived your life in the limelight, the chance of that happening was far too great.

Walking away was the smart choice. The right choice.

"Let me ask you something," Charlotte said, breaking into his train of thought. "Do you really think that never playing music again on stage is going to make you happy?"

"What does that have to do with anything?"

"Seriously? Julian, you're entitled to be happy. You had a crappy thing happen to you and it sucked. There. I said it," she said dramatically. "But that one crappy thing doesn't have to dictate the rest of your life! Go and play music! Record, tour. Be happy! It's not a crime!"

"It's not about being happy!" he yelled, more than ready to be done with this entire conversation. "This is about peace of mind. This is about self-preservation. This is about not being able to trust the people I work with ever again! And if you don't get that, then that's your problem! I don't owe anyone an explanation here, Charlotte! This isn't about you or the guys or the fans or anyone else except me! I need to be able to sleep at night. Do you think it was easy to know other men were screwing my fiancée? You have no idea how freaking mortified I was every time I walked into a party after one of her affairs was exposed—it felt like everyone was looking at me and pitying me. And the gossip and the laughter—it was emasculating! I won't do it again. Not even for you!"

Breathless, he realized everything he had just said.

Tears were in her eyes and he felt them down to his very soul. There was no reason to take any of this out on Charlotte—his anger, his frustration, his paranoia—but apparently, until he learned to deal with them himself, she was going to continue to be an unwitting target.

And he knew there was only one thing he could do.

"I think you should go," he said, his voice thick and low. It hurt to say the words, but he had to.

First one tear fell, then another, and Julian had to hold himself back from reaching out to her. She took a step back and wiped at them herself, then nodded. "I think you're right."

While he thought she was going to turn and walk out the door, she actually went toward the bedroom. He stood, dumbfounded, for a moment before following.

And found her packing.

"What are you doing?" His throat was raw and though he knew what he'd asked her to do, for some reason Julian didn't realize this would be part of it. He wasn't asking her to leave for tonight, he was asking her to leave. Period.

And damn if that didn't feel like a knife to his heart.

"I don't have much here, but I think it's best if I take it all now," she said, her voice trembling. "Just give me a few minutes, and I'll be on my way."

"Charlotte…" he began, but he had no idea what he was going to say after that.

"I'd rather not do this with an audience," she said quietly. "Please."

With a curt nod, he walked out of the room and out of the house. On the back deck, he stared out at the ocean and wondered how everything had gone so wrong. And not just today, but with his life.

Fourteen years ago, he'd come to LA with Shaughnessy and the whole world was wide open to him. He'd made smart business decisions, smart investments, and had toured the world and seen things he'd never thought he'd see. Playing music for millions of fans, winning awards...it had been everything.

Until his own stubbornness had caused him to stop enjoying all the things he'd worked hard for.

Had he loved Dena? Yes. But not for very long.

Did he love music and playing for the fans? Always.

Did he love Charlotte? More than he thought possible.

But it wasn't enough.

The three months he'd spent on the road had been to clear his head, but it hadn't. There was still more he needed to do for his own mental health and well-being. Until he got his shit together, he was just creating another toxic relationship.

And Charlotte didn't deserve that.

Off in the distance he heard the front door close, and his gut clenched. Part of him was thankful she hadn't come out here to say goodbye. He wasn't sure he'd be able to handle that. But another part of him wanted to run after her, chase her down and beg her to stay—to love him despite his faults and hang-ups and all-around messed-up view on his life.

He didn't.

Instead, he stayed where he was and stared out at the water and wished he was anyplace else but here.

———

So, this is what hell must feel like.

That was Charlotte's first thought the next morning when her alarm went off. She hadn't slept, hadn't eaten anything, and basically had spent every moment since she'd walked through her apartment door crying.

Her Uber driver had asked her at least a dozen times on the fifteen-minute drive if she was okay, and all she'd been able to do was nod.

A good ugly-cry had always done the trick in the past when a relationship had ended, but this was the ugly-cry that wouldn't quit.

Like she was some kind of emotional overachiever.

It was six in the morning and already she knew there was no way she could go in to work today. The only thing that made her feel okay about her decision not to was the fact that they were a fully staffed office now, and with any luck, no one would be too put out by her absence.

Decision made, she texted her boss and then crawled back into bed.

And started crying again.

Eventually she dozed off and the next time Charlotte's eyes opened, it was noon.

Progress.

Climbing from the bed, she made her way to the kitchen and tried to find something to eat, even though just the thought of food made her stomach rebel.

"Too bad," she murmured. "You're an intelligent

woman and you know you need to eat. You don't have to enjoy it."

Which was how she ended up with a cup of yogurt and a handful of jellybeans.

Breakfast of champions.

It had been so long since she'd had an entire day off with nothing to do that she had no idea what to do with herself. A few weeks ago, heck, a few hours ago, she would have gotten dressed and gone for a walk on the beach. But that was ruined for her right now. Her favorite place to walk would forever remind her of Julian—and the fact that his house was pretty much in full view of where she normally went didn't help things either. Hopefully he'd continue with his house search and move sooner rather than later, and maybe someday she'd be able to go and sit on the beach and not look over her shoulder for him. Or wonder where he was or what he was doing.

Right. Like that was ever going to happen.

In a few short weeks, Julian Grayson had managed to consume her—heart, mind, and soul. For so long, Charlotte hadn't believed there was such a thing as true love—at least not for her—but now she knew better. She'd fallen hard for him when she'd thought he had nothing, and the more she'd gotten to know him, the harder she'd fallen until she was all in.

Imagine how much more there would have been if he had only opened himself up to her and let her see all of him? What if he had bared it all to her—the good, the bad, and the ugly?

She still would have loved him.

She did still love him.

But clearly, love wasn't enough when he was purposely holding so much of himself back. Of course, she could reason that she couldn't possibly truly be in love with him if she didn't fully know him.

And she'd be lying.

Loving Julian had come easily. Easier than she'd ever thought it could.

Now she had to hope that having a life without him would come as easily.

Liar.

Okay, fine. She didn't want to think about moving on, even though—again, logically—she knew it was for the best. There was no way she could live like this and feel like this for any extended period of time. For all of her strength and determination when it came to helping others, Charlotte didn't believe she had it in her to do it for herself.

"Focus on something else," she encouraged herself, even though there was little hope she would. Walking over to the couch, she sat down and turned on the television. Channel surfing wasn't a favorite of hers, but right now it did provide a decent distraction. An hour later she found a documentary on Princess Diana that captured her attention.

That's when the snacking began.

More jellybeans, then popcorn. Luckily, there were some chips in the pantry, and she even managed to whip up some onion dip. Since no one was going to be kissing her any time soon, she was able to add extra onions.

That took her through the afternoon, and by dinnertime, she felt sick. And that definitely took her mind off Julian and how much she missed him.

That lasted until she crawled back into bed, where she started crying again. "A-at…least I'm consistent," she sobbed as she rolled over and turned out the light.

―――ᴡᴡ―――

While Charlotte wouldn't say a week of self-pity was the way to go, it had certainly helped her to get a little perspective on life and to find her focus again. She'd taken the time for some deep reflection and to try to get her life a little more organized. The first thing she'd done was arrange to have her car fixed. Fortunately the shop offered her a loaner car so she wasn't completely stranded.

So, on Monday morning after picking up her car, she walked into her office with a clear mind, a fresh attitude, and a desire to help everyone who needed it today.

And clearly, there were many.

By five thirty, she was exhausted but decided to call Hank and see how things were over at the shelter. Last week she'd avoided it because it was too much of a reminder of Julian. Now she could make herself look at it as part of her job again.

"CeeCee!" Hank said when he answered the phone. "How are you?"

"I'm good, Hank. And you?"

"I'm great, CeeCee. Seriously, great!"

Okay, that was a little overly enthusiastic, so she had to ask. "Wow! What's going on?"

"Well, the shelter is almost empty, which means people have places to live," he explained. "We had some of your musician friends show up here last Thursday night and we didn't have any kids here for them to entertain, but they were more than willing to give us a hand with some cleaning and maintenance stuff. I'll tell you, it was like that first week when Julian came here. It's amazing what a couple of extra hands can accomplish!"

"That's wonderful, Hank. Really. So, what can I do to help this week? Anything? We haven't had a job search seminar in a while, any requests for one?"

"I appreciate the offer, but we've been having a lot of luck around here lately getting people back on their feet. You've given those of us on staff enough training that we've put it to use to help out instead of burdening you."

"Hank," she said, smiling, "it's my job. You're supposed to reach out to me and it's never a burden. You know I love what I do."

"I do, and you have been such a blessing to everyone here, but the shelter is my responsibility. I finally have a full-time staff, and for a while there we were relying heavily on you and that wasn't very fair either."

Hearing him say it reminded her of how overworked she had felt for a while, but after she'd met Julian…

Nope. Not going to go there.

"I didn't mind. I swear. You know how much I enjoy working with you and everyone at the shelter. It's something very near and dear to me, so please don't ever hesitate to ask for help."

"CeeCee, you are always welcome here, and unfortunately, there will always be a need for your services. But for right now, things are good here."

They talked for a few more minutes about some of the families she'd met there and where they were now, and by the time she hung up, she was feeling good.

Positive. Good things really did happen for people even after something bad.

Something she needed to remember for herself.

Leaning back in her chair, Charlotte contemplated how she was going to get back into a normal pattern of life that didn't involve…well, him. She glanced around her office and saw a picture tucked far down on the corkboard that hung next to her desk.

Tami.

Her friends.

That's what she needed right now! A night out with her friends! Feeling a sense of excitement, she pulled out her phone and did a group text to see if they could all get together one night this week. It was too much to hope that it would happen tonight, but she'd throw it out there and see how it went.

Falling in love had been that exciting roller-coaster ride.

But right now, all she wanted was the steadiness of the merry-go-round.

And her friends.

—⟶⟵—

"You look like shit."

"Good to see you too, Mick," Julian murmured as he shut the door behind his manager. "What brings you here?"

Mick walked through the living room and stopped at the wall of windows. "That's one amazing view, huh? It never gets old."

He rolled his eyes. "Yeah, yeah, yeah. It's magical. Why are you here?"

Looking over his shoulder, Mick leveled him with a glare. "I see your mood hasn't improved."

And why would it, he thought. His life was a mess, he hadn't slept in a week, and right now the last thing he wanted was company. He looked at the folder in Mick's hand. "Is that about the house?"

With a sigh, Mick turned and handed him the folder. "It's a done deal. All you need to do is sign and you'll no longer be a homeowner."

Wordlessly, Julian took the folder and emptied its contents while he searched for a pen. Two minutes later, he handed it all back. "Done."

"How about a drink to celebrate?"

"No thanks."

Mick tossed the folder on the couch and slid his hands into his trouser pockets. "We gonna talk about this?"

"Nothing to say."

This was how they did things—Mick tried to draw him out, Julian resisted, and eventually Mick would calmly say his piece and then leave him alone. It worked for them.

Until now.

One dark brow arched at him, and if Julian wasn't mistaken, there was a bit of an evil smile on Mick's face.

That was new.

"I have a couple of guys who are interested in the gig with the shelter. One's a bassist and one does vocals. They're young and eager and part of an up-and-coming band out of San Francisco I'm interested in representing." He shrugged. "Anyway, I wasn't sure if you were going to be doing anything more with the project since you and Charlotte are no longer dating, so I sent them directly to her."

His jaw was clenched so tight that Julian was certain he was going to split a molar.

"You remember what it was like to be young and hungry for any exposure with the music, right?" Smiling, Mick walked over and sat down on the couch next to the discarded folder. "They want representation and I need to get to know them a bit more. Either way, I figure Charlotte will work closely with them and maybe even find them some work. That's what she does, right?"

"She helps people who are unemployed, Mick," he said stiffly. "She doesn't find jobs for wayward musicians."

"We'll see. When I talked to her yesterday, she didn't seem opposed to the idea. You know a lot of these kids move to LA in hopes of getting a record deal. They play all night and sleep all day, but it doesn't pay their bills. I'd like to get someone who can work with them to find them jobs so I'm not buying their groceries, but I know they won't be living on ramen and beer."

"You…you talked to Charlotte?"

Nodding and smiling smugly, he said. "Just yesterday. Probably again later today after she meets the boys. Well, they're not boys, really. They're men. Young and anxious."

And while Julian knew full well that Mick was trying to bait him, all he could do was hold himself still and refuse to react.

"Boys will be boys," Mick added. "But I think what Charlotte did for you was great. She got you out and playing music again—even if you won't admit you're ready to rejoin the band—and I think she deserves something for her time. You know, for, um…services rendered, if you know what I mean." He winked and the lecherous grin was the last straw.

The next thing Julian knew he was diving over the coffee table and had his long-time friend and manager by the throat. The couch flipped over as every curse he had ever heard flew from his mouth. Mick did his own share of verbal sparring, but Julian was so blind with rage, the words barely registered.

Glass shattered, the coffee table went flying, and it was a free-for-all. It was gratifying to have flesh meet bone as he pounded his fist repeatedly anywhere he could reach on Mick. It didn't feel so great to be on the receiving end of some blows, but he was bigger and stronger and knew how to deflect better.

Pushing up, he pulled his arm back to deliver another blow when he realized Mick wasn't moving. He was conscious and breathing, but…he was also simply lying there and taking the beating. What the hell?

Julian jumped to his feet and stalked across the room, trying to wrap his head around what he'd just done.

Breathless, he grabbed the fireplace mantel and did his best to regulate his breathing and clear his head. Somewhere behind him, he heard Mick come to his feet, groaning. He was too ashamed to turn around and see what he'd done.

"Do us all a favor, Julian," Mick said, his own voice breathless and strained. "Go deal with your shit. It's time you confronted Dena and got this off your chest already. We're all tired of it. And maybe then you'll get your head out of your ass and make music again."

"This wasn't about her," Julian said, his throat dry.

"You keep telling yourself that. You've made everything about her and because of that, you've lost the best thing that ever happened to you."

That made him turn around. "I don't consider the band to be the best thing to happen to me."

With a mirthless laugh, Mick picked up the folder he'd arrived with. "That wasn't what I was referring to."

And then he was gone.

———

It was hard to come off like a badass when all you could think of was how it felt like you had butterflies in your belly, Julian thought.

Yeah, not the manliest thought he'd ever had, but there it was.

He was sitting in a corner booth of one of his favorite restaurants in downtown LA late Thursday afternoon and wishing he was anyplace else but here.

"Hey, Julian."

Dena.

Looking up, he realized that for the first time in a long time he felt...nothing. He'd thought long and hard about what Mick had said, and about all the things Charlotte had said to him as well. This had gone on long enough. It was time to deal with it as an adult and... here he was.

Motioning for her to sit, Julian stayed firmly in his seat. He didn't give a damn about being a gentleman or any of that crap. He wasn't here to impress anyone; he just wanted his life back.

"I was surprised to hear from you," she said carefully as she sat. "You seemed pretty adamant about not talking to me."

"What are you doing here, Dena?" he asked, cutting to the chase.

"You called me."

He shook his head. "No. Back in California. I believe

I paid you enough to make sure you left and wouldn't come back."

"No, your manager paid me," she corrected with a bit of a snap in her voice, which she instantly corrected. "I needed to talk to you."

"If you're going to ask for more money or for another chance, it's not gonna happen. We're done. For good."

And then something strange happened. The woman sitting across from him—the beautiful, confident woman—almost seemed to shrink before his eyes. It was then that he realized she wasn't wearing the heavy makeup she usually did or the large, flashy jewelry. She looked a lot like the woman he had originally met.

Only older.

"You may not believe this, but…I wanted to thank you."

Um…yeah. He didn't believe that, but rather than comment on it, he waited her out.

"I didn't realize just how much I had spiraled out of control until I was faced with it at the wedding. That video was a real wake-up call, and believe me, if you wanted to humiliate me, you succeeded." She let out a breath and reached for the glass of water the waitress had brought.

"I had this idea in my mind of what I wanted to be—*who* I wanted to be—and you were the one I thought could make it happen. What I didn't realize was…I didn't like the person I had become. I was hateful and petty and…" She gave him a helpless look. "I was horrible."

No arguments there.

"But I'm not willing to take all the blame," she went on. "You fed into the craziness just as much as I did. We were a textbook case of a codependent relationship."

Again, no arguments; he simply nodded.

"I kept searching for that thing—just that one thing—that would make me happy. I kept telling myself if I just had this or if we just did that, I'd be happy. And you know what?"

"You weren't," he replied.

"Exactly. Julian, why did we waste so much time?"

He let those words sink in for a minute and it was almost a relief for him to hear it was the same for her too.

When he didn't respond, she posed a question to him. "I know what my reasoning was for staying. What was yours?"

"Stubbornness," he said after a long moment. "My mother once told me she wished my father had fought more for her, for their relationship."

"But…they're still together," she commented curiously.

He'd never shared with Dena the details of his parents' marriage. And he didn't think he should, either. "They had a lot of issues, and my father—who I'm sure you've noticed—isn't the most emotional man. My mom always wished he was. She used to tell me how much it would have meant to her if he had put more effort into their relationship. So that's what I thought I was doing. I thought I was doing the right thing."

"And you were," she said softly, an understanding smile on her face. "You were just doing it for the wrong reason. Or should I say for the wrong relationship?"

He felt himself relax as he laughed. "It never should have gotten to the point it did." Swallowing hard, he said the one thing that had been bothering him the most about the entire situation. "You made a fool of me, Dena. You screwed around with people I knew—people I worked with and trusted. I'm a laughingstock in this business because of you."

She shook her head earnestly. "No, Julian. That's where you're wrong. I'll admit I acted horribly. I was calculated in who I pursued, but you should know…I was the aggressor, not them. Every one of them—and how horrible am I that I can't even remember names?—they all sort of caved because I was relentless. At the time, I wanted attention from you. I did those things because you were so involved with the band that I felt neglected and I chose a very childish way to get even. But all those guys hated me. I meant nothing to them, and believe me when I tell you that each of them told me how much they regretted what we'd done. Why? Because you're this amazing person—a real leader in the music industry, and I was just…I was just this whore you couldn't get rid of."

Wow. That was…totally not what he was expecting.

"So, you can hate me," she said, a tear rolling down her face. "I deserve it. I more than deserve it. But after the wedding, so many people—everyone, really—they all took your side. It was all 'good riddance, Dena' after you left. You're not a joke, Julian. And you're not a fool. And I'm so sorry I messed up your life so badly. I really am."

Here was his opportunity to rant, rave, and really go off on her and tell her what her actions had cost him, but…he didn't. What would be the point? She already knew what she'd done and had apologized for it.

"I don't expect us ever to be friends," she said, interrupting his thoughts. "But I hope you don't look at our time together and have it ruin the rest of your life."

He looked at her quizzically. "Why would you even say that?"

She let out a small snort. "Please. I may be a pretty self-absorbed person, but I spent enough time with you that I know how you think and react. The fact that there has been no announcement of Shaughnessy getting back together tells me you're the one holding out. So what's going on?"

"It's not that simple to explain," he said gruffly.

"Then make it that simple," she retorted. "We both know how much you love music. You played, you wrote, you sang nonstop for all the years we were together, Julian! And you are so gifted and talented, and the thought of you not making music again makes me sad. Don't do it to punish me."

"It wasn't to punish you."

Leaning forward, she boldly placed her hand on his forearm. "Then don't do it to punish yourself. Playing for the fans always gave you the greatest joy. I used to hate that. I was jealous of the masses and there was a time when I would have done anything to distract you from getting up on stage for them, and I did. The only one holding you back now, Jules, is you."

And then they talked.

For hours.

They talked about where he went for those three months and where he hoped to see himself in the future. And for the first time, he was excited to think about it. Dena told him she was living back in Arizona with the guy from the wedding video.

Go figure.

She was working in a salon and happy and truly in love. She was looking forward to having a life outside of Hollywood. And the thing was, he believed her. She looked happy. Honestly, she really did resemble the girl he'd met and fallen in love with, but he was no longer the same man—and while she resembled that girl, he knew she wasn't her anymore, either.

They had grown and grown apart.

And that was okay.

Actually, it was more than okay.

Conversation was dying down and she looked at her hands, which were folded in her lap. "So, who's the girl?" she asked shyly.

"What girl?"

The look she gave him told him how much she hated when he played dumb. "The girl you were with at the restaurant. We've been sitting here talking for what seems like forever and not once have you mentioned her."

And just the thought of Charlotte was enough to make his heart ache. Mindlessly, he rubbed at his chest. "Nothing to tell. It's over."

"Oh," she said softly, her expression going serious, contemplative. "I'm sorry, Julian."

"Really?"

She nodded and then looked thoroughly pained. "I'm not trying to sound egotistical or anything…"

"But…?" he prompted.

"But…don't let what happened between us affect your relationships." She sighed. "Trust me when I say that what we had was dysfunctional, but it is possible to have a good and healthy relationship."

This time he did snort with disbelief. "Dena, you can't sit here and tell me that the things you did don't affect your current relationship. Hell, you cheated on me with him! He clearly knows your history. You don't think he's watching you like a hawk to make sure you don't do to him what you did to me?"

Yeah, okay. The words were said with more heat than he wanted, but they still needed to be said.

She grimaced. "Stephen and I are in counseling. We started almost as soon as I moved. At first I thought it would be a joke—like, how could anyone possibly try to make sense out of the crap I'd done when I still didn't want to own up to half of it." She looked at him sadly. "People spit on me," she admitted quietly. "I tried to defy Mick and stay in town. I didn't think it would be a big deal. I thought the media attention would sway in my favor a bit—don't ask me why I thought that, but I did. I was walking down Rodeo Drive and people spit on me and called me horrible names. That's when I knew I'd hit rock bottom. I had to change."

For a minute, he almost felt bad for her. His stunt at the wedding had been to humiliate her, but no one deserved to be spit on, for crying out loud.

"Whose idea was it to see a counselor?"

"Stephen's," she admitted. "I left town without him—convinced that what we had was just like what I'd had with all the other…well, you know. But he followed me. He swore he was in love with me, and I didn't believe him. He refused to leave, and when he suggested therapy, I thought he was crazy. Now I'm glad I went. I think it's helped so much. It's the reason I came to see you. I needed to see you and talk to you and look you in the eye and tell you how sorry I am. For everything."

Wow.

"So, this is part of your therapy? Sort of like a twelve-step program?"

Shaking her head, she gave him a small smile. "Not exactly. It was suggested that I do this, and at first I said I'd never do it. I knew you'd be so angry and how much you hated me, and I didn't want to put either of us through it."

"What changed your mind?" He was genuinely curious, because if the tables had been turned, he would have refused.

The tables had turned.

And he did refuse.

"I know this sounds corny, but if I'm ever going to move forward and have a life with Stephen, then I had to put this—this whole situation between you and me—behind me. I couldn't do that without us trying to find some closure that wasn't so hurtful or hateful."

Now he felt like crap. Scrubbing a weary hand over his face, he sighed. "Dena, look. Maybe I went about everything the wrong way—"

"No!" she immediately cut him off. "I know why you did it, Julian. Don't get me wrong, I hate it. I still have nightmares about it. But you did it because I wasn't getting it. I know I bulldozed you into a wedding, into a life you didn't want…so many things. The only way this express train to hell was ever going to end was if one of us did something drastic." Tears filled her eyes again. "I'm just sorry it had to be like that."

"I am too." And he meant it. He was a private man and doing what he did with that video meant he was letting the whole world know how messed up his life was. It had humiliated them both—only he hadn't realized just how much damage he'd done to himself until much later.

And all of it was hitting home right now.

They sat in silence for several moments, when Dena

reached for her purse. "There is one more thing I need to do, Julian," she said. Slowly, she pulled out an envelope and slid it across the table toward him.

Without moving, he looked at it and then at her. "What's this?"

"This is a check," she said, her voice a little stronger than it had been a minute ago. She seemed to straighten, like she was building up to something. "Mick showed up in my dressing room in the hotel after all the chaos had died down that day and handed me a check." She shook her head. "I always knew he never liked me, but it had never been clearer than on that day. He told me to take the money and go away—that I could take whatever I wanted from the house but I had twenty-four hours to do it before the locks would be changed."

Julian knew the terms Mick had presented. He had written them himself.

With a small, humorless laugh, she went on. "I remember scurrying around the house in the middle of the night collecting my things. Looking back, I'm so ashamed, because I was no better than a common thief. I took things I had no right to take."

"Everything in that house was yours, Dena. I never wanted most of it."

The look she gave him showed she was grateful he wasn't berating her any further than she had already berated herself. "I can't possibly have the life I need to have, knowing you've financed it. That's not fair to you. Or Stephen," she added bashfully. "So, this is a check for the exact amount Mick gave me. And I promise to pay you back for all the rest—the furniture, the jewelry, the car—"

He held up a hand to stop her. "Those were all gifts," he said evenly. "And I don't want them back or the money for them." With a brief pause, he gave her a weak smile of his own. "Not everything was bad between us, right?"

She started crying again as she ducked her head. "No. It wasn't."

"If you don't want the stuff, then give it to charity. Donate it to a good cause." Then he laughed softly. "I even happen to know of a couple of organizations you can contact if you want."

"You're being far too generous, Julian," she said, wiping away the tears.

He shrugged. "I have my moments."

Her phone beeped with an incoming text and she looked at it before meeting Julian's gaze. "I need to go. We have a flight back to Phoenix in the morning and I still have to pack."

He nodded and rose from his seat.

When Dena stood, she studied him for a long moment before she picked up the envelope and handed it to him. "I'm sorry I ever took this, but I'm not sorry for knowing you. Thank you for being willing to talk with me today."

"I think it was good for both of us," he admitted gruffly.

This time she nodded. "I wish you only the best, Julian. Be happy. No one deserves it more than you." Then she stood on her tiptoes and kissed him on the cheek before walking away.

Chapter 10

"WAIT, LET ME GET THIS STRAIGHT. YOU WERE DATING a rock star—for like a month!—and I'm just finding out about it now after you've broken up. Do I have that right?"

Charlotte dunked her hundredth tortilla chip of the night into a fresh bowl of guacamole and nodded before stuffing it in her mouth to avoid speaking.

"Unbelievable!" Tami cried and then immediately lowered her voice. They were out at a local Mexican restaurant and clearly decided inside voices were a better choice for this conversation. "So...how are you doing? I mean...now."

When she went to reach for another chip, Tami smacked her hand, setting both bowls out of reach.

"Now? Right now, I'm a little annoyed our girls' night turned into just the two of us, and that after you promised me all the chips and guac I could eat, you take them away!"

Rolling her eyes, Tami slowly slid the bowls back toward the center of the table. "Just know this—I don't care if you talk with your mouth full of food, but I want to know all the details and I've got all night. I already texted Jimmy while you were in the ladies' room and told him this could be an all-nighter."

Great.

While she had originally given her friend the *Reader's Digest* version of her relationship with Julian when they first sat down, it was obvious that now she had to relive it all and give her the extended version.

Which she did.

Thirty minutes and way too many chips later, Charlotte leaned back in her seat and sighed. "So, that's it. That's my tale of woe."

"Holy. Crap," Tami stated. "That's just… Wow. I don't know where to begin. Part of me is so freaking impressed that you put yourself out there and not only found a great guy, but a famous one to boot."

"I didn't know he was famous."

Tami laughed. "I know. That's what makes it even greater. You certainly know how not to boost a guy's ego."

She made a face and waved the waitress over to refresh their drinks. "Lucky for me I happened to find the one guy who didn't want to be known for his fame, so there was that."

"Lot of good it did. Sounds to me like he needs a shrink. And extended therapy."

Charlotte wanted to take offense to that on Julian's behalf, but her friend was right. "Yeah, well… Never going to happen. It's like he knows he has a problem, but he doesn't know. You know?"

Another laugh. "I think you should switch to water. The sangria is making you talk weird."

"Anyway…"

"Oh, right. So yes, part of me is happy you put yourself out there, but the other part is happy you knew when to walk away. It seems to me he had way too many issues and it wasn't going to get any better."

"I know, but—"

"Nuh-uh," Tami cut her off. "No way. No."

"What?" Charlotte asked with confusion. "You don't even know what I was going to say!"

"You were going to say that maybe he just needed time and how you could help him and blah, blah, blah!" She sighed dramatically. "Seriously, Charlotte, you have a tendency to try to fix everyone and you don't realize that sometimes people have to fix themselves!"

"Well, drat. That does sound like me and what I do." She eyed Tami for a minute. "Are you sure you didn't get the psychology degree and not me?"

"Trust me," Tami replied. "I barely got my high school diploma. I've known you since we were twelve and I think I've picked up on a thing or two about you."

That made sense too.

Dammit.

"Here's something else I know about you," Tami continued. "You give everything and everyone your full heart. I know this breakup is fairly new, but I've never seen you like this. Ever."

Charlotte shrugged. "I don't think I've ever felt like this. I keep waiting to wake up and feel better and I do, but…there's an emptiness that wasn't there before." With her hand over her heart, she went on. "It's like a constant ache. I can distract myself all day long with work, but it will just take one thing—a flash of something we did together or something Julian said—and then I feel like I'm dying."

And now she felt exactly like that.

"Oh, sweetie," Tami said as she reached over and took one of Charlotte's hands in hers. "I'm so sorry. I hate that you're going through this and I hate that you're trying to handle it alone."

"I really thought he'd realize he needed help—that it wasn't healthy to keep repeating the same patterns of behavior he had with his ex. But he would get so angry whenever I tried to talk to him about it." She felt her frustration building. "What was it about her that she still has such a hold on him?"

Holding up a finger, Tami took out her phone and began typing and scrolling. Charlotte had no idea what she was looking for, but she waited silently.

Tami gasped and murmured something under her breath, then quickly put her phone away.

"What?" Charlotte demanded. "What was that all about? What were you looking up?"

"It's nothing," she said quickly. "Seriously, nothing. How about we order some dessert? They have great fried ice cream here!"

Not wanting to be deterred, Charlotte almost crawled across the table to reach for Tami's phone. "Come on! You can't go and get all dramatic and then act like you didn't!"

"Fine," Tami said defiantly. "But this wasn't what I thought I was going to find." Pulling her phone back out, she went back to her search and turned the phone toward Charlotte.

It was a picture of Julian and Dena.

From yesterday.

"Oh no," she spat out, her stomach roiling. "How? Why…?" And then anger set in as she cursed under her breath.

REUNITED! DRUMMER JULIAN GRAYSON AND
FIANCÉE HE LEFT AT THE ALTAR BACK TOGETHER!

Sun, moon, and stars, my ass. One week of her being out of his life and he ran right back to the woman who completely messed him up! Well, good riddance!

"Char, you okay?" Tami asked cautiously. "You look a little green."

Her stomach pitched as she pushed Tami's phone away, unable to look at the picture anymore.

Although it was probably burned into her brain.

"Seriously, Charlotte, are you okay?"

One minute she was and then the next—

"I'm going to be sick," she hissed as she slid from the booth and made a mad dash for the ladies' room—cursing Julian the entire way.

When she walked out of the restroom fifteen minutes later, she felt better and worse at the same time. Chips and guac may be good going down, not so much coming up.

"Ugh," she moaned as she slid back into her seat and immediately reached for her purse to find a piece of gum.

"Better?"

Charlotte shook her head. Nope. Not better. She'd probably never be better again.

"I paid the check," Tami said, her voice soft and cautious. "We should probably go."

She agreed, so they gathered their things and made their way to the door. Once they were outside, the fresh air helped a lot. She breathed deeply several times until her head felt a little clearer.

"Do you want me to drive you home?"

With a weak smile, Charlotte looked at her friend. "Thanks, but I think I'm going to be okay. There's absolutely nothing left in me. It was just…"

"I know. I know." Tami pouted. "Dammit. I hate how

I ruined our night. I never should have tried to Google Julian. That wasn't helpful at all."

"Actually, it was," she said sadly. "Now I know there wasn't anything I could have done to change him or help him. Julian's determined to stay stuck in a cycle he knows is bad for him. Instead of pining for him, I can only pity him."

"And there's no way you think you can work it out?"

"I can't," she said sadly. "I don't want only a part of Julian. I deserve someone who is willing to give himself totally to me. That's what I did. There wasn't anything I was holding back."

"Sometimes it's not that simple."

"Would you settle for only part of Jimmy?" she asked. "If you knew there was a part of him he was refusing to share with you, would you settle for that?"

A sad sigh was Tami's only response.

They hugged and walked across the parking lot to their cars. "Let's try this again next week and see who else we can drag out with us," Charlotte suggested, hoping she sounded upbeat. "Anyplace but Mexican."

With a laugh and another hug, they went their separate ways. Charlotte stayed in her car until Tami pulled out. It was early—barely after eight—and her big plans for a girls' night out had gone down in flames. Typical for her life right now.

Maybe someday she'd be able to get her life together. Maybe she'd find her Mr. Right and get her happily ever after.

Hey, a girl could dream, right?

Sighing, she pulled out of the parking lot and made her way home.

—◆—

"Fucking tabloids," Julian muttered.

"Don't shoot the messenger," Riley said from the other end of the phone. "Just checking on you because… well, I think I sort of threw up a little in my mouth when Savannah showed me the article."

"I had no idea anyone was paying attention to us."

"So? What were you doing out with her? Is there any truth to this, because the article said the two of you looked cozy."

Julian snorted with disbelief. "Trust me, there is no truth to anything in that story other than the fact that Dena and I were sitting together. There's no reconcili-ation, there's no nothing. I just…it was time. She came back to LA to talk to me, and I knew that if I'm ever going to get my life back, I had to face her."

"Okay. Whew," Riley said, relieved. "Okay then." He paused. "So…do you want to talk about it?"

Hell no, he didn't. For the better part of twenty-four hours he'd been thinking about it and playing it over and over in his head. He was pretty content with how he felt, and now he was ready to put it behind him.

"Look, let's just say I'm glad I went. I'm glad we cleared the air and…things are good." Yeah, he was being vague and maybe someday he'd share it all with his friends, but now wasn't the time.

"Okay."

"You keep saying that."

"I don't know what else to say, Jules," Riley said with a nervous laugh. "You're not giving me much to work with."

He chuckled, because that was true. "So what about you?" he asked, turning the tables. "What's going on with you? How's Savannah and the kids?"

And you know what? He really wanted to know. For months now he had asked everyone else how they were, but he wasn't listening when they told him and really didn't care, because all he could focus on was his own pain and misery. This time, he reached for his cup of coffee and sat down on the couch to listen to Riley talk about family life.

Afterward, Riley said, "I think we all need to sit down and talk. You, me, Matt, and Dylan. This anniversary show is still happening and we've accepted the invite to play, but…"

Julian knew what he was getting at, and yes, it was time to deal with that too.

"Is Matt going to be in town?"

"Dude, if you agree to talk with us about playing the show, then I'll drag him here myself if I have to."

"Sounds like a plan."

"Have you thought any more about not retiring?"

"Lately, my plate's been kind of full with a lot of other stuff, Ry. But I promise I'll give it some thought."

"Jules."

"It's the best I can do, man. I'm not going to make promises I can't keep. Between breaking up with Charlotte and then this whole Dena thing…"

"Wait, wait, wait—you broke up with Charlotte? When?"

Great. Another can of worms opened.

"A little over a week ago. The day after Dena showed up at the restaurant."

"She was pissed about it, huh?"

Putting his coffee down, he leaned back against the cushions and closed his eyes. Not that it helped. He could still see the sadness on her face. "No. She was pissed at me for trying to apologize."

"I'm confused."

"Join the club."

"There's got to be more to it than that. Come on. It's not like you tried to buy her forgiveness or anything, right? I mean, you wouldn't start that trend up again," Riley said with a nervous laugh and when Julian didn't answer, he groaned. "Dude, seriously? Have you learned nothing?"

"It wasn't like that!" he argued, jumping to his feet. Stalking across the room, he opened the sliding doors and walked out on the deck. It was an overcast Saturday morning and the beach wasn't too crowded. It was a little on the chilly side and he contemplated going inside for a jacket, but something caught his eye.

Or someone.

"I gotta go," he murmured into the phone and even as he heard Riley protest, Julian hung up. Tossing the phone on the lounge chair, he walked as if pulled by an invisible force toward the stairs and down onto the beach.

She hadn't spotted him. She was standing farther down the beach—closer to the town—and from what he could tell she had a cup of coffee in her hands. He wished he was bringing her coffee. Then she'd smile at him and kiss him and everything would be okay.

He missed her.

Ached for her.

Wasn't sure how much longer he could live without her.

Each step toward her felt like a mile, and when he was only a few feet away, she finally turned and saw him.

The sadness on her face nearly brought him to his knees.

Wordlessly, he went and stood beside her. He looked out at the waves for a minute until he could figure out what he could possibly say to her that would do justice to everything he was feeling.

"Hey."

Not the greatest start, but at least it was something.

"Hey," she replied softly, turning to look back at the water.

"It's a little cold out here today."

"Yup."

Okay, so his conversation skills sucked. Now what? Finally, he forced himself to face her. "I've missed you."

No response. For a minute, she didn't even blink.

He didn't take that as a good sign.

"Charlotte," he said softly, desperate for her to look at him, desperate to be able to touch her. He thought of the night he came out here and found her and how it had made everything in his world feel right. He wished he could have that feeling again right now.

"You should go, Julian," she said, her voice so quiet he almost didn't hear her over the waves. "I've got nothing to say to you." There was no heat behind her words, barely any emotion at all, and yet it cut him just as deep.

It was foolish to think she'd be waiting here with open arms after everything that had happened, but he had hoped she'd be a little more agreeable to talking to him. "Why don't you come up to the house and we can talk? It's cold out here."

Then she turned and noticed his sweatpants and

T-shirt and bare feet. Meanwhile she was in leggings, a sweatshirt, bulky socks, and boots. Comparatively, he looked like an idiot.

Or like the guy down on his luck she had once thought he was.

When her eyes met his, all he saw was annoyance there—not compassion—and she certainly wasn't considering going anywhere with him.

"Okay, fine," he said, determined to at least say… something. "You were right. About everything. I wasn't handling anything and I was being stubborn about it. I kept thinking that if I didn't hold on to the rage, it would make me weak. I thought that staying angry would keep me strong."

No response.

"But it didn't," he went on. "It was the rage that was killing me. It was ruining my life. It ruined us and what we had. But that's changed now. I swear."

She snorted with disgust and took a sip of her coffee. "Sure, probably because you've gotten back what you wanted."

Yes! She was back and—wait a minute. Little warning bells started to go off in his head. She wasn't referring to herself, she was referring to…

"The two of you looked very *cozy*," she said and there was definitely some snark there. The smile she gave him confirmed it. "Congratulations."

Holding up his hands in surrender, he was quick to try to explain. "No, no, no—that story was a lie. Right now, the PR people are getting it pulled down. There was nothing cozy about it. It was all a lie. I mean, yes, I was out with Dena, but it wasn't to reconcile. I swear.

It was just to…to put things to rest," he explained desperately, wishing he could convince her he was telling the truth.

"Whatever." Another sip of coffee as she watched the waves.

"Dammit, Charlotte, it's true! I went there because you and Mick and Riley and the guys? You were all right! I needed to deal with this and clear the air and… and…just admit that I was angry and hurt and pissed off and humiliated!"

The side-eye she gave him was her only response.

Why was this so damn hard?

This was everything she'd said she wanted. He'd dealt with the problem and fixed it and now everything was good. Right? And he was talking to her about how he felt about all of it! Everything should be able to go back to the way things were before he screwed it all up!

He shivered from the cold and asked her again to come back to the house, but she politely declined as if he was a stranger.

"What do I have to do to convince you that I'm sorry?" he asked, not above begging at this point. "Whatever you want, Charlotte, it's yours."

He knew immediately she took that the wrong way.

"Seriously?" she cried, stomping her foot even as she turned toward him. "You still don't get it! And you know what? I'm tired of explaining it to you!"

"No, Charlotte. What I meant was—"

"We are too different, Julian," she said, ignoring his words. "We are worlds apart, and we're never going to see eye to eye on any of it. I can't live in a world where the answer to everything is to throw money and

expensive gifts at a problem! That's not who I am! I
don't want to live in a ten-million-dollar home that's too
big for anyone to really live in! I don't want a car that
costs more than the average family makes in a year!"

He was going to try to stop her, but she was on a roll.

And at least she was talking to him.

Or at him.

"I work with people every day who struggle to make
ends meet! I'm passionate about helping people less
fortunate, and when I see the level of excess in your
world, I'm uncomfortable with it! I can't drive to work
in your fancy car or wear designer clothes and jewelry
while I'm talking to a woman who is living on the street
with her two kids and believe that she's going to relate
to me!" She paused and shook her head as she turned
away. "And more than that, if you retreated out of the
spotlight and away from the band and the music that
we both know makes you happy..." She looked back
at him sadly. "I couldn't live in that world either. And
not because I want you to be famous or because I want
to be seen with you because of it, but because it would
eventually kill you not to do the one thing you are most
passionate about. Whether you want to admit it or not."

"You don't know—"

She held up a hand to cut off his words. "Do you
have any idea how often you hum or tap on things?"
The change of subject seemed odd, so he simply waited
her out. "All the time. Your hands are never still. There
is so much music in you that you don't even realize it.
I watched you at the shelter with those kids, and those
few times I saw more joy on your face than I ever saw
when we were alone." Pausing, she sighed and then took

a step back. "I want to know that you have that joy with you always, Julian. You deserve it."

"I'm meeting up with the guys as soon as Riley gets back from North Carolina. I'll tell them all right now if that's what you want," he rushed on. "I'll call a press conference today if that's what it takes to prove to you—"

But she shook her head. "Not for me, Julian. It can't be for me. I'm not part of the equation. This is about you."

He watched as she closed her eyes, inhaled deeply, and let the breath out. He knew she did this all the time when she was trying to clear her mind or to find the right thing to say.

When Charlotte opened her eyes—those beautiful blue eyes—he finally saw something there. Compassion. Hope had him in its grip as he waited to hear what she was going to say.

"I never want to be the reason you do something or don't do something. It's a lot of pressure to live with, and I think you have enough of that without me adding to it. I love you too much to end up being one more person with expectations and demands on you." She took another step back. "Be happy, Julian." Then she swallowed hard. "Goodbye."

He couldn't move. It was like he was paralyzed. All Julian could do was stand and watch her walk away. His voice wouldn't work, his limbs wouldn't move, and by the time he finally could, Charlotte was climbing the stairs that led up to the street. If he chased her down, he'd make a scene and no doubt embarrass her.

Be happy.

Did she have any idea how that wasn't possible without her? How it wasn't just playing music at the shelter that made him happy, it was the fact that he was doing it for her? With her? Had he really not communicated that to her at all? Volunteering had been incredibly rewarding and it was something he never would have done if not for her. He'd wanted to help her because she did so much for everyone else and never seemed to get help in return.

How had she missed that? How could he not have told her that everything he did was for her?

Turning around, he looked at the row of houses and sighed. She might say she didn't want to live in a mansion, but she was happy here. The homes weren't over the top by any means, but the view was. He wanted to give her that view. He wanted to give her something—everything—that would give her joy. Because in return, that's what would give him his.

He just didn't know how.

———

It was becoming exceedingly obvious that she was either going to have to change her daily routine or move.

Yeah, those were her options.

Every morning when Charlotte went to get coffee, Julian sat at a table outside the shop reading the paper, sipping his coffee—which he would lift as a way of saying hello as she walked by. He never tried to stop her or get her to sit with him, but when she would leave, he always said, "I hope you have a good day, beautiful," and yeah, it always gave her heart a little thrill.

They crossed paths at the supermarket, at the Chinese takeout place, and at the car wash.

Weird.

And although she couldn't prove it, some strange things were happening all around her and she had a feeling Julian had something to do with them.

There were flowers around the office that were delivered every other day. They weren't addressed to anyone; they were just there to brighten up the place. Someone had even sent lunch to the office twice a week for the last two weeks. And not just something easy like pizza, but sandwich platters and salads and cookies.

Everyone had loved those days.

And then there was the shelter.

The entire exterior had been painted, new windows installed, new landscaping—it looked like a completely new building. And every time she walked inside, something else was being rehabbed.

New kitchen appliances—all top of the line, restaurant-grade.

New furniture in every room.

New computers in the conference room where she and others taught job skills.

On Thursday night she stood in the middle of the rec room, amazed. There was music playing, children laughing, the place looked bright and cheerful, and she barely recognized it.

"CeeCee!" Hank called as he practically jogged toward her. "You're not going to believe this. Come see, come see!" He motioned for her to follow and she did, unable to hide her own excitement over what he had to show her.

There were several storage rooms in the back of the building which normally housed extra boxes of clothes and donated furniture, but both of those rooms now looked like something out of a department store. She looked at Hank in confusion. "I…I don't understand. What's going on?"

"We've got a guardian angel, I think," he said happily. "These are all new clothes and linens for families in need! They were dropped off here earlier along with all the shelves and hangers and everything we'd need to store them for people to go through with more ease."

"That's…that's amazing," she said softly as she walked around the room and saw row after row of men's, women's, and children's clothing in every size imaginable. On the perimeter of the room were shelves that went from floor to ceiling, full of sheets, towels, blankets, pillows—things that were new, so a family getting back on their feet could take them and have a little pride in having something new. Her heart felt ready to burst as she thought of how much families would appreciate that.

"We have a system so no one can take advantage and take more than they need, but there is a monthly order in place for the next twelve months, so the inventory will be replenished with whatever we're low on! Can you believe it?"

Charlotte was still speechless.

"And there's more," he said and boldly took her hand and led her from the room. They walked back to the food pantry. Normally it was stocked with canned goods or boxed goods that were a little banged up or dented, but now the room had new shelves full to overflowing with new merchandise—nothing dinged or damaged— and all brand name.

"When the new kitchen came, we also got more refrigeration units so we can have fresh produce," Hank explained giddily. "I'm telling you, it's a miracle. And like the clothes, there is a standing weekly order in place to restock us." He laughed happily. "In all my years of doing this, I've never seen such generosity!"

Neither have I, she thought as her heart raced.

"Any idea who donated?" she asked hesitantly.

"I can't say with any great certainty, but Julian's been here helping with all the heavy stuff—demolition, construction of the new shelves, cleaning. I'm telling you, he and his team have put in a lot of sweat and time. But he's done that for us before so I didn't give it much thought. And then with the celebrity lineup he's sent through here in the last few weeks, I'd have to say it's either one or all of them combined. Either way, I am thankful for it and I'd love to shake all of their hands and tell them how many lives they've saved with their donations!"

"Wait—celebrity lineup? I mean, I know he brought Riley and Dylan with him a couple of times, but that's it, right?"

Hank laughed. "I forgot you haven't been in when they're here, but it's been like a who's who of the music world in here! Wait, let me pull up the pictures I have on my phone. I've been so star struck and I never know who's going to walk through the door!"

Charlotte scanned the twenty-something pictures on Hank's phone as he shared a story about each of the celebrities he'd met. Why hadn't anyone mentioned this to her? She'd even spoken to Mick several times and the guys he normally sent her way were new to the business and looking for a way to fill their time or find temporary work until their music took off. How could no one have said anything about any of this? Which was what she asked Hank.

"Honestly, I thought you knew! I figured you and Julian had worked this out and you were just busy," he replied. "Are you saying you didn't know?"

"Not a clue," she said, frowning, but then she quickly reminded herself that it wasn't about her. This was a great thing that was happening, and she needed to focus on all of the good it was doing—not the fact that it had all happened without her knowledge or help.

Hank finished showing her all the improvements to the facility and by the time they were done, it was after eight and she was starving. Another night of takeout and she could only pray she wasn't going to run into Julian. After seeing everything that he'd more than likely done, she had a feeling she'd fling herself into his arms and thank him and then beg him to take her back.

So, it seemed the way to her heart wasn't with diamonds; it was helping the needy.

Not a bad thing at all, right?

And it wasn't like he was just throwing money at the problem, he was putting in the time, too, which made what he was doing even more amazing.

"I'm heading out, Hank!" she called out as she walked to the door. People wished her a good night, and when she stepped outside, there was a small mob of people and lights and cameras flashing. What the…?

"*Charlotte!* Is it true the Shaughnessy reunion to raise money for the shelter was your idea?"

"*Charlotte!* How did you manage to get the band back together?"

Wait…what?

"*Charlotte!* Are you the reason Julian Grayson came out of retirement?"

She was surrounded and practically blinded and had no idea what was happening! She looked around frantically, stammering and stuttering while she tried to think of something to say.

"No comment, folks!" a male voice called out and suddenly Mick was there with a protective arm around her to shield her from the crowd. Everyone moved aside as he guided her toward his car.

"But…my car's over there." Charlotte weakly pointed in the opposite direction. Not that Mick noticed, he was too busy fielding questions—and by fielding, all he kept saying was, "No comment."

"Come on, man, just one comment!" someone called out. "Please!"

"There'll be a news conference tomorrow at eleven. You'll get everything you need there," Mick said as they kept walking. "In the meantime, why don't you do something useful like donate a meal to the shelter or volunteer to help a kid learn to read!"

He ushered her into the back of a black SUV before jogging around to the other side and climbing in beside her. "Let's go," he said to the driver and then they were in motion.

For a minute, she forgot to be confused and instead got annoyed. "What in the world do you think you're doing?" she cried, turning in her seat to face him. "What was that all about?"

"I'll take you to Julian's and he can explain," Mick said evenly as he reached forward, grabbing a bottle of water and handing it to her. "Here. You look a little flushed."

Without thinking, she took the bottle. "I don't want to

go to Julian's, Mick. I want you to tell me what's going on. And I need to go back for my car!"

He gave her a very serene smile. "I like you," he said. "And trust me, I haven't liked anyone from the get-go like I have you. On top of that, you're good for him."

Was she in some sort of alternate universe or something?

"Right now, I really don't care who likes me. Why were all those people outside the shelter and what does Shaughnessy have to do with it?"

"Like I said, I'll take you to Julian's so he can explain it. He's really looking forward to being able to share it with you."

"I'm not going to Julian's," she said defiantly. "I want to go back to my car. Now." She did not like having someone dictate what she had to do or hijacking her the way Mick just had.

But all Mick did was smile. "If you give me your keys, I'll have someone go back and get the car. It will be at your place within a couple of hours."

She rolled her eyes. "Thanks, but no thanks. I don't think you're understanding me. It's been a very long day and a confusing night and right now, I just want to go home."

Mick tried to interrupt her, but she quickly cut him off.

"And not like this!" she cried. Taking a deep breath, she let it out and tried to be reasonable. "How did those reporters know who I was?"

"Julian mentioned you in the press release," Mick said casually. "He told them about your work with the unemployed and the homeless, and I guess they did their homework and went to see you. I'm surprised there weren't more of them there."

"It must be a slow news day," she murmured.

"Look, Charlotte, this wasn't quite the way we envi-sioned tonight going. We knew there might be a few reporters around, but I thought I'd get there in time. That's on me and I'm sorry. But Julian can explain the rest, I swear."

Would it really be the worst thing in the world for her to go and see him and just get this over with? Although, remembering her earlier thoughts on what she would do if she saw him right now came to mind. Maybe she should stick to her guns and go home. Her emotions were too all over the place for her to go and see him, and she had a feeling there would be very little talking and a lot of her crawling all over him.

Yeah. That was the better plan.

She hated how logical her mind could be even when her body was crying out for some attention.

Mick's phone rang and he immediately answered. "Yeah. Uh-huh…exactly. No problem. Thanks."

The whole thing took all of ten seconds.

He slid his phone back into his pocket. "I'll take you home and I promise to get your car to you. We're already on our way, so it's crazy to go back."

"Oh. Okay," she said hesitantly. Why the sudden change of plans?

"It's late," he said a moment later. "Have you eaten yet?"

"I…I had plans to grab something on the way home."

He nodded. "Call in whatever you want and we'll swing by and pick it up on the way to your place."

Why was he being so agreeable all of a sudden? And why did that annoy her too?

Right then her stomach growled, so she was going to blame it on hunger. Pulling out her phone, she called in her Chinese food order and then sat back stiffly, wondering what she was supposed to do now.

Oddly enough, Mick started talking to her about her job. They'd discussed it over the phone and in person the few times he'd come to see her about the volunteers, and it was kind of nice to focus on something that was comforting for her and…normal. After the last hour, she could definitely use some of that.

They talked and laughed, and as much as she was dying to ask more about what was going on with the band, she kept that to herself. The driver ran in and paid for her food—something she protested, but fortunately Mick allowed her to give him cash to repay him—and the next thing she knew, she was home.

No paparazzi.

No questions.

No Julian.

"Well, this sucks," she murmured as she let herself into her apartment.

Alone, she ate her dinner and picked up her Kindle to finish reading a Christmas romance she'd started a few days ago that had recently been turned into a TV movie.

The book was better.

When the book was done and her dinner gone, Charlotte gave in to the urge to go online and try to figure out what in the world was going on with Shaughnessy.

SHAUGHNESSY REUNITES!
SHAUGHNESSY—THE INFAMOUS BAND ON THE
RUN—IS FINALLY HEADING BACK TO THE STUDIO!

JULIAN GRAYSON'S NEW LOVE THE
REASON BEHIND BAND'S COMEBACK?

Her eyes began to glaze over as page after page after page of stories came up under her search. It was hard to know where to start, and then she had to stop and ask herself if the internet was really the best place to get information or if she just should have gone to Julian's.

Jumping up, she went to grab her purse and then she remembered—no car.

Opening her front door, she walked out and looked to the parking lot, but the car wasn't back yet. She cursed her own stubbornness, because now she'd either have to wait, call an Uber, or call him. And calling him felt both safe and scary at the same time.

"Just do it," she scolded herself as she headed back in and found her phone. "It's not like he's going to hang up on you. He wanted you to come and talk to him." All this was said as she paced and tried to figure out what she was going to say. "Okay. You got this. Just be… casual. See how he sounds and go from there."

And with that, she pulled up his number and hit send.

It rang.

And rang.

And rang again.

"Hey, this is Julian. Leave a name and I'll call you back." *Beep!*

Seriously? He wasn't answering his phone? And she knew he specifically wasn't answering, since it didn't go immediately to voicemail, so…she was thoroughly confused.

"Um, hey, Julian, it's Charlotte. Mick brought me

home a little while ago and I just wanted to know what was going on, so call me, okay? Thanks. Bye."

Her heart was hammering so hard in her chest that she was practically breathless as she put her phone down. Then she sat down on her sofa and figured he'd call her back.

Channel surfing killed some time, and when she looked at the clock, she saw it was after ten and frowned. He could still call her back.

The eleven o'clock news ended and she glared at her phone, still trying to reason with herself that he could call her back tonight.

When *The Late Late Show* ended, Charlotte turned off the television and chucked the remote across the room.

He didn't call back.

And the thing was, she wasn't sure who she was more pissed off at—him or herself. If she had just gone to his house like Mick had insisted, she wouldn't be sitting here alone and miserable, still trying to figure out what in the world was going on.

Now she had two options—she could go back online and read the articles and piece together what was real and what was just conjecture, or she could go to sleep and try to see Julian tomorrow. Of course, it would have to be after work, since Fridays were usually a little chaotic at the office. But by that time the band would have had their press conference and she'd be able to see video footage of it and hear from the guys themselves about what was going on.

"Sleep it is," she said, stretching.

When her alarm went off in the morning, it felt as if she had just fallen asleep after the restless night she'd had.

And as was her usual luck, nothing went as planned. Her shower drain backed up, she burned her hand on her curling iron, and there wasn't any coffee in the house so she had no choice but to stop and get a cup on her way to work. It was her usual stop, but today she just wanted to get to work and get the day over with.

There were a ton of cars lining the street, and she had to wonder what would have all these people in town at this early hour. Finding a parking spot was a bit of a nightmare, but one opened up miraculously after she'd circled the block multiple times.

"It's going to be that kind of day," she murmured as she climbed from the car. Turning the corner, Charlotte cursed.

The line was easily fifty people deep coming out of the coffee shop.

"What in the world?" she cried softly.

The guy in front of her turned around and smiled. "Free coffee today," he said.

"Seriously? Why?"

He shrugged. "Some guy came out earlier and said there was free coffee for anyone who needed it today. Kind of loud about it too," he added. "You can imagine how fast word spread and people were lining up."

Charlotte looked at her phone and knew that if the line didn't start moving, she was going to be late for work. The thought of the one-step-above-instant coffee at the office made her decide being a few minutes late would be worth the inconvenience.

It didn't take long for her to realize she may have

underestimated how late she'd be when a news crew pulled up and headed into the coffee shop.

"Must be another slow news day," she murmured, and the guy in front of her chuckled.

"Either that or they really wanted the free coffee and used their gear as a ploy to cut to the front of the line!" he said.

That was one way to look at it, she supposed.

Twenty minutes later she was finally walking through the door. Her head was down as she looked at her phone and quickly typed out a text to her boss to say she was running late and would be there as soon as possible. Their exchange went back and forth as she moved forward, and it wasn't until she heard someone call "next" that she looked up.

And saw Julian standing behind the counter next to the cashier.

Charlotte looked around in confusion before focusing her gaze on him.

"I believe the lady will have a caramel Frappuccino and a blueberry muffin," Julian said to the cashier, but his eyes never left Charlotte's.

"Ma'am? Is that correct?" the cashier asked.

All she could do was nod.

"If you could step down to the end, your order will be out in a moment."

She did as she was asked and expected Julian to move with her. But he didn't. She looked at him and saw the amusement on his face. After a moment, he walked over to meet her.

"Julian, what in the world?" she asked quietly, not wanting anyone to think she was having a panic attack.

Even though that was exactly what she was having.

"I'm paying it forward," he said and then looked over his shoulder toward the line. "I'd love to stay and talk, but I need to get back to the register and greet everyone. Who knew so many people were in need of coffee, right?"

When he turned to walk away, she reached out and touched his arm. He immediately turned around, his expression so soft and warm and wonderful, and a far cry from the man she had first met here two months ago.

"I don't understand what's going on," she admitted, moving in closer to him. "I tried calling you last night and—"

"Why didn't you let Mick bring you over?" he asked softly, his eyes scanning her face like a caress.

"I...I was confused and nervous, and those reporters really freaked me out. Everything happened so fast and I just kind of panicked. Then I realized how stupid I'd been and tried to call."

Julian moved just a little closer and she could feel the warmth of his body; she wanted to burrow in close to him and never move away. He touched her hand gently as he smiled down at her. "What are you doing for lunch?"

Lunch? Wait...what time was it?

"I don't have any plans." Hope began to bubble up inside of her.

"Now you do," he said. "I'll pick you up." Then he turned to walk away but stopped and looked at her. "And make sure you're online at eleven."

This time he did walk away and she had to call out after him. "What am I looking for?"

With one last glance over his shoulder, he smiled again. "The link is waiting in your inbox."

And then he was back behind the counter and the barista was handing her the coffee she'd ordered. Head spinning, Charlotte somehow managed to make it out the door and back to her car, but work was the last place she wanted to go. She wanted to stay and watch him do this crazy stunt and then be with him when he went to whatever it was he was doing next.

Beside her, a reporter was speaking to the camera. "Drummer Julian Grayson is giving away free coffee here until ten this morning and reminding people to pay it forward. There's some speculation on why the normally private rocker is suddenly making such a public display. Hopefully we'll find out later this morning when Shaughnessy holds their press conference. In the meantime, everyone, let's all take a page from Julian's book and do something nice for someone today."

If her heart hadn't already been full to capacity before, it was now.

Not only had he remembered her words from their first meeting, he was reaching out to the masses in the hope that they'd do something good for others.

And that was the greatest gift he could ever have given her.

Chapter 11

"THIS IS FREAKING AWESOME!" DYLAN SHOUTED AS HE high-fived Matt. "Do you hear the crowd out there?"

Beside him, Julian stood with Riley and waited for their cue to take the stage. It wasn't a concert. There were no instruments, just a long table with five chairs behind it up on a stage facing a crowd of about a hundred people.

"I'd like to hear the roar of an arena crowd," Matt said and then laughed. "But this is a great start!"

The day after Riley and Savannah had returned home from North Carolina, the four of them had gotten together to talk about the band's future. There hadn't been a lot to talk about—Julian was the lone holdout to them getting back together.

And now he wasn't and here they were.

"You're sure about this?" Riley asked casually.

"A little late to change my mind now, don't you think?" Julian replied just as coolly.

"I'm serious, Jules. It wasn't so long ago when I stood beside you and asked if you were sure about something that was going to change your life. If you're not in this one hundred percent—if you're doing this out of some misplaced sense of loyalty and it's going to make you miserable, just say the word and we'll call it off."

For a moment, Julian was too stunned to speak. Frowning, he looked at Riley and realized he was serious. If Julian had any doubts in his mind about taking this step, Riley Shaughnessy would have his back. Dylan and Matt stepped in close and nodded—clearly having heard Riley's words. And what he saw on their faces was the same look Riley had on his.

These were his friends at their best.

No. They were his brothers, and as always, they had his back.

And now it was time to have theirs too.

"There is nothing else I want more than to start making music with the three of you again," he said, his voice thick with emotion. "The years we've spent playing together have been the best of my life."

And just like that they were huddled together in a group hug.

When they broke apart, Dylan nudged him with his shoulder. "Nothing else you want more?" he teased. "Does that include Charlotte?"

Rolling his eyes, Julian chuckled. Leave it to Dylan to stoop to juvenile teasing. "That's on a whole other level and it's completely separate from this," he stated honestly. "And after this press conference, I'm going to get the girl and convince her we can make this work. So just know that I am not to be bothered for at least seventy-two hours."

"Someone thinks pretty highly of himself," Dylan murmured.

"Mighty optimistic of you," Matt said right after him.

"Make sure you have some Gatorade on hand," Riley added with a laugh.

"I'm serious," Julian said, even as he laughed and shook his head. "We're here to do this and we agreed to an hour. I hope Mick and the publicity people can handle things after that, because—"

"Yeah, yeah, yeah," Mick said as he walked over. "We know. You've got to go grovel and convince Charlotte that you deserve her. But, if you ask me, she's too good for you." Then he grinned and slapped Julian on the back good-naturedly. "It's good to see you back where you belong."

Once again emotion clogged his throat. "It's been a long road," he said and then looked at his friends, his brothers, his bandmates. "For all of us."

Everyone nodded in agreement.

Mick looked at the four of them and stood like a proud father. "Here's how this is going to go—you'll be introduced one by one and when you're all on stage, pictures will be taken. I'm only allowing five minutes for that before you'll be shown to your seats. Once you're situated, I'm going to come out and talk to the crowd and let them know what's going on. After I read the statement we all agreed on, I'm going to open the floor to questions. That's where the bulk of the time will be spent."

They each nodded. "We know the drill, Mick," Riley said with a grin. "This isn't our first rodeo."

"I know it's not, but this is the first one you're doing after several turbulent years," Mick said seriously. "We're going to try and keep everyone focused on what's coming up, but you have to be prepared to answer questions about where you've all been. That includes struggles with writer's block, career failures, rehab, and emotional breakdowns." He studied each of them as he said the words. "If you're not prepared to deal with the questions, tell me now and I'll shut them down. Personally, I think if you each lay your story out on the line—especially those of you who haven't talked to the press already—then it's going to make moving forward that much easier. The more secretive you are, the more rabid they'll become."

More nodding.

"So, are we ready?" he asked.

"As we'll ever be," Julian said, more to himself than the group.

Riley put his hand out and said, "Let's do this."

And just like old times, Matt, Dylan, and Julian placed their hands on top of his as a show of solidarity. Mick touched in at the end and looked at them with a wide grin.

"Let's go tell the world we're back."

Charlotte did her best to focus on her work, but she was entering information for the client sitting in front of her and it was almost eleven. Her nerves were frazzled and she had no idea how she was going to watch the press conference if she didn't get this done. The computer was slow and if she could just get the file to submit, she could rush this gentleman out the door.

She tapped her fingers, her toes, and was basically bouncing in her seat when the screen changed and showed that her file was accepted.

Yes! Finally!

"Okay, Mr. Martinson," she said quickly as she rose to her feet. "That's everything. Renee at the front desk will have a printout for you in about five minutes with a list of jobs that match your search requirements. I'd like you to make an appointment to come see me next week."

Holding out her hand, Charlotte shook his and almost sagged to the floor with relief when he walked out.

Swiftly, she moved around her desk and shut the door. Everyone knew that when her door was shut it meant she was in the middle of something important and not to be disturbed unless it was an emergency.

Luckily she'd set that precedent years ago and no one questioned it.

She nearly tripped over her own two feet to get back into her chair and then it was like she was all thumbs as she tried to get into her personal email account for the link Julian assured her was there.

At ten fifty-nine, she held her breath and waited.

On the screen, she saw a stage with a table on it and cards with all the names of the guys in front of their seats, and then a woman went to a podium off to the side of the stage.

"Ladies and gentlemen, I give you the men of Shaughnessy!" she said with enthusiasm. She introduced the guys one by one, with Riley coming out first and waving to the wildly cheering crowd, then Matt, then Dylan, and finally, Julian. Her heart skipped a beat at the sight of him.

She hadn't noticed this morning that he'd trimmed his hair and that his perpetual five-o'clock shadow was looking a little fuller than usual, but none of it mattered because he was perfect. Standing on the stage and smiling in a pair of faded jeans, a black T-shirt, and a bit of attitude, he was every inch the man she loved.

Next, Mick came out and announced that the band would be heading back into the studio for the first time in five years, and once the album was complete, they would tour. Charlotte's hand flew to her chest as tears filled her eyes. He was doing it. He was finally ready to do it.

And she was so damn proud of him.

Questions were being shouted from all over the room and she held her breath, hoping no one was going to bring up the wedding or the video or anything that might send Julian into some kind of tailspin. Although she had a feeling he was ready to handle it now in a way he hadn't been before.

Riley fielded the first two questions, which were specifically directed to him—first about how he felt being back as a band after a successful solo album and tour, and the second about Savannah's upcoming book.

Sweet, she thought.

Then questions came to Matt and Dylan about their solo work outside of the band.

Also nice questions.

"Julian!" someone called out. "You went on a sabbatical and came back to do a lot of charity and volunteer work. Tell us about it."

Charlotte didn't breathe, didn't blink. She sat and listened to Julian talk about how they'd met, and how he came to find out about the plight of the homeless firsthand, and how fulfilling it had been to get involved. He then encouraged everyone in the room to do something to help out—donate food, clothing, or their time. He was emphatic when he spoke of how most people thought they'd have to give too much or wondered how could they give when they thought it would cost them too much money to make a difference.

"The first time I stepped into the shelter, I helped

unload a food truck and moved some shelves around and swept floors," he said. "It didn't take too much time or effort. But to those people who worked there day in and day out and were feeling overwhelmed? It was a gift. That's when I knew we were looking at charity the wrong way."

"Tell us about the music program!" another reporter called out.

Slowly she let out her breath and felt tears roll down her cheeks. No one was interested in talking about the painful stuff these four men had gone through in the last several years. No one cared about their struggles and their mistakes. They were there because of a shared love of rock and roll and the music Shaughnessy played.

For another forty minutes, each of the guys answered questions, and then Mick stood and thanked everyone for their time before motioning to the band to exit the stage. The reporters were still calling out questions, and that was when Mick brought back the woman who had originally introduced them all and told the crowd she'd be handling the rest of the questions. Charlotte had no idea who she was but apparently she handled PR for the band. She felt sorry for her and imagined how over-whelmed she must feel at the enthusiasm of the reporters for more information.

Closing her browser, she immediately stood and reached for her purse, and ran to the ladies' room to freshen up. No doubt it would be at least an hour before Julian showed up, but she didn't want him to see she'd been crying—even if they were happy tears.

For thirty minutes, she did busywork and was anxiously watching the clock, when her boss came into the office.

"Would you care to explain why there is a horde of reporters out in front of the building asking for you?" Jennifer Roberts looked like someone's sweet grandmother, but still managed to strike fear into you with one look.

"Um..."

"Is there something going on, Charlotte?" she demanded. "Are you in some sort of trouble or involved in some kind of scandal? Because we can't have that here! The people who come to us are trying to get their lives together, and I can't have someone who's causing problems in the public eye sitting behind a desk helping them."

"It's not like that, Jennifer. I swear," Charlotte said, her voice only mildly trembling. "There's no scandal, but—"

"Then why are reporters here? Do you hear how loud they're being? I bet whoever just walked in the door was scared to death to walk through that crowd!" She gave Charlotte a disapproving glare. "I think you should pack up and go home for the rest of the day. And we'll see if things are quiet on Monday." She paused. "On second thought, stay home on Monday too, just to play it safe."

"That works for me."

Charlotte gasped as she heard Julian's words and saw him leaning against the door with a sexy grin. Nothing and no one had ever looked better to her.

"Who's this?" Jennifer demanded. "Is he the reason you're in trouble?"

While Charlotte grabbed her phone, her purse, and her laptop, Julian looked at Jennifer and smiled politely. "There's no trouble, ma'am. I'm just here to get my girl."

Stepping around her desk, Charlotte took the hand

Julian held out to her and wished her boss a good weekend, happily following him out the door.

And stopped short at the crowd of reporters.

"Julian, I…"

Tucking her in close to his side, he whispered in her ear, "Smile and wave and keep walking." When she looked at him with wide eyes, he added, "Trust me."

And she did.

She truly did.

Together they made it to a waiting SUV—probably the same one from last night—and he helped her in before climbing in beside her. Without waiting for any instructions, their driver pulled out of the parking lot, and she felt herself breathe normally for the first time all day.

Julian still held her hand as he kept her close.

"Did you see the press conference?"

"I did. You did great. All of you did great."

He nodded. "I was pleasantly surprised. I think I was expecting a little more drama."

"Every time someone started asking a question, I held my breath and prayed they'd behave. I'm so glad they did. And not just to you, but to all of you."

"Yeah, like I said, it was a surprise, and now that it's over, I'm even happier that we did it. We were prepared to answer whatever was thrown at us, no matter how personal. I'm glad it didn't come to that. This was a good experience, and it's nice to see the support we already have from the media."

As they drove on, Charlotte rested her head on his shoulder and listened to him talk about the conversation he had with the guys and what their plans were for the new music. None of the specifics mattered to her—it wasn't as if she understood the music business anyway. All that mattered was listening to the excitement in his voice as he talked about his future. It was hard to imagine that this was the same bitter, angry man she'd originally met. The two barely resembled one another anymore, and that was a miracle in and of itself.

When they drove through town and didn't stop, she straightened. "I thought we were getting lunch."

Beside her, Julian chuckled. "Don't worry. I know how important eating is to you. I just figured after such a crazy morning, you wouldn't mind a more…private lunch."

All of her girly parts wanted to stand up and cheer and then sing the "Hallelujah" chorus. Smiling shyly, she said, "Sounds perfect."

Within minutes they pulled up to Julian's house and as soon as they were out of the car, he waved to the driver and ushered Charlotte inside—seeming as anxious to get her alone as she was to be alone with him.

They had always been in sync like that.

Inside, with the door closed and locked behind them, Julian took her by the hand and led her directly to the kitchen. The table was set and food was out—all of it looked delicious, but she couldn't help glancing over her shoulder toward the bedroom and feeling just a teeny bit disappointed.

Tugging her in close until they were toe to toe, chest to chest, Julian rested his forehead against hers. "Patience."

Yup. In sync.

Her stomach growled and she reminded herself that it would probably be a good thing for them to take the time and eat now, because if she had her wish, they wouldn't have the time or energy for food until much, much later.

Maybe even tomorrow.

So she let him lead her to the table and took a seat.

They ate as she listened; he talked more about how he felt about the press conference and heading back into the studio. And then she knew they would have to address the elephant in the room before they could go back to what they had before.

"Tell me about your meeting with Dena," she said carefully.

With a chuckle, Julian finished the last of his sandwich, taking his time before answering. "You know, I actually kind of like it when you pose a question like a shrink. At first I didn't, but now I think it's kind of cute."

It was the most ridiculous thing she had ever heard, but she realized it was exactly how her words had sounded. "Sorry. Habit, I guess."

"Don't apologize. It was just the first thing that came to mind."

It was possible he was trying to avoid the topic, but then he surprised her by talking.

And talking.

And talking.

By the time he stood to clear away the dishes, Charlotte almost felt like she'd been there in the restaurant with them that day. He'd held nothing back, and she had to say—on both a personal and professional level— what had transpired had been pretty healthy. For both of them. And while she'd still like to have five minutes alone with the woman responsible for messing up so much of his life so she could get a few things off her own chest, that was never going to happen. Eventually, she'd be okay with that.

Julian sat back down and smiled, looking completely at ease and relaxed. It was such a transformation for him that she couldn't take her eyes off him.

"Tell me what you've been up to," he said, reaching for her hand and caressing her palm.

How in the world was she supposed to concentrate on forming words when his touch was already turning her inside out?

"Nothing at all like what you've been up to," she said, hoping to move things along. "You know, work, sleep, work again. Nothing exciting at all."

"Hmm…"

"I saw the improvements at the shelter, you know."

He nodded, but he was studying her hand and running those talented fingers over her wrist now. "And what did you think?"

There were zero thoughts in her head other than feeling his hands on other parts of her.

"Julian?"

His dark eyes looked at her and she saw all the heat and want and need that she knew were mirrored in her own. "Hmm?"

"I think I'd very much like to take this conversation inside," she said boldly, coming to her feet. "To the bedroom," she added for clarification.

In the blink of an eye, she was scooped up in his arms as they strode from the room.

"Thank God," he said with a husky laugh, and it was the greatest sound in the world to her.

—⁓—

Having Charlotte back in his arms, his bed, his life was even better than all the success Julian had ever had. Nothing had ever felt as satisfying.

He had promised himself he'd bring her home and they'd spend time talking, and he wouldn't pressure her or push her for more than she was willing to give. If that meant taking things slow and starting over, then he'd be okay with that. But judging by the way she was tearing at his clothes with the same fervor he was moving hers aside, he felt pretty confident that slow was out the window.

And he'd never been more thankful in his life.

They rolled onto the bed—each vying for the top position but Julian eventually won out. His prize? He got to gaze down at his beautiful girl with her hair sprawled across the pillows and wearing nothing but ice-blue lace. She simply took his breath away.

She panted his name and it sounded like a plea. He understood completely because he wasn't above begging right now either.

He wanted to savor this and make up for lost time, but the need for her was too great, his desire too strong.

"I promise round two will be better," he vowed. "But I can't wait, Charlotte. I've missed you so damn much."

Her long legs wrapped around his waist as her arms circled his shoulders. "No one's asking you to wait. I was ready about an hour ago. I wasn't sure how much longer I was supposed to wait."

That was his girl. His sweet, sexy, sassy girl.

"The wait is over, sweetheart," he said gruffly, reverently.

What followed was wild and frantic and so perfectly them, and when he held her close afterward and helped her shimmy under the sheets with him, he felt like the happiest man in the world.

He was home.

He was healed.

"Do you remember the night I saw you on the beach?" he asked softly, kissing her temple.

"Which one? There were two of those nights."

"The night a few weeks ago."

She nodded. "I do."

"Do you remember what you said to me?"

"Right now, I can barely remember my own name, Julian," she teased. "You'll have to refresh my memory. I was so mad at you, I'm sure I said something bratty."

He laughed and hugged her close. "There were a couple of bratty comments, but that's not what I was referring to."

Pulling back slightly, she looked at him, her brow furrowed and confusion on her face.

"From the moment I met you, Charlotte, you never asked for anything. You gave, and you gave selflessly. No one's ever done that for me before. Ever."

"Julian…"

"I'm serious. At first, I had no idea what to do with you or about you. I kept waiting for you to do or say something that would prove you weren't who you seemed." He paused. "But you're the most sincere and genuine person I've ever known."

She sighed and looked like she was about to say something but stopped herself.

"But more than that, you felt my pain like it was your own. I didn't…I didn't get that. It wasn't until you told me you loved me too much to end up being one more person with expectations and demands on me that I realized that. I know I don't deserve you, Charlotte, but I love you. I want to be the man who is worthy of you."

Stopping because, for the second time today, he couldn't believe how emotional he was feeling, he kissed the top of her head and smiled when she relaxed against him.

"Then I started thinking about that and realized I felt the same way about you too—I see how hard you work and how much of yourself you give to the things you believe in and how you try to ease people's burdens. Most of the time no one thanks you for it or you don't get to see how thankful they are. I wanted to do something to help you so there would be fewer expectations and demands on you. So maybe you could relax a little at work or have a night off where you weren't feeling stressed about a family you'd helped or the shelter."

"No one's ever done that for me before," she admitted quietly. "I mean, I get volunteers, and my friends and family help out or donate to a cause that I suggest. I think they do it more to make me stop talking about it than for the people they're helping. What you've done in the last two months, Julian? The effects of that are going to be felt for years. And that makes me both happy and sad at the same time."

He knew exactly what she meant and loved her all the more for it.

In each other's arms, they seemed lost in their own thoughts for several long minutes before Julian spoke again. "So you were in trouble with your boss, huh?"

She laughed softly. "Jennifer has two moods—neutral or fully annoyed. I think you can guess which she was today."

"Would it help if I said I was sorry?" he asked with amusement.

Playfully swatting him, Charlotte said, "I guess I figured it was one thing for reporters to show up at the shelter—after all, it was the place you referred to. And then today I thought everyone would be at the press conference. I'm not newsworthy enough for them to track me down at the office."

"Well, to be honest, they followed me to your office."

Lifting her head, she looked at him.

"When I was leaving the building, there were a few reporters outside who asked if I was heading to the studio to start working on the new music, and I told them no. I had to go and get the girl first."

Her eyes went wide. "You did not!"

But he nodded and grinned. "Sure did. So we had a bit of a caravan following us that somehow grew along the way. I hope some people stayed to the end of the conference. Our PR team had a ton of information to share and answer questions about. I certainly thought that would be more interesting than me showing up and taking the woman I love to lunch."

And yeah, he'd said it twice now and she hadn't, and he wasn't sure how much more prompting she'd need to say it to him.

He really wanted her to say it to him.

"Hmm... I wouldn't find that particularly interesting either," she said mildly. "Except maybe they were hoping for a little PDA for their video."

"You think they followed me all that way just to see a kiss?" he asked, totally amused by her theory.

"It's a possibility. You never know."

Shrugging, he did let his mind wander to that, but it still seemed crazy to him.

"Here's something I can tell you about the average person—you know, the ones who don't live in mansions on the beach or who tour the world as a rock star," she added for clarification. "We all have a mild curiosity to watch a train wreck. I don't know why, but it seems to be a fact. And when that train wreck comes in the form of someone's downfall, the more interesting the story becomes."

"Great," he murmured.

"However," she quickly went on, "we all love a happy ending. For years the press has been watching you and the guys have your own versions of train wrecks. Now they're ready for all those happy endings."

His chest tightened at what she was implying.

"And you think this here—us—is going to be one of those happy endings?" he asked cautiously.

"Oh, yeah," she said softly, practically purring as she leaned in close. "I believe that very much."

Now he was desperate for the words.

"Why, Charlotte?" His voice was so low and so unsure he almost didn't recognize it.

"Because I love you, Julian Grayson. I loved you when you were being completely unlovable. I want to watch you step back into the music world with confidence. I want to be by your side when you have amazing success and I want to be by your side when you come home at the end of the day or at the end of a tour and hear all about it."

It was possibly the most amazing thing anyone had ever said to him.

Ever.

"You're mine, Charlotte Clark. And there isn't another woman in the world I want with me as this new phase of my life begins, because you make me want to be a better man. You make me want to do more on a completely different level than I ever knew existed. I love you."

The kiss they shared was soft and reverent.

Just like their words.

"This was what the reporters wanted to hear," she said, smiling sweetly at him.

"Well, too bad. They'll have to wait and hear it another day. Your boss told you to stay home until Tuesday, so if anyone wants a sound bite from us, they'll have to wait until then."

The sun was rising and Charlotte didn't think she'd ever get enough of watching it from this vantage point—wrapped in Julian's arms with a blanket around them while they sipped coffee on the sand.

"You know you're spoiling me, right?" she asked softly as the coffee warmed her on such a chilly morning.

"You deserve to be spoiled. And you can't really put this on me. Mother Nature is the one doing all the work here. I'm just along for the show."

"And what a show it is."

"I don't know, I kind of like the show we had going on inside—you know, where it was warm and we had a big bed and more blankets and no audience."

She laughed. "It's only us and the seagulls out here right now."

"Yeah, well…they're watching," he grumbled and took a sip of his own coffee.

"That's ridiculous." But then one of those seagulls started to walk by and stopped to study them. "You're not helping here, bird."

"Told ya."

They laughed and Julian hugged her close as they enjoyed the peacefulness of the early morning.

As much as Charlotte would love to have this feeling, this view, every day, she knew it wasn't possible. For starters, this wasn't her home, and technically, it wasn't Julian's either. For all she knew, in the last few weeks, he had decided on where he was moving to and it wasn't going to have an ocean view address.

Then again, neither did hers.

Last night they'd stayed up all night talking, making love, and eating, and she knew they both needed some sleep, but that didn't stop her from touching on the topic.

"How much longer is your lease on this house?"

"Mick said I could extend it if I wanted to."

"That was nice of him." She paused and drank a little more of her coffee. "How has the house search gone?"

Behind her, he shrugged. "I've seen a couple of places online that interest me, but I haven't been motivated to go look at any of them."

He went quiet and she had a feeling he had more to say, so she waited him out.

"I was going to look at places on the East Coast," he said quietly, and Charlotte stilled. "Without you, there wasn't anything keeping me here. I grew up out there, and Riley's got a vacation house there, Matt's living there full-time…it was an idea."

Charlotte had been born and raised in Malibu and never considered living anyplace else but here. Even when her family vacationed, it was to other parts of California or in the Pacific Northwest.

"I've never been to the East Coast," she said casually. "I hear there are some beautiful beaches there." As she rested her head back on his shoulder, she could almost feel him smiling. "Then again, you can't believe everything you read, right?"

He chuckled. "Depends on what you're reading."

"I have some vacation time coming. Maybe I'll have to go find out for myself if what I've read is accurate. I may even ask Riley about his brother's resort on Hilton Head. That might be nice to see."

"Oh yeah?"

She nodded. "I trust Riley more than I do a travel brochure. And I doubt he'd brag about the place just because his brother owns it."

That made Julian laugh. "Then you don't know Riley very well. He's got a lot of siblings and if you listen to him, they're all brilliant."

"Well, his twin brother is, isn't he?"

Nodding, Julian said, "Owen. Who is now the father of two sets of twins."

Charlotte gasped and turned in his arms, smiling. "They had the babies?"

"Last week. They induced Brooke and she and the babies are fine—perfectly healthy."

"And? What did she have?" she asked excitedly.

"One of each this time."

"And they have twin boys already, right?"

"Three boys and one girl. They're going to have their hands full."

Charlotte was actually a little envious. Not that she was eager to have multiple sets of twins, but thinking about having a big family and knowing that the entire Shaughnessy family must have been there to celebrate the twins' birth made her feel hopeful. She would love to experience something like that for herself. Even if she didn't have the big family, she did have a lot of friends.

"What are you thinking about right now?" he asked as he nuzzled her neck, his breath warm yet causing chills.

"Thinking about how lucky they are. All that love and new babies and…" She stopped and sighed. "It just sounds like a lot of happiness."

"How would you feel about that kind of happiness?" he asked with a little more nuzzling.

She could play dumb and make him spell out exactly what he was trying to say, but this was far too important of a topic. Twisting all the way around in his lap so she was straddling him and being very careful to keep the blanket in place and not spill the coffee, Charlotte met his very serious gaze.

"I want that kind of happiness. Very much."

A slow smile spread across his face. "How soon?"

So much joy bubbled up inside her that she couldn't help but wrap herself even tighter around him. "How soon are you offering?"

"Sweetheart, I'm ready to take you inside right now and get started if you're up for it."

Was she? Were they seriously talking about this already? Were they being just a little impetuous?

Julian must have sensed her inner questions because he pulled back and looked at her before reaching up and cupping her face. "There's no rush, Charlotte. We don't have to decide right now or today or even tomorrow." His thumb stroked her cheek. "Just promise me something."

"Anything."

"That we will make those plans someday. Because baby, I don't want to waste one more moment of our lives."

"It's the same for me, Julian. Always."

Slowly he maneuvered them so they were both on their feet. "How about this, we go inside and catch a couple of hours' sleep and maybe start making a few plans over brunch out on the deck."

"That sounds like the best plan yet."

Taking her hand, Julian began to lead her back to the house. "Sweetheart, that's just the beginning. You ain't seen nothing yet."

And she truly believed him.

Epilogue

Two months later…

"I'M NERVOUS. IS ANYONE ELSE NERVOUS?"

"I'm doing okay."

"Never better."

Charlotte took a deep breath and accepted the glass of wine Savannah handed to her. "Thanks."

"You need to relax. This is all a good thing. Trust me."

"How can you be so sure? The last time something like this happened was, what—years ago!"

Paige laughed softly as she sipped on a glass of water with lemon. "Personally, I'm excited. I've watched old footage and it was amazing. And kind of a turn-on. Dylan had no idea why I jumped him that night." And with a naughty grin, she moved away to greet some people.

"I saw them live years ago. It was the night I managed to sneak backstage and kissed Matt for the first time," Vivienne said, sipping her own glass of wine.

"Seriously?" Charlotte asked. "That's kind of cool!"

"Nah, not so much. Turns out he didn't remember it," she said blandly.

"He did eventually," Savannah prompted. "But yeah, no points for Matty on that one."

"Ladies!" Mick called out as he strode toward them. "You all look beautiful, and I have an usher here to escort you and the rest of this massive VIP group out to your seats."

They were standing in a grand lounge along with most of the Shaughnessy family, Dylan's parents, Matt's father, stepmother, and little sister, Vivienne's brother Aaron and his fiancée, Emilie, and Julian's parents. Tonight was the first public performance for Shaughnessy in years. The anniversary gala was a star-studded event, but Shaughnessy was the headliner and the media had been buzzing about it for weeks.

It was a little like an out-of-body experience for Charlotte. All of her time with Julian had been fairly off the radar, and to be thrust into the spotlight and walking a red carpet had been beyond intimidating.

But she was kind of loving every minute of it.

Just like she was loving every minute of their life together.

A life they were moving to North Carolina as soon as Shaughnessy's album and world tour were completed. Julian had been anxious to do it all now, but she had argued it would be better to stay grounded where they were for the time being so he could be close to the studio and the guys. She would also be able to keep working while he was on tour.

The discussion hadn't gone quite the way she had envisioned, and they'd compromised—they would stay put in Malibu while the album was being finished and she would keep working, but he wanted her to resign sooner so she could see the world with him.

How could she say no?

And to sweeten the deal, the name of the tour and the album was *Pay It Forward*. A percentage of the tour revenue and record sales were being donated to a foundation whose goal was to end homelessness.

So for the first time in her life, Charlotte Clark was going to see not only the country but the world. Julian had opened her eyes to the fact that it was time for her to live a little for herself—that there was no crime in her doing so. It didn't take away from the work she did to help those less fortunate; if anything, it invigorated her. She knew she'd spent far too long working tirelessly and realized how much more effective she could be if she allowed herself some time to recharge once in a while.

Amazing what the love of a good man could do. And one of the things he did to show he loved her was to be concerned for her mental and physical well-being. He never asked her to stop working, just to take some time for herself once in a while.

This had been a year of many firsts for her and she was thankful for all of them—especially for the man who was making so many of her dreams come true.

—⁂—

"I'm nervous. Is anyone else nervous?"

Julian threw one of his drumsticks at Riley and told him to shut up. The man was practically bouncing on his toes in excitement, and he knew their front man had never been nervous a day in his life.

They'd worked hard, the four of them. They'd spent every day in the studio for almost two months straight and the album was nearing completion. They were fortunate that they were four strong composers who knew one another so well that they had the same vision for their newest musical collaboration.

Julian sat on the sofa and let his head fall back and closed his eyes. He was in the zone. He was ready. It was funny how he didn't realize just how much he'd missed this and needed this until he had it back. The thought of never doing this would have been like losing a limb, and he was grateful that he'd finally got himself together and out of his funk before it was too late.

Lifting his head, he scanned the room and looked at his friends.

Matty Reed. Once a cocky and arrogant little punk who thought he had more talent than the four of them put together. He'd learned a hard lesson with his Broadway flop, but that lesson had helped him finally mature and had led him to Vivienne. Despite Matt's turbulent upbringing, it was nice to see a smile on his face almost all the time. He was calmer now, more thoughtful, and finally at peace with his past and his family and ready to start one of his own.

Dylan Anders. It was a wonder he was still alive. Julian could look back and think of the things Dylan used to do, and all he could say was that his friend had one hell of a guardian angel. The funny thing was how even at his worst, Julian had always considered him one of the most gifted musicians he had ever encountered. But then when he started jamming with a sober Dylan? Man, this clean and sober version was brilliant. And now he was going to have a kid of his own. Julian could only hope the kid inherited some of his father's musical gifts.

"Why isn't the clock moving?" Riley called out to no one in particular.

Riley Shaughnessy. The reason any of them were

even here. A scrappy kid from a large family, with a big personality and a voice like an angel.

Yeah, he'd said it.

No one could sing like Riley, and when he sang a capella? The man was capable of giving even the biggest music cynic chills. Riley had formed this band so many years ago and they had all given him grief about naming it after himself. Turned out it really worked for them because Riley was the heart of this band. None of them could do it on their own, and without him at the helm, it wasn't even worth doing. It had been tough watching him struggle to do this whole thing on his own, but Julian felt it had been a great experience for Riley. It had strengthened him and given him a confidence he didn't have before.

And then there was himself.

He was all of them rolled into one. Except with a heaping pile of attitude and stubbornness thrown in. Most of his life Julian had told himself he was a loner— that he would be okay and even happy on his own. But it was a lie. Without these men, he would be miserable. They completed him and brought out the best in him as a musician.

He firmly believed his heart was split equally in two—one half belonged to Shaughnessy and the other to Charlotte.

And he was happy to give it to each of them.

The door to the dressing room swung open and Mick walked in with a couple of bodyguards behind him.

"Let's do this!"

No one said a word as they walked the winding hallways that led to the backstage area. It was dimly lit and loud, and there seemed to be people everywhere. It was familiar and intimidating all at the same time.

Nervously, Julian twirled one of his sticks in his right hand and waited for their cue. The stage manager led them out behind the curtain, where all of their places had been marked. Stepping behind the drum kit he loved, Julian caressed the wood and smiled. In front of him to his left was Dylan. He was flexing and stretching his fingers as one of the stage crew adjusted his guitar strap for him. To his right, Matt was putting his ear piece in and listening to something Mick was telling him.

And out in front behind the microphone stood the band's namesake.

They were back.

No more running.

No more hiding.

And as the curtain rose and the crowd went wild, Julian counted them in and let the music take them.

About the Author

Samantha Chase is a *New York Times* and *USA Today* bestseller of contemporary romance. She released her debut novel in 2011 and currently has more than forty titles under her belt! When she's not working on a new story, she spends her time reading romances, playing way too many games of Scrabble or Solitaire on Facebook, wearing a tiara while playing with her sassy pug, Maylene...oh, and spending time with her husband of twenty-five years and their two sons in North Carolina.

MAGNOLIA BRIDES

These women have marriage on their minds
and love in their hearts…and in this small
Georgia town, anything is possible

By Lynnette Austin

The Best Laid Wedding Plans

When Jenni Beth Beaumont inherits
her family's beautiful antebellum home,
her dream of turning it into a wedding
destination feels closer than ever. But
former crush Cole Bryson plans to buy
and tear down the house. Good thing
Jenni will do whatever it takes to keep
her dream—and protect herself from
falling for Cole all over again.

Every Bride Has Her Day

Sam Montgomery thought he'd have
no trouble finding peace and quiet
in the small Georgia town where he
inherited a rundown house. Until his
effusively optimistic neighbor, Cricket
O'Malley, storms into his life—and
his heart.

Picture Perfect Wedding

Beck Elliot thought he'd never again see the woman who broke his heart. But when divorced single mom Tansy Calhoun moves back to Misty Bottoms to open a shop, she's impossible to avoid…and so are his old feelings.

"Lynnette Austin has made her mark on contemporary romance."

—Night Owl Reviews for Picture Perfect Wedding

For more Lynnette Austin, visit:
sourcebooks.com

MUST LOVE BABIES

Bachelors find themselves with unexpected bundles
of joy in this heartwarming series from
award-winning author Lynnette Austin

Brant Wylder is a bachelor and loving it. He's found the
perfect location for his shop restoring vintage vehicles:
Misty Bottoms, Georgia. Supporting his family and
running the shop, he's convinced he doesn't have time for
a relationship. Until he meets Molly Stiles.

For Molly Stiles, it's nose to the grindstone establishing
her bridal boutique—not the time to meet Mr. Right. But
Molly can't help her attraction to Brant. And when an
accident leaves his seven-month-old nephew in his care,
Molly won't turn her back on them.

"Romance that has it all!"

—Fresh Fiction for *Every Bride Has Her Day*

For more Lynnette Austin, visit:
sourcebooks.com

A NEW LEASH ON LOVE

First in the fresh, poignant Rescue Me series
from award-winning debut author Debbie Burns

When Craig Williams must take his daughters' adorable new puppy to a shelter after the holidays, it's just another painful episode in the fall-out of a miserable divorce. Getting grief from the fiery woman running the shelter is the least of his problems.

For Megan Anderson, it's hard enough to run an underfunded no-kill animal shelter without taking on the problems of a handsome man with a troublesome puppy. But as Craig and Megan are drawn closer together, they realize the magic of unconditional love can do anything—maybe even heal a broken heart.

SIT, STAY, LOVE

In the second Rescue Me book from award-winning debut author Debbie Burns, the dogs aren't the only ones in need of rescue

For devoted no-kill shelter worker Kelsey Sutton, rehabbing a group of rescue dogs is a welcome challenge. Working with a sexy ex-military dog handler who needs some TLC himself? That's a different story.

Kurt Crawford keeps his heart locked away from everyone but the dogs who need his help…and always have his back. But as Kurt gets to know the woman he's been assigned to work with, he can't help but feel a little puppy love…

For more Debbie Burns, visit:
sourcebooks.com

COME BACK TO ME

THE MONTGOMERY BROTHERS

Samantha Chase, *New York Times* and *USA Today* Bestselling Author

Return to You

James Montgomery has achieved everything he'd hoped for in life...except marrying the girl of his dreams. Now Selena Ainsley is back, but how can she face the man she loved and left behind?

Meant for You

Summer Montgomery wants to be taken seriously almost as much as she wants her brother's off-limits best friend, Ethan. But it only takes one night away from watchful eyes to make impossible dreams come true...

I'll Be There

Zach Montgomery lives by his own rules and doesn't answer to anyone. But his assistant, Gabriella Martine, has no intention of backing down.

Until There Was Us

Megan Montgomery can't stop thinking about her sexy hookup with Alex Rebat at her cousin's wedding. Alex can't stop thinking about her—and now that Megan's back in town, Alex hopes she'll take a chance on a future they can only build together.

"Charming...Chase's three-dimensional characters leap off the page."

—Publishers Weekly for Until There Was Us

For more Samantha Chase, visit:
sourcebooks.com

Also by Samantha Chase

The Montgomery Brothers

Wait for Me

Trust in Me

Stay with Me

More of Me

Return to You

Meant for You

I'll Be There

Until There Was Us

The Shaughnessy Brothers

Made for Us

Love Walks In

Always My Girl

This Is Our Song

A Sky Full of Stars

Holiday Spice

Shaughnessy Brothers: Band on the Run

One More Kiss

One More Promise

One More Moment

Holiday Romance

*The Christmas Cottage /
Ever After*

*Mistletoe Between
Friends /
The Snowflake Inn*

Holiday Spice

Life, Love and Babies

The Baby Arrangement

Baby, I'm Yours

Baby, Be Mine